BEFORE THE FALL

Across the channel, the Great War rages; in London's East End, with her husband fighting, Hannah Lockwood struggles to hold everything together. But when Hannah takes a job in a café, she discovers a glimpse of freedom away from her needy young children, her spiteful sister and desperately ill father. While the conflict drags on, Hannah battles with the overwhelming burden of 'duty'. She has sacrificed so much for a husband who left her behind, a husband who may never come home. Then, when she meets Daniel – thoughtful, intelligent, quietly captivating – Hannah finds herself faced with the most dangerous of temptations...

BEFORE THE FALL

BEFORE THE FALL

by

Juliet West

Magna Large Print Books
Long Preston, North Yorkshire,
BD23 4ND, England.

British Library Cataloguing in Publication Data.

West, Juliet
    Before the fall.

    A catalogue record of this book is
    available from the British Library

    ISBN   978-0-7505-4031-5

First published in Great Britain in 2014 by Mantle

Published in Large Print 2015 by arrangement with
Macmillan Publishers trading as Pan Macmillan Publishers Ltd

Magna Large Print is an imprint of Library Magna Books Ltd.

Printed and bound in Great Britain by
T.J. (International) Ltd., Cornwall, PL28 8RW

For Mum, Dad, Alison and Rob,
with love.

Author's Note

Before the Fall is inspired by real events that took place in London during the First World War. The documents quoted in the novel are based on police statements and newspaper reports of the time; however, all names and some details have been changed.
This is a work of fiction.

I seem but a dead man held on end
To sink down soon...

'*The Going*', THOMAS HARDY

Part One

Part One

Leman Street Police Station

18th day of July 1918

Statement of Herbert Tilling
Motorman

I am a motorman employed by the Metropolitan Railway Company. At 5.49 a.m. on 18 July 1918 I was running my train into Aldgate East Station when a man got up from a seat on the platform and jumped in front of my train. When I saw the man jump, I applied the emergency brake.

I got down from the train and searched for the man and found him lying between the negative rail and the inside running rail immediately under the first carriage. I saw that the man was alive and moving. I told him to remain still until I got to him. I moved him to between the first and second carriages, then helped him over the negative rail into the six-foot way and eventually onto the platform.

I saw that his head was bleeding from the back.

He said: 'Will you give me a drop of water?' I caused some to be fetched. I then left him in charge of other officials.

1

I can't help looking down as I cross the bridge over Bow Creek. The high tide heaves, rising with the Thames, grey oily water sucking and slapping against the muddy banks. This water can swallow you in an eye-blink, whether you want to be swallowed or not. Women trip on trailing skirts; dockers overstep in the fog. Too long in the pub and even a lighterman could find himself falling.

People forget that water needs air to survive. *Aitch-two-O.* As I look in the river, I think of Beatrice and I wonder whether her drowned breath still breaks the surface, swirled up somehow with the coal dust and the rotten cats and the centuries of London filth.

After Beatrice died, I refused to cross the water. Six years old and stubborn, I would sink onto the cobbles wailing at the sight of a bridge. Instinct told me it went against nature, keeping things up with nuts and bolts. I couldn't understand this peculiar magic, however much Dad tried to explain. It was surely only a matter of time before the bridge collapsed, I thought. Why not at *that* moment, the very moment I was stepping across?

For a time I conquered my fear.

A gust of wind batters in from the east and now the bridge seems to shift, a lurch downwards. I

17

put my hand on the iron parapet and try to shake the dizziness away, the sense that I am falling. There's a little trick I play. I imagine Dad teasing me in the way he always did – *Daft old Hannah-Lou, daft old Hannah* – and I chant the words silently, over and over, as I cross to the East India side. It comforts me as I hurry along, past the Blackwall Tunnel, over the dock bridges, until finally I'm in Cubitt Town.

A ship's whistle sounds as I turn into East Ferry Road. The wind is sharp, demented; it tugs at my hair and flings grit into my eyes, so I have to squint and hold my hat down hard on my head. An old greengrocer is standing in front of his shop, arms crossed, with his apron flapping in the squall. I walk up to him, smiling.

'Yes, miss,' he says, smiling back and jangling the coins inside his apron pocket.

'I was just calling about a job.'

'What job?' He's frowning now and the coins fall silent.

'Just any job.'

'Sorry, dear,' he says, turning to rearrange a display of small apples. A terrier pads out from the shop and the greengrocer shoos him back inside.

'Thank you, anyway, sir.' I carry on walking, head held high.

I try the newsagent two doors down, then the chandler's and even the sweetshop on the corner. No luck.

At the crossroads, I turn right into Glengall Road. I've not been this far down the Isle of Dogs in ages, not since Dora dragged me to a bazaar at the Liberal and Radical Association because a boy she liked was running the dipping tub. That was a warm spring day, but this morning everything is darker. Two men in oil-specked waistcoats lean against a wall outside the George pub. Beyond them rise the blackened arches of the railway viaduct. 'Morning,' one of them says, while the other whistles a long, low note. Lecherous beggars, they are. Got to be careful with men like that, keep your eyes straight ahead.

There's a cafe opposite the pub, double-fronted and the windows busy with advertisements and chalkboards so that it's hard to see inside. Sticking out of the roof guttering is a crooked tin teapot. Flowers are growing from the spout, those pink jobs you see all over the show. Vandal root, we call it – posh name valerian. Supposed to be good for the nerves.

I cross the road towards the cafe and the closer I get to the teapot, the further I crane my neck up to see it. I should know better, really I should, because it sets off that feeling again, the sense of falling. I steady myself against a lamp post, try to breathe in deep, but all I get is a lungful of kipper stink from the fish shop nearby.

What I need now is a cup of hot tea, plenty of sugar. There's a sign in the cafe window that says, NESTLE'S MILK. OPEN. When I push the door, a tiny bell rings.

It's busy inside, the air all chewy with tobacco smoke and grease. Squat dockers with thick wrists and sloping shoulders stare at me over half-raised spoons. I make for the woman at the counter.

'Morning,' she says. She's older than me, forty-ish and fat, wearing a plain apron over a high-necked blouse. Her hair is folded into a white net, and when she smiles, her wide-spaced teeth and little pink-rimmed eyes put me in mind of the Lipton's pig.

'Cup of tea, please.' Soon as I've said it I wonder where I'll sit. Might be easiest to stand at the counter, keep my back to the men.

Next to a jar of pickles on the counter is a plate piled with currant buns. A small square of cardboard rests against the plate – BUNS ½d, written in pencil. I take out my purse and put a coin on the counter.

'I'll have a currant bun 'n' all,' I say.

'Good girl.'

The woman claws at the top bun with a pair of tongs and places it on a plate.

'Marg?'

I nod and there's a *whoosh* inside my mouth. Ravenous, I am.

The woman slices the bun, then spreads each half with margarine – *flick, flick* – all smooth and graceful, like the bone-handled knife is part of her body, an extra finger. She turns to a high shelf behind the counter and picks a china cup rather than the tin mugs lined up on the shelf below. From a huge pot she pours my tea; the steam curls from the spout in a lazy mist and suddenly my legs feel weak. I have the curious feeling of wanting to lie down right there on the floor and sleep for a long time.

'Sugar?'

'Please.'

She adds two heaped spoonfuls, pushing the second spoonful down so that the wet crystals crunch in the bottom of the cup.

'Lovely as you like,' she says under her breath, with such private satisfaction, surprise almost, as if this might be the first time she has ever served anyone tea and a bun. She looks up. 'And you'll be wanting a seat.' She nods towards the table nearest the counter.

A man is sitting there. His shirt sleeves are rolled up, and he's reading the *Daily Mirror*. This man, he's not like your average docker. He's well built all right, strong like you have to be, but there's something unusual about him. A word comes to my mind – *elegant* – and I tell myself not to be so daft. It isn't a word I've ever thought before, let alone said. He's just a plain old labourer. You can tell from his ragged fingernails and the hairs on his forearms, laced with dirt.

The woman sees me staring. 'Don't you worry about him,' she says, leaning forward so that I can smell her tea-sweet breath. 'Soft as kittens they are, these boys. Would never insult a lady.'

The man looks up at me, straight-faced. His hair is too long and falls across his forehead. At the corner of his eye, a pulse jumps, like there's the tiniest creature under his skin.

'Just leaving anyway,' he says, tucking the newspaper into his jacket pocket. He doesn't wear the jacket, though, just holds it, all bunched up in his fist, not bothering about the creases. As he walks past, there's the sharp smell of metal and something softer: peppermint, could it be? He touches the peak of his cap in our direction, but

21

I don't smile.

'Good day, Mr Blake,' says the woman, and the bell jangles him out.

The silence in the cafe lifts. An old boy coughs into a handkerchief, and two men near the window laugh. 'God's honest,' one of them says. 'Found 'er up the Commercial Road.'

Mr Blake's chair is still warm. I think about moving across to another, because it doesn't seem proper, soaking up the heat of him, but I stay put, sipping my tea. I eat the bun slowly, aiming for dainty, savouring the sweet stickiness of the currants, the cold layer of marg and the hot, heavenly tea cutting through it all.

'Not often we see a young lady in the shop.' The woman is leaning over the counter again and I have to turn sideways, try and face her to be polite. 'Unless they're looking for work, of course. And then they don't bother buying nothing.' She shakes her head as she wipes down the counter, her greying rag swishing damp circles into the wood.

'Well, since you mention it...' I say, placing the last piece of bun back on the plate. I can feel the blush rising, but I can't pass up the chance. 'Since you mention it, I *am* looking for a position.'

'A *position*, is it? Well, I'll tell you, Miss...'

'Mrs Loxwood.'

Her eyes flicker to my left hand and for a second I'm tempted to produce the wedding ring from the chain round my neck. Instead I raise my hand to my throat, press the curve of the thin gold through the wool of my buttoned-up coat.

'I'll tell you, Mrs Loxwood, Mr Stephens – he's the proprietor – Mr Stephens *has* been considering an extra assistant. My knees are playing up and the prospect of another damp winter–' she twists her lips together and sucks in a stream of air '–it don't bear thinking about. You local, dear?'

'Poplar born. Just over the creek now, in Canning Town.' Her nose wrinkles in a tiny sniff. She thinks she's a cut above, here in Cubitt Town. Don't blame her.

'Husband work at the docks?'

'East India. Did work there, I mean. He's joined up.'

'Oh, bless you, dear. You must be very proud.'

I don't reply. She stares at me, her head to one side.

'But no nippers, I take it, little slip of a thing like you. You're no age.'

'I'm twenty-four, and I've got two children, boy and a girl. My sister'll look after them. When I get a job, I mean.' I think of Jen laying down the law with Alice and Teddy. She'll look after them all right, even if it turns her red hair grey.

She asks whether I've ever worked in a shop or a cafe before and I tell her no, but I was a kitchen maid at a house in Chelsea before I was married.

'Well, that's useful, at least,' she says. 'But can you write, Mrs Loxwood? Only you'd have to take down orders, and there's the totting-up.'

'Oh yes, I won prizes for my handwriting. Headmistress wanted me to stay on, but...' I trail off. She doesn't want to hear my sob story.

'You'd be amazed how many girls come in here

23

unlettered. Heaven knows what they got up to at school.'

They didn't bother going, I want to answer, but surely she's seen the children just as well as I have, mudlarking at low tide, scrabbling in the sludge for scrap iron or a good length of twine. Still, I sometimes wonder what's worse, never having a chance, or thinking you had one, then finding it got taken away.

Lipton's lady smiles. 'I'll put in a good word with Mr Stephens. You come back same time tomorrow and we'll see about a position.'

'I'm much obliged to you, Mrs...'

'Stephens. Mrs Stephens, for my sins.'

Mrs Stephens disappears into the kitchen and I stand up, slipping the leftover morsel of bun into my coat pocket. When I get back to Canning Town, I'll divide it between Alice and Teddy, tell them to shut their eyes and open their gobs and then they'll have a surprise.

Walking home, the sun comes out, flashing on the shop windows and the drain covers so that the street looks almost cheerful. At the top of East Ferry Road, glass glints up from the rubble of Beasley's milk yard. Mr Beasley wouldn't leave the yard, my friend Dora said, not even when the Zeppelin was cruising right overhead. 'What killed him wasn't the bomb itself; it was the flying glass from his milk bottles, great big shards of it. That's Dor's account, anyway, but she always has been prone to melodrama. She'd be right at home on the stage; everyone says so.

Vandal root is flowering around the edges of

24

the rubble. Gets everywhere, this stuff. I never could resist a posy, so I bend down to pick a few sprigs, digging my thumbnail into the juicy stalks – *squeeze, snap* – and threading them into the buttonhole of my coat. When I walk back past the grumpy old greengrocer's, I smile, jaunty as you like with all that sugar in my belly and the tiny pink flowers nodding from my buttonhole. 'Up yours,' I whisper, and the wind takes my words, lifts them high above the Thames.

A wool ship is locking into South Dock and the barrier comes down to shut off the swing bridge. Rotten luck to catch a bridger. I could be stuck here for twenty minutes now, and this is the very last place I'd choose to wait, this shadowy stretch of Manchester Road, not ten yards from the exact spot where they laid out Beatrice.

The swing bridge creaks as it turns a half-circle across the basin. A crowd gathers on the pavement around me: a gentleman in a bowler, an old Chinaman sucking on a pipe, three girls from Morton's smelling of pickles. One of the girls smiles at me and rolls her eyes, as if to complain about the hold-up, but I don't want to get involved in their chatter. I keep my eyes fixed straight ahead as the ship clears the lock and slowly the girders swing back into place. The crowd surges across the bridge, but I hang back. The footway is ever so narrow: too much of a crush and you could lose your balance. *Daft old Hannah-Lou.* I'd rather be daft than drowned.

Someone is crossing from the other side, a tall man who's reading a folded-up newspaper as he walks. He grasps the paper tightly, and his shoulders are set, as if he's trying to pour his whole body into those flimsy pages. When we pass on the bridge, he doesn't look up. It strikes me then why this man seems so familiar. The cafe, of course. Mr Blake.

By the time I turn in to Sabbarton Street my flowers have wilted and the clouds are threatening rain. I think of Jen inside the house, poking coals in the stove, sweating and sighing, Alec skulking in the doorways, the children bickering and telling tales the minute I walk in the door.

The piece of bun is like a jewel in my pocket and it dawns on me that what Alice and Teddy have never known they'll never miss. I take out the bun, doughy from the heat of my fingers, and push it into my mouth.

George's letter is propped up against the button box on the hall shelf, a dusty footprint stamped across the front of the envelope. All those mornings I've been stuck indoors wondering what the postman might bring. Minute I go out, a letter comes, and it gets trodden on for good measure.

'Any luck?' yells Jen from the scullery.

I pick up the letter and walk through. She's slicing bread, sleeves rolled up to show her arms, all dimply and mottled. Her hair's the usual mess, gingery curls escaping from her bun. Jen doesn't look at me standing there, just keeps slicing with a tight grip on the loaf and a frown on her face.

'Not exactly.'

'What do you mean, "not exactly"?'

'I mean nothing definite. But there might be a

job in a cafe. I have to go back tomorrow.'

'You'll be wanting me to mind the children again?'

'If that's all right.'

She sniffs, and right on cue a howl starts up from the yard. I squeeze past Jen and step through the open door. Alice is standing in the corner of the yard, back pressed against the sooty brick wall. Her right hand is stretched up high above her head, dangling Teddy's Ducky. It's a little sock puppet that George brought back from the training camp on his leave. He'd stitched it together himself: two odd buttons for eyes and a yellowish piece of sacking for the beak. Teddy takes it everywhere, and now he's started to call it Daddy.

'Want Daddy, Daddy,' he's shrieking, but Alice is still waving the puppet above her head, her black curls teased by the wind.

Teddy sees me and rushes over, grasping me around the knees. I run my hands through his knotty hair, press the damp heat of his head.

'Alice Loxwood, give the baby his duck,' I say.

Alice cackles louder, and although she leaves off the dangling, she keeps Ducky close to her chest.

'I didn't do nothing,' she shouts. 'It was him what kicked me.'

'He's two years old and you're four. You should know better. Now give it back or you'll get a smack.'

'Back, smack. Back, smack,' Alice chants. 'You done a rhyme!'

I know Jen will be looking at me through the

27

scullery window. Something about Jen's way with the children always makes them see sense. I swear they save all their playing-up for me.

'I ain't telling you again.' My teeth are clenched and my head feels tight, like someone's lifting my scalp with a fork. The vandal root winks up at me from my buttonhole. Good for the nerves? What a joke. 'Give it back *now*.'

Alice throws the puppet onto the cobbled ground near the privy. It lands on a patch of moss, yellowed after the dry summer. Teddy breaks away from my knees and toddles across the yard, lunging at the puppet so that he tumbles right onto it. 'Daddy,' he says, screwing up his small hand and putting it inside the sock. He lies on the ground, rubbing Ducky against his cheek, but his eyes are open all the while, watching Alice, guarding.

The rain starts, just a few blustery drops that blow in on the wind, smelling of autumn. Half a mile away, children are shouting and singing in the playground at St Luke's, a peculiar ghostly sound. Alice is still stuck in the nursery class, mornings only. She's longing for January, when she goes up to the infants.

'I'm 'ungry, Mummy,' she says, then springs her skinny legs up against the yard wall in a handstand.

'Play nicely and I'll get you some bread and sugar.'

'Or you'll have your uncle Alec to answer to.'

I hadn't heard Alec come into the yard. He's like that. Always creeping up.

I spin round and attempt a smile. 'That's right,

Alice. Your uncle Alec don't want to come home to a racket.'

Alec is standing close behind me now, so close I can hear the wheeze of his chest.

'And it's ever so dark in the coal 'ole,' Alec says, winking and blowing a stream of fag smoke past my ear. 'Don't make me put you in there, little Alice.'

Alice doesn't say anything. She's still upside down, toes pressed against the brick wall. Her dress has fallen right over her head so that her drawers are on show. She'll be poking out her tongue underneath that skirt; I'd put money on it.

I turn to go inside, but Alec is blocking my path to the back door.

'Letter from George, is it?' he asks, nodding down at my hand.

'I haven't read it yet.' From the look on his face I reckon he expects me to open it there and then, read aloud so he's first in the picture. Nosy beggar. 'I'm saving it for the evening,' I say, 'once the kids are in bed.'

'Saving what?' calls Alice from under her dress.

'Never you mind.'

There's nothing for it but to brush past Alec. As I step towards him, though, he stands aside, bending low in a fancy bow like I'm some grand lady of the house and he's the footman.

'After you, madam,' he says, and though he keeps his hands to himself, I know he's looking at my backside. Sizing me up.

Alice and Teddy are tucked into bed. I stand

against the bedroom door, watching them now they've finally dropped off: little Teddy flat on his back with his arms clasped behind his head, snoring. He's the spit of George, with his high forehead and wide mouth, the bottom lip protruding in that gormless way George has. Alice is on her side, spine arched towards Teddy and a tangled curl draped over her cheek. There's a small palliasse on the floor where Alice is supposed to sleep, but she won't stay down there. 'Lumpy and cold,' she says. 'Spiders under the floorboards.' I want to tell her that spiders ain't the half of it, but best to keep my trap shut. So every night I find myself sharing the creaking iron bedstead with the two of them, squashed along one edge of the mattress. It's a good job the war has turned me so skinny. Can't even keep my wedding ring on my finger these days. I ought to nip in the waistband of my skirt, tighten the seams of my blouse, but I like my clothes loose. Loose means less for Alec to stare at.

Through the bedroom window I can see the banks of Bow Creek, thick mud gleaming in the September dusk. A rowing boat rocks on the water as an old man leans over, scooping up flotsam for winter firewood. If he leans any further, he'll be in the creek. He stretches slowly for a jagged plank, grasps it and bends his body back into the boat. Delicate, measured. He's an expert, this old boy. Understands the weight of things, the art of balance.

Beyond the creek rise the chimneys of the treacle refinery and the ironworks, black as the swelling tide. George is wrong. I'll never get used to living in Canning Town. I'm stranded out here, the wrong side of the water.

Downstairs, the front door slams. That'll be Alec, out to the pub. Now Jen will spend the evening getting the scullery straight; then she'll go up to bed with a warm milk if there's milk spare and a copy of the *Pictorial*. She'll blow out the candle when she hears Alec sway back home, steel herself for her husband, because if there's one thing she wants more than to be left alone, it's a baby.

Alice stirs as I shake creases from her pinafore and fold it over the end of the bedstead. I undress as quietly as I can, slip on my damp nightgown and pull it close around me to warm the cold cotton with my skin.

In the corner of the room is an upturned barrel that serves as a washstand. I've put George's unopened letter in an old toffee tin underneath the barrel. It's not much of a hiding place, but it's the best I can find. I don't think for one minute that Jen or Alec haven't unearthed that tin and had a good old poke around.

There's enough daylight to read by. I take the wash things off the barrel and slide the tin out. You can still smell toffees when you open the lid. George's letters are at the bottom, under my herb book with the flower remedies and the copy of *Barter's Guide to Beautiful Handwriting*. George promised he'd look at *Barter's*, but he never did, not once, so I always have to read his writing a few times before I can work out his peculiar spellings and the tiny letters that he squishes up so close. When I open this latest letter, a couple

31

of fag cards for Teddy drop out and a purple ribbon, which I guess is meant for Alice. Where he gets hold of these things in a war I couldn't say.

There's been a flare-up, George says, but it's all settled now. Nothing to worry about. *Hot sunshine and plenty of rashons*, he says. *The lads are a smashing bunch.*

2

The whore in the room next door is noisy tonight. Anyone would think she was enjoying herself. The thought intrigues him, which leads to the next thought, and then he can't help himself. Afterwards he washes in the freezing water that is still standing in the bowl from this morning. The cloth catches on a chip in the china and water sloshes over the sides. Now there are murky pools on the old wooden stand. He uses his cloth to wipe up the spill, though the washstand is already covered in watermarks and scratches: the carelessness of tenants past.

He is naked, but not cold, and the flush of his cheeks is still visible in the pocked oval mirror that hangs from the picture rail. The landlady was particularly proud of the mirror when she showed him round the room. 'Only two rooms has got a looking glass,' said Mrs Browne, stroking the curve of the oval so that the mirror rocked gently on its string. 'You can wash and brush up beautiful with this. Not that you need any help, fine-looking feller like you,' and then Mrs Browne appeared to wink.

The murmur of voices from the whore's room, the sound of a door closing quietly. He stands at the window to watch her customer leave the house. There is something confident in the soldier's step as he strides across the road, past the public baths and the bronze statue of a long-dead philanthropist patting his pet dog. The soldier's arms swing loosely by his sides; they are not drilled into coat pockets or wrapped around his body as if to deny the pleasure he has just taken. No, this punter may as well be whistling.

Gaslight shines on dewy cobbles. A cat picks its way across the road, pausing when it reaches the other side, its back arching so that he can see the silhouette of inky fur, raised in matted spikes. The cat twists down an alley near the railway station, its body so close to the blackened bricks that he soon loses sight of it.

The whore is now singing to herself. Sonia, was it, her name? Terrible tuneless voice, she has. He can't make out the melody. He wonders whether he should knock on the partition wall. Knock on her door, even? She'd make him welcome; he's sure of that. Sonia doesn't seem to be anyone's doxy; she is a free-trading tart, if such a thing exists. He counts out his money and doubts it will be enough. Another night, perhaps.

He takes his nightshirt from the back of the chair and shakes it. A large spider drops out and scuttles into a crevice between the skirting and the floorboards. Bad time of year for spiders. So many creatures coming in from the cold.

The candle is very low now, but there should be enough light to read for an hour, perhaps two. Then it will be dawn, and if he still cannot sleep, there will be light from the window. Next to his bed is a stack of tattered volumes: books he has bought or bartered; books he has been given by Lady Tolland; books he has borrowed but intends to return.

He sleeps, finally, and dreams of Esther. Her hair has turned wavy in the rain, and she is standing in Lady Tolland's garden, rocking the third baby. He calls, but she seems not to hear, and then she wades into the lake, the autumn-brown reeds catching on her skirts, her sleeves, the baby's feet, as they disappear under the surface.

3

On Wednesday I walk over to Poplar to call in on Mum and Dad. Jen's keeping an eye on the kids. Dad's not so good and Mum doesn't like the children to see him when he's ill.

They live in a tenement block now, on the fourth floor. It's only half a mile from where we grew up, but it feels a world away from the Ellesmere Street terrace with its sunny backyard where Dad would grow vegetables and flowers in half-barrels filled with earth. Sometimes Mum complained about the barrels – they took up too much room, she said, got in the way of the washing when it was drying on the line – but she loved the flowers all right, dainty snowdrop posies in February, daffodils in March and by August the brazen sunflowers growing taller than the privy roof.

My breath starts to catch as I reach the fourth floor. I hate to think of Mum and Dad perched up here with so many stairs to climb. There's danger in these tall buildings; you only have to look at the rusting banisters, the rough plaster over the stairwell cracks. They have their own front door at least. It's quieter than usual on the landing, only the drip of a pipe from the communal tap.

'Mum,' I call, soft as I can, because Dad might be sleeping.

The key turns in the lock and Mum appears, an index finger pressed to her lips. She steps out onto the landing.

I glimpse Dad through the half-open door. He's curled in his bed under the tiny window, his back to me. It's only a week since I last saw him, but he looks shrunken. On top of his blanket is the rag rug from the floor. He must have felt cold in the night. This person, it isn't really my dad. It's a kind of dumb creature, something wounded you have to care for. It's not even a proper ailment – rheumatism or heart trouble or the gallstones that killed Dor's dad. 'Nerve weakness' was old Dr Evans's diagnosis. Then there was the fancy doctor who had a fancy name for Dad's condition but no cure either. 'Circular insanity,' Mr Bloor-Stephenson said, and that's all we got for our two pounds.

'Shocking night,' whispers Mum. '"The crows,"
he kept saying. "The crows. They're leaving the
tower." And he was trying to get out of bed,
crawling over to the door. I had to hide the key in
the end. He's asleep now, thank God.' She fingers
the gold chain round her neck. 'It's no good,
Hannah – I'm going to have to take him down
there again.' With the back of her hand she wipes
her eyes; they seem to have sunk even further
into her face, red-rimmed, with oil in the
wrinkles where she's rubbed in her ointment.
'But it's jam-packed down there, I'm told. Full of
soldiers. Some of them don't recognize their own
mothers. Do you remember Ciss from Ellesmere
Street, Hannah – Ciss with the piano? Her boy
Peter is in a terrible way. I saw her on the tram
and she was half mad herself with the worry.'

It upsets me to think of it. I was fond of Peter
before I went up west. When I was barely fourteen
and he was a couple of years older, he winded me
with a snowball the year of the heavy snow. He
put his arm round my shoulder till I got my
breath back and for months I would conjure him
in my daydreams, imagine him playing piano for
me, his delicate fingers on the keys. It's terrible to
picture him in that hospital, the bright white walls
that hide so much darkness. And then I think of
George. If he came back touched, I have no idea
how I'd manage, what sort of a wife I'd be.

'Peter was always a nervy sort,' says Mum. 'Not
like your George. You heard from him?'

'There was a letter on Monday. He seems to be
all right. Hot sun and plenty of rations, he said.'

'Well, let's be thankful for that.'

'And I've just got a job, Mum, in a cafe down Cubitt Town. Called in Monday and went back yesterday and they offered it to me there and then. Waitressing and kitchen work, meals included...'

She's staring off into the distance beyond the railings. There's no view to speak of, only the rows of greasy windows and the shifting grey laundry of the tenements opposite. I'm not sure if she's heard a word I said about the job. Her hands are clasped together, crooked and knobbled from working the Singer.

'Mum? Waitressing work. So there'll be a bit more money coming in. I can help you and Dad out.'

'You'll do no such thing,' she says, facing me now. 'You'll keep every penny for those children. I won't have them going short.' She shivers and pulls the rolled-up sleeves of her blouse back down to her wrists. 'You'd better come in for a cup of tea. Dad's bound to wake up soon and he'll want to see you.'

I wonder if that's true. Last week he barely seemed to know me. But I follow Mum inside. The room is tidy – Mum is forever fussing around – but however hard she works at keeping the place decent, somehow the squalor blows in. Newspaper is laid over the floor to keep the draughts down. Mould creeps from a corner near the window. Behind the front door, piles of finished shirts are folded neatly into tailors' boxes. She's been busy, trying to keep up the rent on this wretched room.

Mum strikes a match for the gas and Dad starts

awake. He sits up in bed and wipes a dried crust of saliva from his mouth. He blinks at me. 'Beatrice?' he says. 'Whatever are you thinking of?'

4

Dor calls round on her way back from work. Says she can't face going home because her mum's in an evil mood and the little ones are driving her spare. She's the eldest of seven – two girls and five boys – and no dad because of the gallstones.

'Spare any milk?' she says. She's never shy to ask for anything, but that's one of the best things about Dor. She knows how to stand up for herself. She wasn't afraid to stand up for me either when we were at school. I was the smallest in the infants' class, only came up to Peg Riddle's armpit, whereas Dor could stare Peg down any day of the week.

I pour half a cup of milk into a glass. Alice and Teddy crowd round Dor in the scullery. They're hoping she'll twirl them round or make them laugh with one of her daft rhymes, but I tell them to hop it because it's time for bed.

'It's still day!' moans Alice, dangling a cat's-cradle string from her thumb.

'And soon it will be night. Now toddle off and leave us in peace.'

Dor has gulped her milk before we've even sat down in the parlour. Jen looks up from her mending and manages a smile. Dor opens her mouth as if to say hello, but a loud burp comes out. She's always burping. She eats too quick, drinks too quick, talks too quick. 'Pardon me,' she laughs, patting her chest through the brown overalls. Her hands are the colour of custard. Dor notices Jen staring.

'It's the dynamite,' she says, holding her hands out and turning them over, like she's wearing an expensive engagement ring we're supposed to admire. 'At least it don't bring me out in a rash, though. Some of the girls are suffering terrible. What about me 'air, then?' She takes off her cap, pulls the pins from her hair and shakes it loose. There are bright yellow streaks all the way through.

'I like it, Dor, very glamorous,' I say. Her hair does look pretty. Makes up for the strange tint to her skin.

'Good, ain't it? Not so good if you're grey, though. Grey hair turns green.'

'So I've heard,' says Jen.

'But as for ginger, I ain't sure, Jenny. I'll keep me eye out and let you know.' Dor burps again.

Jen stiffens and folds her mending into the basket. She never has warmed to Dor, not since the family became neighbours in Ellesmere Street all those years ago.

'I'll leave you to it,' says Jen, and disappears into the scullery. There's a loud clanking as she takes the dirty pans out to the yard.

'I've never known backache like it,' says Dor, sinking down into Jen's chair and circling her shoulders so that you can hear little cracking noises in her bones.

I sit on the hearth rug.

'You found a job, then?' asks Dor.

'Waitressing in Cubitt Town three days a week, meals included.'

'You've struck lucky there, Hannah. Shame you couldn't get anything closer, though.'

'I don't mind the walk. Clears my head after I've been cooped up with the children.'

'Know what you mean,' she says, rolling her eyes. But she doesn't know what I mean. You can't truly know about children until you've had your own. Brothers and sisters are all very well, but it's not the same. I can't help envying Dor sometimes, all the freedom she has. It seemed like the end of the world when Len threw her over – on a postcard from the training camp like that too – but now I reckon she's well rid. She doesn't have to worry about Len being blown to pieces in France, or coming back gaga, or spending the rest of his life with stumps for legs.

Dor reaches into her overalls pocket and pulls out a tin of Nut Brown. There are five cigarettes in there, some a bit ragged and some fatter than others because Dor is still getting the hang of rolling them.

'Got a light?' she asks. 'They won't let us take matches in the factory.'

'Should think not.' I look at the yellow gunpowder under her fingernails.

'I have washed them, you know,' she says. 'This is as clean as they get. Don't worry – I'm not going to explode on you. Then again...' She lifts her backside from the chair. 'Nah, let you off this time.' She sits back into the seat, laughing.

40

I strike a match to the end of her cigarette, pretending to be cross. 'Whenever are you going to learn to be ladylike, Dor? No wonder Len dropped you.'

'I was *always* a lady with him,' she says, winking. 'A perfect lady.' She holds her cigarette with her wrist bent outwards, takes a drag and blows out the smoke with her lips all pouty like a film star. Then her shoulders slump and suddenly she has a sulk on. She didn't want to be reminded of Len, of the fact she's single again.

'You'll soon find someone else, Dor.'

'Fat chance when there's nothing but grand-dads and invalids left in the whole of bloody London.'

'Seemed to me there were plenty of decent fellers down on the Isle of Dogs.'

Dor sits forward in her seat. 'That right?' she says. 'Dockers, you mean?'

'Cafe is full of them. I wasn't taking much notice, of course, but it struck me that some of them were younger men. Dock work is protected, you know.'

Dor gives me one of her dry smiles. 'I do know, lovey. That's what your George told you, wasn't it, until he took it upon himself to join up anyway. What was her name? Pavlova?'

'Pandora.' She's got me back for mentioning Len. 'My point is, Dor, there are still plenty of men out there. You want to come down the cafe and see for yourself. I'll give you extra sugar in your tea if you promise not to show me up.' As soon as I've said it, I wonder whether I should have kept quiet. I'm not sure what Mrs Stephens

41

would make of Dor.

She laughs and stubs out her cigarette. 'I might just wander down there next week. Best behaviour, I promise.'

I can't sleep for the song circling in my head, droning in time to Teddy's snores. It's Dor's fault for reminding me of Pandora. I try my usual trick for dropping off, which is to recite the rhymes from *Barter's*: '*Let all your letters slope alike and equalize your distance/Attention pay to form and size and you'll need slight assistance.*' It's no use, though – the tune keeps coming back – so I give in to the memory, the words of the song they struck up at the music hall that night, '*We Don't Want to Lose You, But We Think You Ought to Go*'.

November 1915, it was, a cold night nearly a year ago. The children were playing outside before tea: Teddy just walking, toddling around with his chubby legs, holding on to Alice's pinafore and covering it in mucky fingerprints. George seemed excited when he came back from the sawmill, and there was an ale moustache above his lip. It wasn't like him to go drinking after work. His jacket was slung over his shoulder, and his waistcoat was opened so that you could see his saggy braces.

'Get your glad rags on, Hannah, love,' he grinned. 'You and me's going out tonight. Free singsong down at the Queen's.'

'You what?' I dropped a half-peeled potato back into the bowl. 'What about the children?'

We were living in Poplar then. Two rooms in a basement in Alton Street, clean and not too damp.

'One of the girls upstairs will mind them.'

I hadn't been to the Queen's since before Teddy was born. Hadn't done much at all except clean and cook and mind the children and worry about Dad.

'Go on, then. I'll knock and see if Mary's about.' I tugged at the bow of my apron and I felt a little giddy as the strings came free.

It was dark as we walked to the Queen's, the street lamps all dimmed and no sign of the moon. In front of us, a couple giggled, arm in arm. George reached out and held my hand. I squeezed his fingers and thought that life wasn't too bad.

'Perfect night for a Zeppelin,' said George.

'Thanks. Just when I was starting to enjoy myself.' I looked up into the darkness. You don't see them until they're upon you, fat black ghost ships, droning in the sky.

'Nah, we're all right. It's been quiet for a few weeks. Reckon we've scared the Germans off. The war's going our way.'

It was odd to hear George express an opinion like that. He was generally quiet about the war or politics or union matters, never chatty at all, in fact, unless you got him started on different types of hardwood or the best way to fit a chine to the end of a barrel. Still, I hoped he was right about the war, and I tried not to look too closely as we passed another street-corner shrine, the wilting posies and the chalked-up names of dead sons and husbands.

When we arrived, the theatre was nearly full. We sat near the back, George on the central aisle and me next to him, with a girl I'd known from school on my left. Mabel Murray was her name, and she was a year or so older than me. At school Mabel always had terrible breath, which she tried to mask by sucking humbugs. Now she smiled and her teeth were brown as boot leather, and sure enough, there was the whiff of humbugs.

'Hannah White!' she said.

'Hannah Loxwood now.'

Mabel raised her eyebrows, took a sidelong glance at George and then settled back in her seat. 'We'll soon sort the men from the boys,' she said. She opened her hand to show me a fistful of white feathers, then nodded towards the red velvet curtain across the stage. There was a soldier standing by a little door at the side of the stage. He was a high-up, I guessed, because his uniform was bright with medals and stripes. He was beaming out at the audience, ever so friendly-looking. The side door opened and several more soldiers marched out, the one at the front banging a drum. There was no spotlight on these soldiers; they just filed into line and stood on the auditorium floor in front of the orchestra. Evidently we were in for a patriotic night. Bloody impossible to escape the war.

The theatre fell silent as the curtain rose and there at the centre of the stage was the most glamorous woman I'd ever seen, all done up in sequins and feathers, beautiful shiny hair with a diamond clip that made you blink, it was so dazzling. The compère came onto the stage in his bow tie.

'Ladies and gentlemen, we have a rare treat for you tonight. Please welcome our special guests of honour from the London Regiment. And not for-

44

getting our very own ... our ravishingly talented ... Pandora Pavelle!'

I looked at George and of course his eyes were popping. This Pandora Pavelle didn't leave much to the imagination. She started the show with 'God Save the King', then disappeared into the wings. We all sat down and the next act came on – a sword-swallower who somehow guzzled a bayonet. A second-rate magician followed; then Pandora was back, draped in a Union Jack this time and holding a small tin shield across her chest. She started on the patriotic songs: 'Rule Britannia', 'It's a Long Way to Tipperary' and then a new one I'd heard drifting from the pubs and sung in the crowds when the recruits marched down Poplar High Street: 'We Don't Want to Lose You, But We Think You Ought to Go'. Whether that's the title or not, I couldn't say, but that's the line you remember. One of the dancers strutted onto the stage with a board showing all the words, so that the audience could sing along.

It's easy for us women
To stay at home and shout,
But remember, there's a duty
To the men who first went out.
The odds against that handful
Were nearly four to one,
And we cannot rest
Until it's man for man
And gun for gun.
And every woman's duty
Is to see that duty done!

45

During this last song the soldiers put up trestle tables at the front of the stage, the chorus girls still singing behind them. Then Pandora Pavelle waltzed right down into the audience and began inviting the men onto the stage. Dozy cow I must be, because I took a moment to clock what was happening, namely that the men were supposed to walk up to the trestle tables and sign up for France there and then. I elbowed George, ready to raise my eyebrows, to grumble at the cheek of it, but he was too busy watching Pandora walking slowly down the aisle, smiling and beckoning, arse swaying, the tin shield now strung on a strap across her shoulder and her pink cleavage quivering above the sequinned bustier. One by one the men stood up and filed onto the stage – even a few clapped-out old boys and a tiny chap with a built-up shoe who was never going to stand a chance. I recognized some of them – Ernest Taylor from the chandler's near North Street and Tom Steer who once went out with Dor. Occasionally you'd see a man shake his head at Pandora, mutter something you couldn't hear, and every time that happened Mabel twitched her fistful of feathers.

I felt smug at that moment, knowing we'd got a free night out but George wouldn't be signing anything because he was already doing his bit down at the docks. *Starred occupation, crucial for the war effort.* We couldn't care less if Mabel dropped him one of her stupid feathers.

What a fool I was.

When Pandora touched George on the shoulder, he couldn't get out of his seat quick enough.

He said nothing to me, just a too-hard squeeze of my knee as he stood to attention. His chair seat flipped upright and I felt the vibrations shudder down my back. Off he went, following Pandora up the aisle, while the orchestra reprised the national anthem to round off the night.

Mabel leaned in towards me and the brims of our hats clashed.

'Good on 'im,' she said, nodding towards George. He was in the spotlight now, pen in hand.

I looked at her and I thought I had never seen anyone so grotesque. She was like a wild animal with her blazing eyes.

And so it was all decided. We would give up Alton Street and I would move in with Jen and Alec – for company, and to economize. It was what families did, George said, and Jen would help with the children, which would be nice for her, wouldn't it, seeing as how she didn't seem to be popping out any of her own.

Now, here we are. Squashed up in the back bedroom. Teddy stirs and I turn to face him, propped on my elbow. I stroke the softness of his right eyebrow. Little Teddy, don't ever be a soldier.

5

The smooth water shivers as he sinks his cloth into the washbowl. Outside, a blackbird sings, though dawn is still an hour away. He rubs pomade into his palms and attempts to tame his hair. Perhaps Sonia has a pair of scissors he could borrow. He resolves to ask her, next time they pass in the hall.

The photograph of Esther is propped on a small shelf under the mirror. She is seated on a straight-backed chair, a vase of wilting marigolds on a table at her side, and a space behind the chair where he should have been standing. When he had arrived at the studio an hour late, another family was busy brushing up and straightening clothes in the full-length glass. 'Your wife left several minutes ago,' said the photographer's assistant, his smile disdainful as he handed a comb to a fussing young mother.

Now the damp of the lodging room is leaving its mark. The photograph has curled at the sides, casting an extra shadow on Esther's face. It troubles him to see the shadow, because there was nothing Esther liked more than to sit on a park bench, tilting her face towards the sun. He remembers the day they met – Victoria Park, Whit Sunday 1910, a few days after the old king's funeral. Most of the girls at the picnic were dressed in black, but Esther was wearing a pale blue shawl over her navy dress. She seemed different to the others and he was glad when Arthur introduced her: a cousin who'd recently moved to London from Leighton Buzzard, a secretary for the GPO. He liked her low, straight eyebrows, her intelligent smile, and it didn't seem to matter that she looked older than him. Esther was different. She was interesting.

He takes the photograph down from the shelf and tries to smooth the curled edges, but the

48

shadows persist, so he slides Esther into the brown envelope in his trunk, alongside her death certificate and the bracelet he is saving for little Maddie.

He dresses quickly, making as little noise as possible because he would hate to wake Sonia. She was busy last night, he couldn't help hearing. He ties a white neckerchief in a loose knot, then buttons his waistcoat. At the window, he rubs a pane of misted glass with the hem of his jacket. The blackbird is still singing, a puffed silhouette perched on the lopsided rowan tree that grows on a patch of green next to the baths. The bird stiffens suddenly, sleeks down his feathers and flies off towards the church.

At Beaumont's yard, he joins the queue of men at the gate.

'Mornin',' says Bryn, and there is that tone again, the sarcastic edge to his voice. 'Read anyfing good lately?'

Shears, one of the older men, snorts a laugh.

'Give us a poem, then.'

He smiles, tries to think nothing of it. They're a friendly lot, in the main. Don't mean any harm. Still, he knows he'll never fit in here, same as everywhere else. Aunt Winch had a word for him. 'Queer,' he once heard her say. 'He's a queer one all right. I blame Lady Tolland for turning his head.'

He wonders about that summer in Dorset. It would have been better, perhaps, if he had never gone, if he had run off down his mate Robbo's shed when Aunt Winch had told him to pack his best short trousers and a set of clean underwear because they were going on a journey. But he had wanted to go on a journey, of course he had. He'd never been further than the seaside on a charabanc.

Aunt Winch no longer worked for Lady Tolland, but as she was once a favourite, she had been asked to accompany the lady on a visit to the country. They would be staying with Lady Tolland's sister close to the Devon border. They were to travel by train, and he was old enough not to be a nuisance. He could even help carry the bags.

Lady Tolland and Aunt Winch sat in a first-class compartment, while he travelled in second class, bread and drip tied up in a handkerchief and a Red Ralph book he'd swapped with Robbo slotted into the pocket of his shorts. The woman in the seat opposite sighed when the train pulled out of Waterloo and crunched hard on a boiled sweet. He took out the Red Ralph story.

He'd read the book twice by the time the train reached Basingstoke. Then there was nothing for it but to sit staring at the soft hills, the dribbles of rain swerving around the window glass as the train swayed along the track.

At Salisbury, Aunt Winch woke him with a tug on his ear.

'Wipe yer mouth,' she whispered. 'Drooling like a baby, you are. Now listen, Lady Tolland says you're to come and see her. Says she's bored, though I don't know what good you'll be to her. Best behaviour, now – don't go showing me up.'

He followed his aunt into the private compartment where Lady Tolland sat with her hands clasped in her lap. Her black dress looked creased and dusty, and the hem was coming down. He wondered why Lady Tolland still mourned her husband, the man who had caused such a scandal. Perhaps the black dress was the only one she could afford.

'Ah, young man. How are you enjoying the journey?' The gold brooch at her throat glinted as she spoke. A tiny pearl was missing from the cluster in the centre.

'Very well, thank you, ma'am.'

'And how have you been occupying yourself?'

'I read me book and then I fell asleep.' Aunt Winch glared at him. 'My book. Ma'am.'

Lady Tolland laughed. 'Quite. I have also finished my book. It's too sad when a book comes to an end, especially a book that one has enjoyed. Don't you agree?'

He nodded. 'Oh yes, ma'am. But you can always read 'em again. I read 'em a hundred times over.'

Lady Tolland looked thoughtful. She reached into a large leather portmanteau resting on the seat beside her.

'I have an idea. Shall we swap? I will lend you my book and you may lend me yours.'

Aunt Winch cut in. 'Oh no, ma'am. It's only a grubby old penny horrible he's reading. It's not what you'd call ... *li-tritch-er*. As it were.'

He wanted to laugh at the way Aunt Winch's chin poked forward when she spoke to Lady Tolland. Her words came out differently too – a fake accent, pretend posh. It curled his toes to hear it.

Lady Tolland raised her eyebrows at Aunt Winch and he noticed there was the trace of a smile on her pale lips. She pulled a thick bound volume from her bag. 'I must say this is rather horrible, and it cost a lot more than a penny. Mr Hardy's latest, quite chilling. How old are you now, boy?'

'Nearly twelve.'

She paused for a moment. 'So tall – I thought you were older. Still, I believe you may be just old enough. Here.'

She offered the book, but as he reached out, she drew her hand away. 'Our agreement, remember? You must fetch me your book first.'

He pulled the worn copy from his shorts pocket. The paper on the narrow spine was torn, and there was a streak of grey fluff stuck to the cover. He brushed the book before offering it to Lady Tolland. The fluff stuck fast, but he handed it over anyway.

She smiled as she read the title aloud. '*Adventures of Red Ralph*. How exciting, and just as I was drooping with boredom. Thank you very much.' She handed him her book. 'And here is my side of the bargain.'

He took her book with both hands and stared at the cover. *Jude the Obscure*. He said the title aloud and then repeated it in his head. He did not understand the meaning of the words, but he liked the sound of them: *Jude the Obscure*, heavy and rhythmic, rolling with the carriage.

'Manners,' Aunt Winch mouthed.

He bowed and thanked Lady Tolland, backed out of the compartment and hurried down the train to find his seat.

How exhilarated he felt, how important, as he sat with the heavy book opened on his lap, 'Mr Hardy's latest', and the woman opposite sniffing as if she couldn't care less.

At the end of his shift he leaves Beaumont's and wanders into the nearest pub, buys a pint of stout and chooses a small meat pie from the tray on the counter. He takes the table in the corner, away from the heat of the fire, and pulls a book from his jacket pocket.

The novel is not a good one, the prose flat and repetitive so that he finds it difficult to concentrate. Is it the writing, or is it him? Perhaps it is not possible to surrender to a story in the way he did when he was a boy. He thinks again of *Jude the Obscure*, of the cold, disbelieving horror that made him sick in the woods behind the Dorset house. He'd read the book in three days, creeping into the woods when his aunt thought he was playing in the field with the dairy farmer's sons.

Aunt Winch had told him not to bother Lady Tolland, but he wanted to return *Jude the Obscure* in person. Perhaps he might even feel bold enough to ask her opinion. He couldn't sleep with the whole thing in his head, the very sight of a cupboard door making his food rise with the memory of the babies and Little Father Time, their limp bodies hanging from two hooks and a sturdy nail.

He found his moment after breakfast one morning, when Lady Tolland was walking around the garden. She had stopped to admire a white flowered shrub, and as he edged to her side, the book clutched in both hands, she turned and smiled.

'Such a delicate hydrangea,' she said. 'The petals are like babies' fingernails.'

He swallowed hard, glanced up at the hydrangea and tried not to think of the fingernails.

'I'm returning the book, Lady Tolland. I'm very grateful for the borrow, thank you.'

'You have finished it already? And what is your opinion?'

'I ... I...' He had wanted *her* opinion. 'I did like it, but it was very tragic. I was wondering, ma'am: why would Mr Hardy imagine such terrible things?'

'I hope the answer is always beyond your knowing.'

'Because it ain't true, is it? The hangings?'

'Who can know? Who can know what poverty and shame may bestow?' Then she bent to sniff the bloom, holding the hydrangea stem between her thumb and forefinger. Her mood seemed to change as she waved her black-gloved hand at the book and, with the same gesture, motioned him away towards the house.

'There's no need to return it to me out here. Lay it on the hall table, would you, and have Immy take it up to my room?'

'Yes, ma'am,' he said. At the mention of Immy's name, he felt a hot blush spread through his body. He bowed and began to walk away, but she called out again.

'If you wish, I'll see to it that you may read from my sister's library during your stay. You'll find a great variety in there.'

In his head there was a kind of reverse explosion: a thousand fragments of possibility soldering into one.

6

I write to George every week, like I promised, but there's been nothing from him for a while now, not even a postcard. You bump into other soldiers' wives and often they'll lower their voices, all confidential, start saying how much they miss the old man and how they're ill with the worry. I join in, of course, say the same things, but the honest truth is, I'm not ill with the worry. I miss him in some ways, it's true. I miss our own rooms. I miss him for the children's sake. But there's plenty I don't miss: his fingers inching up my nightdress, his wet lips kissing me on a Saturday night.

I stoke up the stove and refill the second kettle so that everything is in order when Mrs Stephens comes down from her rest. She's put a fresh pinny on, but when she smiles, there's a strand of beef trapped between her front teeth. I don't say anything, just smile back.

'Many in?' she asks.

'Only a handful.'

'Mondays is always quiet. And it's still raining. You'll get the tram home today?'

I shrug. 'I'll end up soaked just walking to the stop. Might as well save me money.'

'Tell you what...' she says, and disappears back upstairs.

I squeeze out the cloth and wipe down the tables, not that they really need it. It makes me jump when the bell over the door rings and Mr Blake walks in.

'Just a coffee today, Mrs Loxwood,' he says.

He doesn't have a newspaper; instead he pulls a letter from his jacket pocket and starts reading. When I place his cup on the table, he says thank you in an absent-minded kind of way that makes me feel invisible.

'Mrs Loxwood?' he calls.

I turn back to face him, pulling out my pad because I suppose he'll be wanting food after all.

He looks up at me and for the first time I see the details of him. Such truthful eyes. Brown eyes, same as mine, but there are slants of yellow like golden spokes, beautiful as sunlight.

The sound of rain in the street is insistent, pressing.

'Ain't it ... terrible weather?' he says.

'Ain't it?'

I can feel the pulse in my finger as it grips the pencil. Mr Blake's eyes move from my face to my hands. He opens his mouth to speak.

The door to Mrs Stephens's flat bangs and she appears behind the counter. 'You can borrow this,' she says, waving a black umbrella with an ivory handle. 'Now off you pop – it's well past three.'

Mr Blake resumes his reading of the letter. I walk through to the back to collect my coat.

By the time I get to Blackwall, I'm already soaked through, and the vicious easterly has turned Mrs Stephens's umbrella inside out. At the approach to the tunnel, there's a commotion involving a horse tethered up to a van. The horse doesn't want to go in the tunnel, keeps dancing to the side and rearing up, until the back doors of the van fly open and several crates smash out, dumping vegetables across the road. Beetroot, I think, but it's hard to be sure with the rain and the wind battering my face. The driver is trying to calm the horse, leaning in to stroke him, but you can tell the animal is too spooked and he's going to have a hell of a job getting him through to Greenwich. What do you expect without blinkers? That horse isn't stupid.

Truth is, I've never been through the tunnel myself, although I did once *try*.

I must have been five and Jen would have been eight. The tunnel had just opened: on the day of the ceremony we'd seen the royal carriage go past on the dock road and we'd heard the band playing at the rec. Next morning, Sunday, Jen had shaken me from sleep in the bed we shared. 'Wake up,' she whispered, poking her toenails into my ankle for good measure. 'Wake up – we're going on an adventure.'

We left Ellesmere Street ten minutes later, telling Mum we were calling on Granny Hinton, who lived a couple of roads away. We walked right down to the high street, past Poplar Workhouse, where the shadowy windows seemed to have their sights fixed on me. Beyond the workhouse lay East India Dock, its sharp crane hooks

57

and black masts scratching at the sky.

Jen knew I was frightened to walk past the workhouse, but she told me I had to keep going. I wondered if Ruby from the infant school was still in there. Her beautiful black curls all shaved off; that's what they were saying in the playground.

'Scaredy-cat, scaredy-cat, don't know what you're looking at,' Jen chanted, dropping my hand and rushing ahead, so that I had no choice but to follow her along the street, chasing up Robin Hood Lane until the tunnel entrance was in sight. We stood and gawped as a carriage was swallowed into the wide black mouth.

Jen stared at a sign screwed to the red brick of the tunnel gatehouse.

'"Ped-er…"'

'"Pedestrians,"' I said.

She gave me an evil look, then put her hands in her pinafore pockets. 'D'you think we have to pay? Well, we ain't got no money, so we'll just have to chance it. Come on.'

Jen crouched down past the gatehouse window, in case there was someone inside. I was little: I didn't need to crouch. Down the stone spiral staircase we went, into the gloom. The tunnel was lit by flickering electric lamps and the shadows were like coal heaps, sliding and trembling. We were used to smells, the stink of the docks and the factory chimneys, but this was a new kind of smell. There was something so heavy about it, close, like a poisoned rag smothering your face. Again, I wanted to turn back, but Jen held my hand, dragging me on.

'Wally Mills dared me,' she said. 'He's done it twice already. We 'as to count how many electric lamps is on the walls, for proof. Three so far.'

Then came the water. A small drop of water, which fell from the high arched roof onto the top of my nose.

'Can it rain in a tunnel, Jen?'

'What you on about?'

'There's water falling, on me nose.'

Jen turned round, saw the drop trickling down my nose and cackled. 'The Drink's coming in,' she laughed. 'We're all gonna drown!'

The Drink. That meant the sea, the river, the whole bottomless swirl of it, and I knew for sure that all those walls were cracking and the weight of the Thames was about to come crashing down. I turned round and ran, back up the spiral staircase, each breath a sharp pinch, and the sound of Jen's laughter echoing behind.

'Easy, easy.' Now the van driver is walking the spooked horse round in circles, tugging at the bridle to keep his head down so he can't see the tunnel entrance. Some of the beetroot are mashed into the road, pink and muddy, and others have rolled away. A girl runs out from the Tunnel Gardens, swipes a beetroot from a puddle. She shoves it into her pinafore pocket and runs off, startling the horse again as she flashes past.

Alice and Teddy are with a crowd of other children, larking and screeching at the end of the street near the railway line. They're wet through and I can't believe Jen has let them out in this weather. Teddy will catch it with his chest. He's always the first to sicken. When Alice sees me, she runs over, Teddy following, his Ducky wobbling from the waistband of his breeches.

'We found a dead rat, biggest ever,' says Alice.

'All opened up,' Teddy adds, his voice high-pitched, almost hysterical. 'All bleurghy and red.'

'Did you touch it, Teddy?' I try to smile a little. If I sound too cross, he won't tell the truth.

'Alice poked it with a stick. White bits came out.'

'Back to the house, both of you. Where's your Auntie Jen?'

'With Nana,' says Alice. 'Nana came round crying and they had to go off.'

'Go off where?'

'Don't know.' Alice is sulky now, slouching towards the house.

'Don't take on, Alice – I ain't got the energy. Get in the yard.'

Teddy cries while I'm washing his hands. The bar of Sunlight is thin with a sharp edge and when I drop it, it slips straight down the grate. Alice laughs, hopping from one foot to the other in her maddening way.

'Wait there,' I tell them. There's another bar in the scullery, cracked and yellow, but too big at least to disappear underground. I look around for a note from Jen, but there's nothing. Nothing in the hall either, behind the button box. On the parlour table is a cup of tea that hasn't been touched, as if Jen has left in a tearing hurry.

My first thought is to take off to the tenements to try to find Mum, drag the kids along with me.

But it will be dark soon and there's every chance we'd cross paths, end up in a worse muddle. Teddy's little teeth are chattering, and Alice is still hopping around, asking me questions I can't answer, like 'When is Auntie Jen back?' and 'Why was Nana crying?' I get them indoors, strip off their damp clothes and tell them to warm up in bed while their things are drying.

Before long they're messing about, Alice singing and the floorboards banging. I'm about to go upstairs, calm them, when there's a knock on the parlour window and a 'Yoo-hoo.'

Dor.

She comes round the back into the scullery, dripping wet. 'Jen sent me,' she says.

'It's Dad, ain't it?'

She nods, taking off her wet coat and draping it over the mop handle behind the door. She follows me into the parlour.

'What's happened?'

'Disappeared this morning. Your mum popped down the market, forgot to lock up and he walked right out.' She sits in the armchair by the range, reaches into her skirt pocket for her cigarette tin.

'And?' My heart starts knocking. In my head, there's a picture of Beatrice: the poppy-out fish eyes, the purple claws for hands.

'And your mum spent hours looking in the usual places – Ellesmere Street, where she called on me, the workshop – till she ended up at the nick and sure enough they had him in the cells. Public disturbance, they said.'

'But they can't... He's ill!'

'It's all right. They haven't charged him with

nothing. They've sent him to the nuts' ward at the hospital. Jen's gone with your mum to take his things.'

Upstairs, Teddy starts to howl. Alice taunts him. 'Crybaby,' she says. 'Stupid baby.'

'I'll go and sort the kids out,' says Dor, sliding the unlit cigarette behind her ear. 'Jen and your mum'll be home soon. You make some tea.' She nods at the kettle on the stove.

Dor cheers the kids up in no time and has them singing one of her silly songs.

'Have a banana!' Alice starts shouting.

Teddy giggles. ''Nana, 'nana,' he chants.

I stand watching the kettle, and the main thing is that I feel terribly guilty, because I haven't been round to see Dad since before I started at the cafe. The sight of him that day – a dumb creature under a blanket – it did something to me, gave me a queer feeling low down, like my insides were curling up.

Above the mantelpiece, three pictures hang in a column, smoke-stained from the range. I take them down one by one and rub the glass with my sleeve. The first photograph shows Mum and Dad standing behind Jen and me, the four of us wearing our best clothes and Mum in her two strings of imitation pearls. Jen and I are sitting together on a wooden bench, my boots swinging, hers pointing down, the tips just touching the floor. It's 1900. I remember the date because that's why we had the picture taken. 'To mark the turn of the century,' Dad had said, though at the age of eight I didn't care too much for the turn of the century. It sounded like something old and creaky – hardly worth celebrating, or getting pulled into best clothes for, having to stand still while the man disappeared under the cloak of his camera.

The next photograph is Jen and Alec on their wedding day, seven years later, Jen aged seventeen. She is wearing a high collar of lace and a brooch at her throat that looks as if it's killing her. Alec seemed handsome then, in his skinny way. I didn't blame Jen for marrying him. We all thought Alec was a catch, a bit of class from the city with a rag-trade fortune he reckoned to inherit. The charm wore off and the fortune was lost, but give him his dues: he brings in a wage every week – his 'commission', as he calls it. I've never quite found out what he does for a living, but to my knowledge, he's never been behind with the rent.

The last photograph shows me and George on our wedding day, February 1912. Of course, it's only our heads and shoulders that's showing because we had to keep my middle out of view. I held the posy of flowers over my stomach, camomile and fern, with gardenias for purity, a gift from Jen at the last minute. 'Just my little joke,' said Jen. 'No need to look so po-faced.'

Dad had been ill for a few years by then, but he managed to come to our wedding. Oh yes, I'll never forget Dad at my wedding. He was high as a kite – one of his maniacal moods, the mood that always comes before the melancholy. All through the service he talked and mumbled, and at the end he shouted, 'Bravo!' and clapped his hands as if he'd just watched a turn at the music hall.

I spray a fine layer of spit on the glass of the photo – *pfft, pffft* – like I'm cleaning shoes, then rub at it until our faces shine out. Do I miss you, George? I stare at your long, straight nose and your pale skin, smooth like a boy's. What children we are, in this picture. I blush to think of our wedding night, how awkward we were together. We lay apart on the cold sheets. George didn't touch me on account of my condition, though Dor had told me that it was perfectly safe – she had a married friend who'd read it in a book – and in fact I ought to make the most of it because I couldn't fall for another child all the time I was expecting. But how could I tell George that, even if I'd wanted him to touch me? It would have embarrassed us both to talk of such things. Instead I asked him what his dreams were, his ambitions. He replied he'd need to think about it; what were mine? There was no point saying a clerking job, a job where I could use my brain and write words on paper, because no office would have me now that I was married. So I told him my ambition was to be a good mother to our baby. And a good wife, I added, and he patted the top of my shoulder through my cotton night-dress. 'The same,' he said. 'A good dad and husband. Here's to Mr and Mrs Loxwood.' I lay awake after that listening to the tick of our new mantel clock, a present from Mum and Dad. The clock struck eleven, a dull chime, and George began to snore.

Footsteps skip down the stairs and Dor re-appears in the parlour. I hang the photograph back on the wall.

'Reckon they're ready for their tea,' says Dor. 'Want me to peel some spuds?'

'Don't be daft. You've done enough, traipsing over here on such a filthy day.' More than anything I want her to stay, but it's not fair to keep her here. I'm trapped in this gloomy house; I can't expect to trap her too.

'If you're sure, Hannah. But listen, why don't you come down the White Horse on Friday night? I'm meeting some of the girls from the factory.'

'Just you and the girls?'

Dor rolls her eyes to the ceiling, like I'm a terrible prig.

'Unless you can think of any unattached gentlemen willing to chaperone us? Come on, Hannah. Do you good.'

It's so easy for Dor. If she fancies going out, off she goes, and now she expects me to come too. Shouldn't complain, though. I should be thankful she bothers asking.

'I'll see. See how Mum is.'

'Well, if you don't come Friday, I'll pop round Sunday. Might bring some sherry, eh? I can do your hair like Holly Forrester.' She pulls a strand from my pinned-up plaits and curls the hair round her index finger. The loose ringlet falls towards my shoulder.

I smile and she leans over to peck me on the cheek, then takes the fag from behind her ear with a flourish. 'Now cheer up, sunshine, and give us a light.' She holds the cigarette in her film-star pose, pouts her lips, and with her other hand she curls a lock of her yellow hair.

I'm mashing spuds in the scullery when the fingers press onto my waist. The masher jerks away from me with the shock and flecks of potato fly off, landing on the floor and the shoulder of Alec's coat.

'Mind out, girl,' he says. 'Didn't mean to frighten you.'

'You never frightened me,' I say. 'Just a surprise, that's all. Didn't hear you come in.'

'Where's Jen?' He flicks a lump of potato from his shoulder, not caring where it lands.

'With Mum. Dad's ill and he's been taken in. They should be back soon.' I take the potatoes through to the parlour, spoon the mash into two bowls, add some scraps of yesterday's meat and gravy from the stockpot.

'Taken in where?'

'Hospital,' I call back.

'Again?'

'Tea's ready!' I shout up to the children, sliding the bowls onto the table by the parlour window. Steam curls up from the bowls and swerves in the draught.

Alec has followed me in.

'Any tea for me?' he asks, in a little-boy-pleading voice.

'I'll get it in a minute.'

'You're a treasure.' He strokes a hand down my arm, then sits at the table with his newspaper. 'So, your dad's back in the nuthouse.'

The children are gawping in the doorway, naked but for their drawers. 'What's a nuthouse?' asks Alice.

'Never you mind,' I say. 'Now look at you two. You'll catch your death.'

I'd forgotten about their clothes. They'll still be damp, but they'll do. I let down the dryer ever so slowly. I don't like to use it, a heavy thing like that dangling from the ceiling, just four screws in the plaster somehow bearing the weight.

Alec watches me from the table, amused. He knows the dryer makes me nervous. The sour waft of wet wool fills the room as I shake out the clothes.

'Let's get your things back on. They're warm as toast now.' I slip on their vests and shirts, Alice's pinafore and Teddy's little breeches. 'Lovely as you like.'

'Lovely as you like what?' says Alice.

'It's just an expression. Something a lady says at work.'

'Are you going to work tomorrow?'

'Not tomorrow. Mondays, Wednesdays and Fridays. Tomorrow's…'

'Tuesday!' shouts Alice.

'Yes, and you'll have to be extra-special good tomorrow. There'll be a lot to do, with Granddad White being ill.'

'Granddad White's always ill.'

'Well, he's more ill than usual. He's had to go to hospital again.'

They don't ask any more questions, just sit at the table spooning in their mash, quiet for once as if they're mulling it over. Teddy is wearing his Ducky puppet on his right hand, so that it looks like the beak is holding the spoon. The button eyes click on the metal as he eats.

67

After a few mouthfuls he puts down his spoon. 'Daddy in hospital?' he says.

'No, not Daddy. It's Granddad. Daddy's in France. For the war. You remember, Teddy?'

His eyes fill with tears and a smear of potato slides out from between his shiny lips. Alec puts the newspaper down and looks at Teddy.

'But your uncle Alec is right here, Teddy lad, and Uncle Alec might have something for you.' He reaches into his waistcoat pocket and produces a wad of faggies. 'My collection of exotic birds,' he says, winking at me. 'God's honest. Parrots, macaws, the great auk... One of my clients wanted me to have them. "You've got a nephew, ain'tcha, Mr Danks?" asks this old boy. "I have," I says. "A dear boy, and I'm like a father to him now 'is dad's away fighting for king and country..."'

I open my mouth to speak, but Teddy's little face is all lit up and I haven't the heart to interrupt.

'...and the old boy says, "You give him these 'ere faggies, with my regards," and so that's what I'm doing, Teddy. I'm giving them to you, just like the old boy said.'

Teddy starts to get down from the table, but Alec puts the cigarette cards back in his pocket, pats them twice and holds up his hand – *stop* – like a policeman.

'When you've finished your tea, that is. Eat up nicely for your mother.'

Teddy's smile is as wide as Alice's envious scowl. 'And as for madam...' says Alec. 'How will this do?' He produces a paper bag and pulls out a bar of Fry's.

He can be kind to the children, I can't deny it. But I know Alec. He's not kind for the sake of it. He'll be wanting something in return.

Mum has agreed she'll stay with us in Sabbarton Street till Dad comes out. We've been saying that a lot – 'Till Dad comes out' – but I'm not sure any of us is convinced. You can tell it's killing Mum, the relief mixed with the guilt and the sadness. Alec and Jen have offered Mum their bedroom, but she won't hear of it. Instead we make up a bed for her on the parlour floor, with the mattress from their tenement room. Alec turns the mattress over onto its newer side and the imprint of Dad soon flattens against the boards.

A letter comes from George. It's waiting for me on the hall shelf when I get in from work. Jen and Mum are out with the children. Just me here at Sabbarton Street. I can't remember the last time I was alone in the house.

George hasn't written much, only a few lines telling me he's in the pink, not to worry but the regiment is on the move and he can't say where to. *Last night some of the lads put on a show for the troops, a bit like a Pierrot show, and it put me in mind of our trip to Brighton.*

The day trip to Brighton. I haven't thought of it in months. There's a memento in my toffee tin, I'm sure of it – a picture postcard, never sent. I slide the tin from under the barrel and root around until I find that postcard, tucked inside a little sketchbook. We meant to write it out to Alice, but the day went by and suddenly we were

69

on the train back to London.

The photograph shows two Pierrots, one in a blue silk costume, one in pink, standing on the Brighton prom either side of an upright piano. We had watched their show on the esplanade as the sun began to set. On the beach just ahead, two sweethearts were sitting on a red towel spread across the shingle. They were holding hands, staring out to sea one minute, then in the next instant they'd turn to gaze into each other's eyes, smiling and giggling.

George and I sat silently waiting for the show to start, and in that silence a low boom rolled across the water. 'Flanders,' said an old man sitting on the other side of George. Two soldiers, heads bandaged, eased themselves into deckchairs in the front row. 'God help them,' the old man said, making the sign of the cross in the Roman way.

I felt hollowed out by the sadness of everything. Those guns firing while the couple on the red blanket kissed and giggled. Had I ever giggled when George kissed me? Maybe when we first started going together ... although that night in the Captain, I can't remember an awful lot about it. Something possessed me to drink five gin and lemonades, large ones too, and he was knocking back the rum. At closing time we stumbled two streets to his backyard and I let him do what he wanted, let him kiss me and touch me, because he was a kind man, I sensed that. I liked him, the calm, heavy lids of his eyes, the slow blink. After that night George would meet me in Chelsea on my half-day and he'd take me to a tea shop where they served apple cake with thin sugar icing. How

I looked forward to that apple cake, until the sickness started and after that I never touched another slice.

The scullery door bangs open and Alice runs into the hall passage.

'Mummy! Look what Nana give me.'

'I'm up here.' I shove George's letter and the Pierrot postcard back into the toffee tin. Alice appears in a ragged feather boa. She jumps onto the bed, spins and twirls, then dances back out the door, trailing dust and greying wisps of feather. Just like that, silence is stripped from the house.

7

The evenings are drawing in and the lodging room has never felt so dreary. Pictures are what he needs, something to cheer the place up because he'll stay here now, for the winter at least. He takes out the African hanging that is folded at the bottom of his tin trunk: an orange and red patterned cloth he bought from a market stall. Esther had never let him hang it: she said the pattern looked like piccaninnies screaming; it hurt her eyes just to look at it. Not screaming, he'd told her, they're laughing, but she couldn't see it as he did.

Perhaps he should call on Sonia, warn her that he'll be making a racket, banging nails into the wall. But there is no answer when he knocks: she must be out already, working the pubs down Limehouse way.

He takes a hammer and two nails from his toolbox, places one nail between his teeth, then lines the other up against the wall. Three taps of the hammer and the nail goes clean through. The wood partition is thinner than he'd thought; no wonder the sound carries so clearly. He'll have to find a couple of shorter nails. He removes the nail and looks at the mark in the wall. It's not much bigger than the hole a woodworm might make. He steps closer, then presses his face up against the wall and squints through the hole. Sonia's room is almost in darkness, just a smear of grey twilight from the lace-curtained window. His eye adjusts to the gloom. Shapes become clear. Spread on her bedside table is a linen cloth, little wooden beads worked into the crocheted edges, and an empty glass tumbler. There is a vase filled with peacock feathers. The bed has been made, but Sonia has left a chemise or night-dress crumpled on the eiderdown. He stands back and shakes his head, as if that will quieten the sound of blood rushing in his ears.

Surprising, he thinks, that so much can be seen through such a tiny aperture.

Sonia comes in after midnight. Only one set of footsteps up the stairs: she must be alone. He looks at the African hanging for a long time and imagines her on the other side of the wall, slipping the nightdress over her skinny body.

He wakes again at four and knows he will not sleep. Can it really be less than a year since

72

Esther died? Each month, each day has stretched endlessly, like a road of fresh-made bitumen, treacherous and stinking. He shuts his eyes and tries to think of a different time, a different landscape. The childhood trip to Dorset. Immy's face appears, her flat little nose and the wrinkles around her eyes, so strange on a girl who couldn't have been more than sixteen.

Immy had ignored him when he arrived at the house with Lady Tolland and Aunt Winch. She was all curtsies and smiles for Lady Tolland, a curtsey even for Aunt Winch, while he hovered behind them, his tongue poking at a loose tooth, which squelched satisfyingly as he wiggled it back and forth. When Immy was asked to show him to his room, her smile fell. She looked at him and her lips puckered as if she was sucking on an unripe gooseberry. It wasn't his fault, he thought. He didn't ask to be brought here.

They traipsed up the back stairs in silence, and he followed her along the corridor to a box room with a small crooked sash that was propped open with a wooden spoon. The bed was made up with plain sheets, and an eiderdown fell in folds down to the floorboards. Immy walked over to the bed and aimed a kick at the eiderdown. There was the clank of metal. 'Slop bucket,' she said. 'Don't you be using the servants' WC.'

Did she think that would rile him? A slop bucket was nothing. At home he emptied his own into the outdoor privy every morning. And Aunt Winch's, when her back was bad, which was more often than not.

'Thank you,' he said, but she had already turned

to leave the room. A thread from her black skirt caught on the edge of the door. 'Dammit,' she cursed, shaking the skirt free, then disappearing into the corridor.

The thread hung on the splinter, swaying in the warm draught.

He opened his case, took *Jude the Obscure* from it and sat down on the bed to read.

Next morning Aunt Winch told him to make himself scarce. There was a dairy farm along the lane, she said, lads about his age. But he didn't want to spend time with lads his age. He wanted to spend time with his book, with Jude Fawley as he walked the village roads towards Christminster City, tools slung over his back and stone dust in his black curly hair.

He put the book into his haversack and trailed off through the garden and into the wood beyond. It was August and the canopy was heavy, shutting out the sunlight and creating a darkened space, still as a church. Swallows cried in distant fields, but inside the wood there was no birdsong. He followed a path to the right, swishing down nettles with a stick and stopping to pull ivy from a dead tree. As he carried along the path, the silence lifted and now he could hear water rushing. He rounded a steep bank, and when he reached the top, he could see the shallow stream below, the clear water crashing from an opening in the muddy rocks. The air was damp and green. He could taste the greenness on his tongue.

On the other side of the stream, there was a

kind of hut made of branches, a bivouac just like he'd seen in the *Boys' Gazette*. He scrambled down the bank, splashed through the stream and looked inside. Immy screamed and clamped her naked knees together, grabbed at a petticoat that was wedged into a gap in the branches. The boy rolled to one side and scowled at him. He had odd ears. One stuck out more than the other, and the sticky-out one was blazing red.

'Fuck's sake,' said the boy.

He turned and ran, back through the stream, up the bank until he reached the stile that led into the meadow at the far end of the garden.

Something cracked and crunched in his mouth. The loose tooth was out. He spat the bloodied molar into his palm and examined it in the sunlight, the pale enamelled ridges and the blob of pink flesh that had held it in place. There was a molehill just ahead. He poked a finger into the top and let the tooth drop down into the crumbling earth.

8

When I reach Bow Creek, I almost turn back. I stare at the bridge, the stone steps encased by redbrick piers, the solid iron hulking between the banks. The water stretching down, down, who knows how deep? 'Creek', such a harmless-sounding word, like a trickle, a stream you might paddle in. But water's dangerous, no matter how shallow.

Babies drown in tin baths – you hear of them every year. Sometimes it's a clear accident; other times people whisper. *One less mouth to feed...*

My right foot is on the bottom step. I have to carry on. I can't go back to Sabbarton Street, another night in with Jen and Alec. I won't let the bridge trap me.

Dor's mum is putting pans away when I poke my head round the back door. 'Only me,' I call.

'Dor's in the front, love.' Mrs Flynn straightens up from the cupboard. 'She said you might be coming. Oh, you look peaky, poppet. Such a rotten week. How's your mum?'

'She's all right. Staying with us till Dad comes out.'

'That's good. You girls will look after her, I know you will. Now go on through – you're letting the cold in.' She shoos me away from the door with a milk pan.

Dor is squinting into the small mirror above the mantel shelf, lining her eyes with the burned end of a match. She smoothes her eyebrows with a little spit and pinches up her cheeks. The room is hot with banter and bickering, her brothers arguing over a comic book and her sister, Nuala, kicking out at them from the low stool where she's trying to sew.

They look up and say hello, Dor winking with the eye she's not colouring. When she's finished with the match, she picks up a lozenge tin from the shelf, takes out a curled-up flower petal. She rolls it between her finger and thumb, then rubs the petal across her lips.

'Want some, Hannah?' She's holding out the squashed petal.

'Not really.' We used to colour our lips like that as kids, but I've never gone out like it.

'Suit yourself.' She shrugs, dropping the petal onto the hearth. 'You remember Sim Harrison? He's home on leave. Bet we'll find him down the White Horse tonight.'

'Your boyfriend, is he?' asks Harry, looking up from the comic.

'Chance'd be a fine thing,' she says, giving him a little shove. She bends towards the mirror again and pats her cheeks. The confidence seems to drain from her face. 'What a sight, eh, Han? I just can't get these hands clean, and as for my face...' She turns her head to and fro and the lamplight shows up her sickly pallor.

'You look lovely,' I tell her. 'A sight for sore eyes.' I mean it, too. Her skin might be yellow, but she still turns heads when she walks along the street.

She sighs. 'Thanks for saying so. Got to keep trying, eh? Keep making the effort.' She steps over Nuala and brushes a stray thread from my blouse. 'You'll like the factory girls – promise. About time you enjoyed yourself.'

Mrs Flynn hurries into the hall as we're putting on our coats. 'You mind how you go,' she says. 'Keep your wits about you.'

'Don't worry,' says Dor. 'If there's an air raid, we'll go down the pub cellar. Safest place of all. And refreshments on tap.'

'All a joke to you, is it?' says Mrs Flynn. 'I won't sleep a wink till you're home.'

Sure enough Sim Harrison is in the pub, but he already has his arm around another girl. Dor pretends not to notice as we elbow our way to the other side of the saloon bar to find her friends.

There's six of them, crowded round a square table meant for two.

'Over 'ere, Dor,' an older woman says, raising her eyebrows so that her frown lines deepen, thick as pen strokes. 'We'll shove up.'

'You're a dear, Ada,' says Dor.

Ada doesn't look much of a dear. She's like a man, with her blouse sleeves rolled up so you can see the tops of her strong arms. The grey in her hair is tinted green from the factory, and her voice is low and scratchy, as if she's smoked a dozen fags without stopping.

'Introduce us to your friend, then,' says Ada.

'This is Hannah, who I told you about. Known her since I was this high,' says Dor, gesturing towards the floor with the flat palm of her hand.

'And poor old Hannah never got much higher,' says Ada. All the girls laugh, then say things like 'Only joking' and 'Don't take no notice.'

Dor and I have to share a stool, half on, half off, but the more we drink, the less we care. Dor says I should have a fag – do me good after the aggro of the week – and I think I may as well, with the clouds of tobacco smoke already choking my lungs. I hold the cigarette away from me, put it to my lips occasionally and try not to think what my mum would say if she could see me sitting in a pub with a group of girls, smoking and drinking like navvies.

'Dor says your husband's fighting,' says Ada.

78

I nod, stubbing the cigarette into the ashtray. 'That's right.'

'Mine too. Army?'

'Poplar & Stepney Rifles.'

'Fancy – just like my old man.'

It surprises me to learn she has a husband. She's so different, so much *herself*. It hadn't crossed my mind to think of her as Mrs Someone.

'You heard anything recently?' she asks.

'There was a letter this week. They're on the move, apparently, but he couldn't say where to.'

'They're going south – I know that much.' She lights another cigarette, draws deeply and drops the match into the neck of a beer bottle. There's a rash on her wrist, specks of fresh blood where she must have scratched. 'And you know what south means?'

I don't know what south means.

'A-lex-an-dri-a.' She flicks her tongue around the word, revelling in it.

Alexandria.

Alexandria. Is it a woman or a place? And then I remember it from the Empire map on the wall at school. Egypt, is it?

'It's the port of sin, ain't it? Get up to all sorts there,' she says. 'And knowing my Cole, he will find all sorts to get up to, dirty bugger. Long as he don't bring back no unwanted gifts, if you get my meaning.'

She winks and the other girls laugh. I shift in my seat. The edge of the stool digs into my thigh.

'Not her George,' says Dor. 'He wouldn't get up to nothing. Devoted family man, ain't he, Hannah?'

Ada looks at me and scratches at her wrist. I know what she's thinking: that I'm above my station. Hoity-toity.

'Must be your turn to fetch the drinks, Hannah,' says Ada. 'Mine's a barley wine.'

It's busy at the bar, three deep, and I'm pushed up close to a Chinese sailor, so close I can smell the sweet spice of his jacket. Eventually I'm at the bar, clutching my coins and wondering how I'll remember what everyone's having.

'Evening,' a bald man says to me. He's sitting on a bar stool, one elbow resting on the beer-splashed counter. He's familiar, but I can't place him. I'm praying he won't start speaking to me when he turns instead to the person on the other side of him.

'Young man!' he says. 'How the devil are yer?'

The young man doesn't seem too intent on talking either. I sneak a look sideways and I notice his hands first. Big hands, yet somehow elegant. I glance up to his face and he is looking straight at me.

'Mrs Loxwood,' he nods.

'Mr Blake.'

The landlord's wife hands him a flask, a takeout, and he drops coins into her hands. She winks and tells him to mind how he goes.

'Goodnight, Mrs Loxwood. Albert,' he says, touching his fingers to his cap. Then he turns and dips back through the crowd. The heavy pub doors bang shut.

My face flares with the embarrassment of it: Mr Blake seeing me like this, standing in a public house clutching my money at the bar.

'You're a friend of Daniel's?' says the bald man. Under his fingernails is a line of deep red and it dawns on me then: he has a meat stall at Rathbone Market. This is the first time I've seen him wearing anything but a blood-spattered apron.

'Not exactly. An acquaintance.'

The landlord appears in front of me.

'What can I getcha?'

I want to disappear, to turn and run, but I can feel Ada's eyes on me. She'll be getting thirsty.

Dor appears to help carry the drinks.

'Saw you chatting away,' she says. 'Who's your friend?'

'Oh, he's a butcher... Rathbone Market.' I risk a glance back towards the bar. 'Think he's had one too many.'

'Not the old feller – the younger one, bought the takeout.'

'He's a customer from the cafe. Mr Blake, I think he's called.'

'Well, is he married or what?'

'No idea.'

Dor looks hopeful. 'I've been meaning to pop along to that cafe of yours, haven't I?' she says. 'Extra spoonful of sugar, you promised, if I didn't show you up.'

'That's right.'

'And what's the best time to run into Mr Blake?'

'I couldn't tell you. Depends on his shifts.'

'I'll just have to take me chances, then.' She gulps a mouthful of gin and lemon, and licks her lips. 'Come on, Han. The girls are gasping.'

81

It doesn't take Dor long to reel in Mr Blake. She's on a stretch of night shifts, so it suits her to pop in to the cafe at two-ish, after she's had a sleep. She happens to sit at his table; I happen to introduce them. She says she's seen him somewhere before: the White Horse, wasn't it, on a Friday night? I leave them to it. Customers waiting.

The next time Dor sees Mr Blake at the White Horse, she's straight up to the bar, asking him for a light, brazen as you like. He buys her a drink – doesn't have much choice from what I can see – and by the end of the night she's still talking to him at the bar, perched on a stool, her skirt hem riding up to her calves, a shoe dangling from her foot.

It's packed in here tonight. Outside, the December fog is freezing, but the pub doors are shut to the icy draughts, and I can feel my cheeks blazing with the heat of port wine. Shouldn't have had the third glass, but Ada was determined. She's drinking more than usual, which is saying something, and she seems to be all clued up on the Poplar and Stepney Rifles. When I tell her I still haven't heard from George, she can't wait to fill me in.

'They're definitely in Greece,' she says. 'We got a secret code. Set it up before he went, didn't we? It's the first letters of the first sentence tells me what country he's in. See...' She produces a letter from the waistband of her skirt. '"*Greetings to my dear wife.*" That's "G-r" for "Greece". When they was in France, it was "*Freezing cold but out of harm's way*" or some such.'

A code? It had never occurred to me or George to set up a code, and now it's too late. I ask Ada if she thinks they'll be home soon on leave. Christmas is only two weeks away. Perhaps some of them will get time off.

She shakes her head. 'Bugger all chance,' she says, refolding the letter. She seems to get one letter a week. More, maybe. 'Out there for the duration, if you ask me. And it don't look like stopping anytime soon.'

I notice a word pencilled in large letters on the back of the envelope: *NORWICH*.

'What's that?'

Ada rolls her eyes and her mouth crinkles at a wicked angle.

'"Norwich"? You never heard of "Norwich" before? Quite the lady, ain't she, our Hannah?' The other girls smile as she straightens her back and clasps her hands like a toff. '"Knickers Orf Ready When I Come Home."' She says it in a nobby accent. The girls hoot as she takes a cigarette from her tin. 'Trouble is, I don't know if I can wait till he gets home. Especially when you see them two lovebirds over there. Makes you come over all romantic, don't it?'

We look across the pub to Dor and Mr Blake – Dor and Daniel – sitting in the corner near the yard door. She is leaning towards him, her elbows on the table, wearing her new blouse: cream with dark green stripes – cost her a packet in the Army & Navy. The neckline is low and edged in lace, so that you can see her flushed throat and the smooth dipped skin above her collarbone. With one hand she fingers a curl of dynamite-yellow hair, slow and rhythmic, twisting the curl, letting it drop, then picking it up again, twisting. Dor seems to be doing most of the talking, but he is smiling sometimes, chipping in.

'She don't waste no time, does she?' says Ada.

'Dor's always been like it. If she wants something, she generally gets it.' This comes out wrong, like I'm criticizing, and I hadn't meant to criticize. I smile at Ada and the other girls. 'But you can't blame her, can you? I mean, there ain't many men to go around, and Dor's a single girl.'

Everyone nods, everyone except Ada, who scratches at the rash on her wrist. It's spreading up to her elbows, raised like a burn.

'Even so, I can't 'elp wondering about his lordship over there,' she says, jerking her head towards Daniel. 'Why ain't he in uniform?'

'War work,' says Daisy. 'Dor told me he just got another six months' exemption.'

'He's a feather man more like.'

'But if he's exempted,' I say, 'you can't call him—'

'I can call him what I like,' says Ada. She sniffs and squares her shoulders. 'Fact is, he's not doing his bit.'

'But...' I want to defend him, but I can't think how. The port wine has muddled my brain. 'I suppose you're right,' I say, and steal another look at Daniel. His lifts his pint glass, gulps two mouthfuls and glances towards me. He smiles and I turn away, embarrassed to have been caught staring.

I'm bursting for the lav. They've got a ladies-only privy now, out in the yard. I sit there, head swimming, and try to think it through. It seems

84

to me there's something childish, unthinking almost, about this 'do your bit' attitude. I can't explain it to Ada: I struggle to explain it to myself. All I can think of is a playground bully, of Eliot Hever, whose father belted him every Sunday and once tied him to a lamp post, the length of box cord pulled so tight he never lost the tremor in his hands. Eliot liked to teach the smaller boys similar lessons whenever he got the chance. *If I'm in hell, then why shouldn't you be too?* I'm certain that was Eliot's reasoning, and there's a whiff of the same from Ada.

The toilet door rattles, but I push it shut with an outstretched foot. Christ, it's freezing out here.

I want to go back in and say to Ada: 'Maybe it's just as brave *not* to go, to stand up to the white feather brigade?' But the moment I step into the warm pub, I know I can't risk it. What would be the point of arguing with Ada? I know I'd never win.

Just before Christmas a letter arrives from George. It's light, insubstantial as ever. He wonders what we'll be having for Christmas dinner. *I know what they'll give us,* he says, *a tin of Maconochie's stew. You can count on it. All the way from London – maybe you even smelt the beef cooking?*

I read the letter to the children at bedtime. Alice sits up, rocking back and forth on the bed, but Teddy lies on the pillow stroking his nose with the sock puppet, an absent look in his sleepy eyes. It occurs to me that he can't make a connection between the letter and his father. Why would he? He's not even three years old and his dad has been gone almost a year.

'Lie down quietly, Alice,' I say. 'I'm not reading if you fidget.'

She sulks back on the pillow, arms folded across her chest. A gale is blowing outside; every gust rustles the sheets of newspaper that are pasted to the window frames. So much for the newspaper keeping out the draughts. It's as if somebody is in the room, turning pages.

I read the letter slowly, pausing on certain lines: *Tell the children to be extra good for Mummy* and *Don't go playing near the creek*. By the time I've finished, Teddy is asleep, but Alice's eyes are spilling with tears.

'What is it, Alice?'

'There's dads what aren't coming home,' she sobs. Her bony shoulders are hunched right up. Teddy stirs, then buries deeper under the covers.

'Violet told me,' she whispers through little shudders. 'Her uncle is never coming home, not for Christmas or never. The Boche 'as blown him up, she says. What's the "Boche"?'

'It just means the Germans, love. But we don't have to worry – we've got our letter, haven't we?' I hold it up, give it a little shake like a winning raffle ticket. 'Your daddy is all right. Look, he says it's warm and sunny, and he's having Maconochie's stew for Christmas dinner.'

It's not much of a comfort, I know, but what more can I say without making promises that might not be kept? There's hundreds dying every day, thousands maybe. When it's quiet in the cafe, I scan through the casualty lists in the left-behind newspapers. I can't help looking for 'LOXWOOD, Rifleman 592482', just in case there was some sort of mix-up, a letter that never arrived.

'What are *we* having for Christmas dinner?' asks Alice, suddenly hopeful.

'Your uncle Alec has promised he'll find us a chicken ... and I might just have a few treats from the cafe. Mrs Stephens can be very kind, can't she?'

'Lovely as you like,' she says, and we both smile.

I climb into bed and stroke Alice's hair until she's asleep. George's letter runs through my head. He misses us; I know he does. So why did he leave? Why did he abandon us when he could be here now, safe with his exemption papers, just like Mr Blake?

Outside the bedroom window, the north wind shrieks. It rifles off the creek and fires dirty rain against the panes. I think the war is everywhere: in the rain, in the river, in the grey air that we breathe. It is a current that runs through all of us. You can't escape the current; either you swim with it or you go under. In my dreams, I am always in the river, always floundering. Dad is trying to rescue me, but it's no use. I never did learn to swim.

9

His last day in Dorset was a Saturday, and he had no choice but to go out with the boys from the farm. They were walking the five miles to the coast and Aunt Winch thought the sea air would do him good. Charmouth Beach was famous for fossils, she said. Perhaps he would find a souvenir to take home.

They set off after breakfast. There were five boys, the youngest aged eleven, the eldest sixteen – brothers and cousins with matching blond curls, save for the youngest, Vic, whose hair was straight and red.

The weather had been wet in recent days, and a warm mist hung around the fields and the hedges of the vale. They tramped along the lanes, silent at first, then Lester trod on Tink's bootlace, sent him stumbling, and Tink thumped him and called him an idiot. They scrapped as they walked, exchanging insults, until Ralph, the eldest, knocked Lester on the head with the bowl of his clay pipe and told him to fucking shut up.

He trailed behind the five boys, behind Ralph and his tobacco smoke, which drifted in short bursts from the pipe. He recognized Ralph's ears, the way one stuck out more than the other. He knew that Ralph must recognize him too.

To the south, there was a wooded hill and Ralph decided they should climb it. 'Might be a fair crop,' said Ralph to John, elbowing him in the ribs. John nodded and dragged his stick through a wet ditch, hooking up a clump of slime that could have been leaves or a dead frog and flicking it towards Vic so that it landed on the back of his neck. The fighting started again and he wondered whether he could slope off, crouch behind a hedge and stay there until they had forgotten about him.

Too late. Ralph looked back and told him to keep up, said he wanted to talk. Not exactly a conversation, it turned out, more of an inquisition. 'What's it like in London?... Have you ridden in a motor car?... Have you been to a cinema show?' They laughed at his accent, made him repeat particular words and tried to mimic them: *abaht, nuffink, me muvver.*

'You live with that old aunt, then?' asked Ralph. 'You an orphan boy?'

He had nodded, because that seemed easier.

The hill was steep – the highest hill in Dorset, they told him – and he felt hot and heavy when they reached the top. They sat on a dead tree trunk to eat buttered bread and drink water from leather flasks.

When the bread was finished, Lester handed round apples. Ralph and John didn't want apples; they jumped up and began to roam the wood, heads down, searching the ground until Ralph stopped near the trunk of a huge beech tree. He took a large piece of cloth from his trouser pocket and lay it on the ground. They began to pick mushrooms, tiny brown domes, camouflaged in the dead leaves. A mound of mushrooms rose in the cloth. Ralph picked up the cloth by its four corners and walked back to the dead tree trunk where the rest of the boys were still sitting. He offered the mushrooms – five each, he said – and the boys took them, laughing, swallowing them down with the water. Barely chewing.

He shook his head, but they jeered. 'Don't be namby,' they said. 'Five won't hardly touch you.' Ralph counted out five and dropped them in his lap. He gagged as he swallowed, but somehow kept them down.

The boys grew wild as they climbed back down the hill and followed the lanes to Charmouth. He found himself blinking at the green hedgerows, the daisies and the purple vetch, the colours so vivid it was as if his eyes had been stretched to twice their size. A white butterfly appeared, mazy above the hedgerow. He wanted the butterfly more than anything, wanted to capture it and care for it, but when he reached out, the butterfly dipped from his grasp and disappeared into the white sky.

The sense of loss lay coiled in his gut as they tramped towards Charmouth Beach. The butterfly was as beautiful as his mother, and the pain felt sharp as the day she disappeared.

They told him it was prehistoric mud, crumbly with fossils, smelling of dinosaur shit. 'No, we bain't joking,' said Ralph. 'See for yourself. Over there is the best place to dig.' The dairy boys laughed when he reached the mud and began to sink. Then they disappeared and their absence was worse than their laughter. How long would they leave him here, with the tide coming in? The mud was almost at his waist, and struggling only seemed to speed things up.

He looked up to the heavens, but all he could see were the shadowy ridges of Charmouth cliffs. On the cliff ledge, a young seagull cried.

10

Boxing Day afternoon and this house is like the grave. Mum sits in the armchair, looking at Jen's *Pictorial*. Alec is bad with his chest and Jen is fussing around him upstairs. All we hear is cough, cough, cough, pathetic and weak. Jen is up there every hour to burn his asthma powders. The house stinks of Potter's Powders, but they don't seem to help one bit.

I wish we had a piano. Dor and her crowd will be having a fine time in Poplar: the whole family crammed into their parlour; Mrs Flynn battering the piano keys; the room pulsing with their laughter; a bowl of hot punch on the table. Then Dor standing on a chair for her party piece: 'The Boy I Love Is Up in the Gallery', sung saucy as you like, in the style of Marie Lloyd. She'll belt it out chirpier than ever now she has Daniel.

We were almost cheerful yesterday. Alec had made a hobby horse for Teddy from a mop and an old wine box. Teddy was cock-a-hoop: he tumbled around the house with it, shouting, 'Giddy-up,' and getting under our feet until we had to send him out into the yard. Alice looked at the pinafore dress Mum had made and tried to smile. I know she was hoping for a little velvet coat like her friend Violet's, though I'd told her we couldn't afford the brass buttons, let alone the fabric. She soon dirtied the dress outside, chasing after Teddy and begging for a turn on the horse. All the children were out in the street and in the yards and the alleyways, screeching and singing, stirring up the pails of plucked feathers so that the air was speckled with down.

'To Dad and George,' said Alec, as we sat at the table for Christmas dinner. 'May they both come home soon.'

We raised our glasses, trying to smile for the children's sake. The gravy was too thick – it slithered from the jug in clots – and I felt sick to think of my dad lying in a faraway asylum I'd never even visited. Mum had only been to Colney Hatch twice herself; she came home both times with a false smile and her fists clenched knuckle-white around the handle of her basket. 'He's still settling in,' she'd said. 'Don't go along just yet... Wait until the weather's better.'

As I chewed the chicken, I thought of George with his tin of Maconochie's, joking with the lads in the Greek sunshine. Perhaps that was why I didn't miss him too bad, knowing he was getting on all right. If he was still in France, I might have felt different. I wished he'd made more effort for the kids at Christmas. The card he promised never did turn up. Alice asked after the postman every day, on and on, so that in the end I bought a card myself, copied his squashed-up handwriting and told her it was from Daddy. It stands on the shelf now, next to the other cards – one from Mum's sister in Lincoln and the rest from Alec's most grateful clients. They like to keep on the right side of him, especially at Christmas.

'There's a fog coming,' says Mum. She has her back to the window, but you can sense fog without looking: a weight in the draught. 'Time those children came inside. We don't want Teddy getting a chest. It's enough with Alec.' She raises her eyes to the bedroom above.

I stand at the window and scan the street for the kids, squinting through the twilit fog. My head spins for a moment so that I have to steady myself against the window frame. I've drunk my share of Boxing Day sherry – probably Jen's share too. There's no sign of Alice and Teddy, hard as I look. Something pale and light clatters onto the cobbles: the remains of a chicken carcass. A crow swoops down, snatches it back in its scaly claws, rises sideways, off-balanced but determined to keep hold.

'I'll nip out and call them,' I tell Mum, tying my shawl tight and hurrying into the hall. The front door is swollen into the frame; it takes three attempts to pull it open and then I'm running down Sabbarton Street towards the creek, shouting the children's names.

Mrs Hillier opens her front door, holding a lamp.

'Everything all right, duck?'

'The children, have you seen them?'

'They was at my window earlier, making faces at the canary.'

Mrs Hillier's gentleman friend appears behind her, tucking in his shirt.

'Little beggars,' he says. 'I'll 'elp you look. What's their names again?'

'Alice and Teddy.'

He shoulders past us into the street and hollers their names.

A reply comes sing-songing from the other end of Sabbarton Street, up near the main road.

'Yoo-hoo!'

For all the world it sounds like Dor, but the fog is so thick now we can't see more than two yards ahead. Then I make out the shape of her, sauntering along with a small box under her arm.

'Thought I'd wander up and wish you a happy Christmas,' she says. 'Got something for the kids.' She stops and touches my arm. 'What is it, Han?'

'They're not here.'

'I saw 'em not ten minutes ago,' says Mrs Hillier. 'They can't be far away.'

We split up. Mrs Hillier and her friend head towards the main road; me and Dor knock on the neighbours. 'Not here. Sorry, love, not here.'

We call and we call, but still there's no answer.

Sabbarton Street is a dead end; beyond it stretches the railway lines and the creek. There's a gap in the barbed-wire fence leading through to the sidings. A fragment of torn material is caught on the wire. Dor crouches down and eyes up the opening.

'Do you think they would?' she asks. She tears loose the fabric and hands it to me.

It's just a scrap of brown wool. Could be from

94

Alice's coat. Could be from any nipper's coat.

'I'll kill 'em.' My throat is closing with panic. 'They know to stay by the house. Time and again we've said it.'

'They've got lost, that's all. This fog. Can't see a thing, not now it's dark.'

I'll have to go through the fence, can't expect Dor to do it.

'Will you wait here?'

'Don't lose your way, Han. I'll keep calling and you answer.'

When I crawl through, my shawl catches on the wire. Dor unpicks it. I straighten up and inch forwards, boots kicking through rotting newspaper and piles of stinking rubbish.

'Alice! Teddy!'

The smell of wet metal, the taste of soot: I must be close to the railway line now. If they were here, they would answer, wouldn't they? They wouldn't dare to hide. The ground ahead of me shifts and squeaks: a wave of rats cascading towards the creek, their backs shining like ripples of grey water.

Dread paralyses me. It's my fault. I should have called them in sooner. I wasn't watching them. If any harm comes to them, Christ, I'll never forgive myself.

If only I was like Dor. No children to love. No children to lose.

11

Thirteen, was he, or fourteen when Lady Tolland judged he was strong enough to handle the lawnmower? She had sent a note via Aunt Winch, asking him to call the following Sunday. He had walked the four miles, skirting the boundary of Greenwich Park, the observatory majestic on the hill, sparrows calling from neat box hedges.

Royal Grove was on the west side of the park, a quiet road lined with tall Georgian terraces. Lady Tolland's house stood at the end of a terrace, closed in by sharp black railings, the sash windows half obscured by a rampant wisteria. He pulled on the bell, stood up straight when Lady Tolland herself opened the door.

'Let yourself in through the side gate,' she said, glancing at his dusty boots. 'I'll meet you in the back garden.'

The side passageway opened into a long walled garden, so long he couldn't see where it ended. There were flower-beds, a vegetable patch and a great deal of grass, which was overgrown and dotted with dandelions, glaring a sickly yellow in the mid-morning sun. In the shade of the house was a terrace where a stone bench was pushed up close to a small iron table. Moss and lichen crept up from the claw feet of the bench.

He surveyed the garden and decided to station himself by a brick shed midway down, close to the vegetable patch. He watched a robin sing from the branch of a tree. In a nearby church, an organ began to play the opening bars of a hymn: 'There Is a Land of Pure Delight'. He couldn't remember the words, but he hummed the tune, aware of the vibrations low and strange in his throat. His voice was breaking. The robin stopped singing and stared down with a mocking black eye.

It must have been September because the autumn raspberries were ripening. Large white flowers were twined round the raspberry canes and he thought how colourful they looked in the sunshine, the white flowers against the red berries. It was only later that he learned the identity of the flowers: bindweed, enemy of Lady Tolland's garden, to be destroyed at all costs.

After several minutes Lady Tolland appeared through the door of the glazed lean-to at the side of the house. There was no maid, and to his astonishment she carried a tray. She walked over to the terrace, placed the tray on the iron table and beckoned him over.

'Tea and shortbread,' she said, settling herself on the bench. It was chilly in the shade and Lady Tolland pulled her woollen wrap tighter around her pudgy shoulders. 'Sit down, sit down,' she said, patting the space next to her. 'Do help yourself.'

Picking up one triangle of shortbread, he sat on the edge of the bench, the stone pressing cold through the worn seat of his breeches. He took a small bite and chewed. The shortbread felt dry and awkward in his mouth. It didn't seem right to eat while she sat watching.

'Do you still like to read?'

He swallowed, wiped his mouth with his free hand. 'Very much, ma'am.'

'But your aunt tells me that you have left school.'

'Got a job up Billingsgate. Porter's boy.'

'Hard work, I imagine.'

'I don't mind it. I'm strong for me age.'

'Such a tall boy, aren't you?'

'People says so. Me mum was little, so it must've been me dad, but I...'

'You never met him?'

'No, ma'am.' His voice cracked down to a baritone and the suddenness of it surprised them both. It had been happening for a few weeks now; the porters at the market were having a field day, mimicking his up-and-down voice whenever he finished speaking.

The silence was broken by the church organ, the comfortless minor keys of another hymn, one that he didn't recognize. Lady Tolland stood and wandered over to a bed of rose bushes. She sliced through the stem of a dead bloom with her thumbnail, then looked around the garden, shaking her head.

'It's getting a little out of hand, as you can see. I've had to let my man go. Funds are not ... forthcoming. And so I was wondering whether you might be able to help. Just a few hours on a Sunday morning. I think you are more than capable of operating the lawnmower.'

He nodded. He liked the idea of the lawnmower, and Aunt Winch would be pleased with an extra shilling or two. Lady Tolland picked up the plate and offered him another piece of short-bread. 'I can't pay you, I'm afraid,' she said, 'but in return for gardening, you may borrow my books. I don't have a large library, not so grand as my sister's in Dorset...' She looked at his boots again. 'You may as well come and see.'

They went into the lean-to, where pots of spiky plants were arranged along a wooden bench. A watering can lay on its side in the butler sink, and a spider had spun a web from the spout up to the bottom of the brass tap.

Lady Tolland stopped at the inner door and gestured towards his feet. 'If you wouldn't mind...' she said.

He stared down at his boots, puzzled. Then he realized: Lady Tolland would have carpets, posh patterned ones, not the oilcloth mats that lined Aunt Winch's floors. He bent to untie his laces.

12

I haven't let the children outside since Boxing Day. Wandering off like that, I still feel sick to think of it. It was Mrs Hillier who found them; they were following a ginger kitten up the Halls-ville Road, then lost their way in the fog. I should have knocked their heads together, but instead I sobbed and pulled them close. It overwhelmed me, the fact that I'd failed in my duty, let down George.

I check on the children in the bedroom one last

time before going downstairs to meet Dor. They're fast asleep. 'Won't be long,' I whisper.

Dor is standing in the scullery, looking impatient. She's wearing her new black boots with a heel and red satin ribbons for laces. They're too small and they kill her toes, but they were the last pair in the sale at Baker's. She'll be cursing all the way to the Steamship.

I finish tying the laces on my boots and push a couple of extra pins in my hair. The ringlets hang down, tickling my neck. I'd rather pin the ringlets into my bun, but Dor spent so long with the curling irons I haven't the heart. Truth is, I'd rather not go out at all.

Alec appears in the doorway. He whistles softly, under his breath so Jen won't hear. I grab my coat from the back of the door and button it up.

'Look at you two. New Year party, is it?'

'That's right,' says Dor. She puts her arm around my shoulders. 'Don't worry – I'll take care of her.'

'That's a comfort, I'm sure,' he says.

'You celebrating, Alec?' asks Dor.

'Not 'specially. An early night with my good wife.' He winks and then coughs, his chest whining with every breath.

The Steamship is packed and we can't get a seat. I hang back while Dor goes to the bar. There's an accordion player over by the fire, a crowd singing around him. Daisy is there – I'm sure it's her – next to a man in a creased shirt who plays with the glass beads at her neck. No sign of Ada or the other girls.

100

Paper chains are draped around the walls and ceiling, the links cut from pages of a variety magazine. I can make out parts of sentences dangling above me. 'A little bored gesture', 'her hair fine spun and of a wonderful pale gold colour', 'I am mesmerized by her smile.'

'You're away with the fairies, gel,' says Dor, circling a glass in front of my face. 'Here you go. I know you said lemonade, but there's a drop of gin added.'

'Dor–'

'No, don't thank me. Make the most of it while I'm flush. The overtime at that factory is unbelievable.' She glances towards the door, swallowing half her drink. 'Daniel hasn't come in, has he? Oh, I know he probably won't make it. He seemed a bit vague on Friday night.'

She waves across the room to Daisy, but instead of joining her, she spots some people who are leaving, lunges over and plants her drink on their table.

'Bagsy this one,' she says, beckoning me over.

Dor is in the mood for confiding, and there's only one topic she wants to confide about. She talks fast but finishes each sentence slowly, savouring every word, as if the opportunity to speak about Daniel is almost as good as being with him.

'Every time I look at him I ... could ... die. Honest to God. Oh, his eyelashes – did you ever see eyes like that, except on the picture screen? But he's such a bleedin' gent, Hannah. Hasn't laid a finger on me. I tell you, I don't know how much longer I can wait. Do you think I should ask myself back to his place?'

I taste my drink: more gin than lemon. 'Not yet, Dor. You should be pleased he's not like most men. It'll be worth the wait, though, won't it? Just imagine.'

She groans and then strikes her forehead with the palm of her hand. 'Imagining's the problem. But hark at me, selfish bloody ratbag. You've been on your own for months, no George for Christmas and all I'm talking about is myself. Do you miss him and, you know, miss *it*, Hannah?' She elbows me, laughing. 'Ada says she might take in lodgers and charge them payment in kind, if you get my drift. But it's just one of her jokes, ain't it?'

I'm not sure how to reply, but I'm spared the bother because a flare of light suddenly brightens the room. The paper chain has caught fire. The links blaze closer and closer towards the electric light in the centre of the ceiling, cinders fizzling as they drop down onto the sand-scattered floor. A jug of water is thrown, and then another, and suddenly everyone is throwing drinks at the flaming paper chain until the fire hisses out and there's an almighty bang as the bulb explodes.

The accordion player starts up 'London's Burning' and soon the whole pub is cheering and singing in the half-darkness as the landlord brings out more candles.

'Cheers,' says Dor, and we chink glasses. She glances towards the door.

I creep in quiet as I can, but my coat sleeve catches a pan handle and sends it crashing onto the floor. I put the pan back on the side, stand for a moment in the scullery to listen for bed creaks or footsteps upstairs. Silence: the children haven't woken. My feet are so cold I can scarcely feel them and I know I won't sleep unless I can get halfway warm.

It's dark in the parlour. Mum is lying on the mattress, but I'm certain she'll still be awake. I tiptoe towards the armchair.

'I was just dropping off, love,' whispers Mum. 'Do you have to make such a racket?'

'Sorry. Have the children been all right?'

'Not a peep. Busy at the Steamship?'

'Packed.' I open the range door and poke at the coals, chuck in an old tram ticket from my coat pocket. A flame rises.

There is silence for a moment, disapproval in the air.

'I don't like to think of you walking out at night. What would George make of it?'

'He'd hate me to stay indoors moping. He was always saying I should get out more.'

'Well, your dad wouldn't approve, I know that much.'

'Can I see him soon, Mum? Go with you to the hospital?'

She sighs. 'He's not himself, love. He ... he might not know you.'

'He knows *you*, don't he?'

'Can't say he does.' She sits up and takes a sip from the cup next to the mattress. 'He's always talking about Beatrice. Says she's burning in hell.'

'In hell? She didn't do nothing wrong.'

'The way she carried on? Took the easy way

103

out, didn't she.'

'But I thought ... it was an accident.'

'You know what thought did.'

Followed the muck cart and thought it was a wedding.

'Auntie Bea jumped in?'

'I don't know much more than that.' Mum's voice is guarded now. 'She left a note. She was drinking too much, finding it hard to get straight, after Matthew left.'

Uncle Matthew. I remember him a little, the day of the Queen's Diamond Jubilee. Everyone traipsed up London Bridge to watch the procession. Dad gave me a shoulder ride, said Jen was too heavy and she'd have to walk. I sailed above the crowd. From Dad's shoulders I could look down on Uncle Matthew's bald head, the little blemishes and scars, the outline of skull bones underneath.

'What happened to Uncle Matthew?'

'We lost touch with him after she died. I heard he moved away, somewhere up north.'

'Why did he leave her, though?'

'Oh, Bea and her gadding about. She didn't know how to be a wife.'

Above us, Alec starts up his coughing and Jen's heavy limbs shift in the bed. Through the ceiling comes the tired rumble of her voice. She'll be sitting up next to him, rubbing his back now, asking if he wants more powders.

Mum dozes on her mattress. I can't draw my eyes from the glow of the coals and I can't stop thinking about Auntie Beatrice. It's her green satin dress I remember: the enamel buttons, each one painted with a tiny picture of a cat. My favourite was the Siamese; it had a matching green ribbon round its neck. Auntie Beatrice was wearing that dress the time she took me to a pub at Coldharbour, bought me a sherry and lemonade, and made me promise not to tell. Later we stood on the jetty, looking out across the water. 'See, Hannah, the river is smiling,' she said, her eyes misty with joy. Auntie Beatrice was right: I could see the smiles, the little waves bobbing past Bugsby's Marshes like a thousand upturned mouths.

Next time I saw her, she was slumped against the dock wall. Mickey Austen had come to tell Mum, greasy cap in hand and his one buck tooth wobbling as he stuttered out the news. Mum rushed out the house, told us to stay inside and wait for Dad, but Jen said we should follow, fifty yards behind so Mum wouldn't spot us.

Auntie Beatrice's skin was smooth and red as a yew berry, not wrinkly from the water like you'd imagine. She had poppy-out staring fish eyes, until the constable bent over to force her lids down. Ribbon slithered down her neck, and her hands were swollen, purple fingers curled like claws. The cat buttons glistened on her green dress.

'Third one since Christmas,' the constable said, fingers drumming on his notebook. Mum nodded, her hand up to the side of her face so she didn't have to look at the body.

The constable leaned in towards Mum, lowering his voice. 'Had there been any ... trouble?' he asked.

Mum said something we couldn't hear. Jen put her finger on her lips and we crept out from behind the police van. I remember how pale Jen looked in the cold dusk light.

The copper spotted us, of course. He raised his eyebrows at Mum and nodded in our direction. She turned round and frowned.

'Jen! Hannah!' she said. 'Get home this minute. Go on – your dad'll be back soon.'

The constable glowered at us: me, a scrawny six-year-old; Jen, chubby in a too-tight pinafore, wild ginger hair frizzing from her plaits. 'You heard your mother,' he said. 'Now 'op it.'

We ran back along the high street, then slowed to a nervy pace, taking the shortcut through the bowling green and the graveyard until we reached the rec. We were in no hurry to get back home. We didn't want to be the ones to tell Dad that his sister had drowned.

I never saw the river's smiles again, though I often tried. Poor Auntie Beatrice. Not an accident, then. I wish I had been older, wish I could have talked to her or known something of her troubles.

Mum sighs in her sleep. The fire has almost died. *She didn't know how to be a wife.* The wedding ring feels cold round my neck. I slip my hand through my blouse and warm it with my fingers.

13

Lady Tolland has never given him a key, so there is no choice but to break in. The lean-to door is always left unlocked, and from there he can climb onto the butler sink and force up the sash window, which has a loose catch. The window opens into the large kitchen at the back of the house. He squeezes through, tilting his broad shoulders, arching his body to avoid the low table stacked with mixing bowls and tarnished jelly moulds. He drops down onto the floor, the soles of his socks slipping on the tiles. He steadies himself, then leans against the table, surveying the kitchen and listening for unexpected footsteps.

He is certain the house is empty: Lady Tolland is still in Dorset. The Zeppelin raids have played hell with her nerves and she has vowed to stay out of London until the end of the war. A neighbour's maid is looking in twice a week to air the rooms and check the traps for mice. She is unlikely to come on a Sunday.

All the gardening jobs are done, what little there is to do in the winter: water the greenhouse plants; make sure the apple store is dry; dig over the vegetable plot ready for spring sowing. Today he felt the garden stirring: humming, almost, the snowdrop shoots pushing through the leaf-mulched earth, delicate and fearless.

The kitchen has barely changed since he first

visited on that warm autumn day so many years ago. Everything has its place – the copper pans, the pickling jars, the three sets of weighing scales. The clutter still fascinates him; he finds something comforting in the busy rows of shelves, the dresser crammed with gilt-edged crockery, the trappings of a wealthier past. Over the years Aunt Winch had gossiped snippets of the story: how Lord and Lady Tolland once owned a mansion in the best square in Knightsbridge. After his lordship died, the gambling debts emerged, along with his two mistresses and their several bastard children. Lady Tolland was forced to move, went from twenty-eight rooms to eleven, if you included the entrance vestibule of the Greenwich house and the attic room with its tiny skylight. She was almost penniless, and if it were not for the generosity of her brother-in-law, she wouldn't have a London house at all.

He sniffs the shut-up air, the familiar smell of damp dog, though Lula has been dead for months now. He misses Lula, her whorled black spaniel fur, the way she padded behind him on the lawn as he pushed the roller up and down, up and down, imprinting the vertical lines that Lady Tolland found so pleasing.

On the windowsill, a pink cyclamen blooms in a green-glazed pot. The neighbour's maid must have watered it.

For the first time in over a year – the first time since Esther died – he senses possibility: a shred of something less bleak. Is it wrong to imagine this other woman, to picture her standing before him, hair loose around her shoulders?

108

A tap drips and Esther floods back into his mind, a guilty reproach, and it is as if his dead wife's palm is pressed again in his. Her hand was still damp when the orderlies came to wheel away her body. Christmas Eve, such a cruel date for a death. When their son woke on Christmas morning, he couldn't bring himself to say the words. Instead he dangled a white sugar mouse by its tail, told Sam that Mummy was still poorly, but that she sent her love and this little Christmas treat. '"Make it last," Mummy says. "Make it last, Sam!"'

Maddie was just a baby: the memory of her mother's milk would fade soon enough, and Ellen insisted she had more than enough milk for two. It made him queasy, his sister with her enormous breasts, clamping Maddie onto her nipple, her own baby sleeping in the cradle nearby. Capable in a crisis, dear Ellen. Very capable.

He thinks of their third child, a boy, born too soon and never named, the only trace of him recorded on Esther's death certificate: '24th December 1915. Cause of death: 1. Incomplete abortion. 2. Septicaemia.'

Was it his fault, allowing the pregnancy to happen so soon after Maddie?

He had carried Esther most of the way to the hospital, her blood-soaked skirts staining his hands and coat so that when they arrived, the nurses weren't sure who to treat first.

'The womb is not a machine,' the doctor had lectured in the hospital corridor as a nurse took Esther's temperature. 'A woman's body needs time to recover, however pressing one's desire.

Think of fornication as a bus ride... Are you with me?'

He had nodded. His throat was too dry to speak. He knew about the bus ride, of course he did. Standard advice for eager lads.

'So the trick is to bump along and then to jump off the bus one stop before the one you want. All right? Capital,' and the doctor had patted him on the arm as he turned away. Christ, the nerve of that man.

His fingernails have dug into the edge of Lady Tolland's pine table, leaving a pattern of tiny crescents. He walks over to the large window overlooking the back garden, fixes his eyes on the snowdrop shoots until the memory subsides.

In Lady Tolland's library – a small, crimson-papered room between the kitchen and the drawing room – he unloads four books: one from each trouser pocket and two from the saggy lining of his jacket. Lady Tolland is very old now, over seventy, he's sure, but her eyes are sharp as ever. What would she say if she discovered him here? He imagines he could win her round... They could drive a fresh bargain. She has always liked a bargain. In any case, he has kept his side of the pact: the garden is well cared for; the wisteria no longer invades the windowpanes; the bindweed is as good as banished. Lady Tolland's promise, however, escapes her each time she goes away. She should trust him with a key.

Slowly he paces the shelf-lined walls of the library, slotting the books back into their original places, until he holds a single volume in his hand. He traces the gilt lettering of the cover: *Satires of*

Circumstances, Lyrics and Reveries. He has written out all Hardy's poems, keeps the papers in a trunk. Still, he turns the pages until he reaches 'The Going':

Well, well! All's past amend,
Unchangeable. It must go.
I seem but a dead man held on end
To sink down soon...

He shuts the book, clasps it tight for a moment, then slides it onto the shelf. *A dead man held on end*. Surely this year will be different? It is 1917 and he wants to feel alive.

As he passes back through the kitchen, he looks at the calendar nailed to the wall. Next birthday he will be thirty. He thinks of Sam and little Maddie, how happy they seemed this Christmas at Ellen and Alf's house, playing with their cousin, patting Ellen's enormous belly and asking would the stork come soon. When they went for a walk in the woods, Sam had run ahead, called out, 'Daddy!' when he spotted a strange fungus growing from a tree trunk. 'Coming!' he and Alf had called in unison. Sam turned and glanced between them, picked up a stick and jabbed at the fungus so that it crumbled from the tree in a cloud of spores.

A grating sound echoes from Lady Tolland's hallway. A key turning in the door? He lunges towards the open sash window, then pauses when he hears the first chime. It was only the grand-father clock, gearing up to strike midday.

Sunlight hazes through the cloud as he leaves the house. The day feels more like April than January.

111

By the park gates, a young woman is helped from a carriage by an older man: her father, perhaps. The hem of her yellow dress is trimmed with white lace. He glances up and finds that the woman is looking at him. He smiles, touches the peak of his cap. The woman casts her eyes down, a blush rising on her pale winter cheeks.

Downhill he strides, down towards the river, King William Street with its pubs and trinket shops. He stands at the riverside and looks over the railings. The tide is out and there are children crouched along the muddy banks, sacking tied round their ankles to protect their feet. The smell of silt rises up, rank and salt-stained. One of the children lifts a small lump of flat mud towards her mouth, spits on it and rubs until the shape of a coin emerges. The copper catches the sun and the girl smiles at her good fortune.

14

After the morning rush a woman walks into the cafe on her own. She's about my age, wearing grubby cornflower-blue gloves and a creased old coat. But she's posh-looking for all that, and when she opens her mouth, you know she's not local.

'Are you the proprietor?' she asks me.

Vernon Cridge looks up from his fried bread and snorts a laugh.

'You'll be wanting Mrs Stephens,' I say, 'but

she's gone out. She's on a ... special delivery.'
She's taking pies and sandwiches round to her
friend Mrs McCarney on Galbraith Street. Mrs
McCarney's son has been killed and all the aunts
and cousins have trooped down from Archway.

'If I could perhaps leave you one of these, to put
up in the window?' She opens her leather satchel,
takes out a cardboard folder and pulls a poster
from it. 'It's for a meeting next week, not far from
here.' She smiles and shows her white teeth.

I look down at the poster. PEACE MEETING,
20 RAILWAY STREET, POPLAR. SPEAKER:
JACK FENWICK, THE NO-CONSCRIPTION
FELLOWSHIP. STRIKE A BLOW FOR FREE-
DOM AND RIGHT! At the bottom of the poster,
there's another line, written smaller: UNDER
THE AUSPICES OF WSF: SUFFRAGE FOR
ALL!

I've heard of them, the Workers' Suffrage Fed-
eration. They've set up shop down the Roman
Road, led by one of the Pankhurst lot. Dor
thought she was marvellous, What's'er-name
Pankhurst, went along to a couple of suffrage
meetings before the war. I might have gone too,
but Teddy was just born and it was a job to leave
the house. Of course, Dor lost interest when the
war started and this Pankhurst sister turned out
to be against the fighting. Dor was very keen on
the war at that time. She was still seeing Len,
thought he was the bee's knees in his uniform.

The woman gives a polite cough into her gloves.
'A couple of posters in your window are out of
date, if you don't mind me saying so. A Christmas
bazaar at the Liberal Association, well...' she

laughs brightly, 'well, Christmas just seems an age away once we get into January, don't you agree?'

'I suppose.'

'If you like, I can paste that up now...' She reaches out for the poster, but I pull it close to my chest.

'I'll check with Mrs Stephens, if it's all the same.'

'Of course.' She buckles up her satchel, then smiles right at me. 'And perhaps you might be interested in coming along yourself?'

'P'r'aps.'

Just as she's walking out, Vernon Cridge belches loudly. She pauses for a second, then quickens her pace to the door, tries to open it, but pushes instead of pulls. Then she gives the door a hefty swing back, setting the bell jangling. She hurries out, almost colliding with Mrs Stephens, who's coming in the opposite direction.

'Excuse *me*,' says Mrs Stephens, turning to look at the girl's back. 'Miss High-and-Mighty.'

'She's brought a poster,' I say, holding it up from behind the counter.

Mrs Stephens raises her eyebrows, then looks towards the poster, eyes screwed up. 'My spectacles are upstairs, she says. 'You'll have to read it me, Hannah.'

I recite it word for word, and when I get to the part about striking a blow for freedom and right, Mrs Stephens folds her arms across her chest.

'She wants to know if we can display it in the window,' I tell her. 'Meeting is next Thursday, January 25th, I think...' I scan down to the date. I wonder if I might go along, listen to what they've got to say. Peace is what we all want, isn't it? Maybe I'll mention it to Dora. Peace would be right up her street, now she's met Daniel. I don't know how she'd cope if he went off to war.

'Give it here,' says Mrs Stephens, holding out her hand

'Shall I mix up some paste?'

'Shall you mix up...?' She doesn't bother finishing the sentence, just rips the poster in half, then half again and drops the pieces onto the counter. 'You'll put that filth where it belongs – on the fire. Paste it up? I might as well spit in poor Mrs McCarney's face! Peace meeting, for heaven's sake. Shirkers' meeting, more like. Waltzing down here in her fancy gloves...'

Mr Cridge drains his mug of tea and mops up the bacon fat with his fingers.

'One or two shirkers frequenting your establishment, Mrs Stephens,' he calls out, his voice grim.

'Whatever do you mean, Mr Cridge?'

'I'm saying there's young men drinking tea in here what should be putting the boot into the Boche.' He sticks out his tongue to lick the fat from his fingers.

Mrs Stephens turns her back on him, lifts the countertop and steps into the kitchen next to me. She lets the counter drop with a bang and the torn-up pieces of poster flutter to the floor.

'I don't know about that, Mr Cridge. I'm not acquainted with all our customers' private circumstances,' says Mrs Stephens. 'Some people have good reasons ... medical or whatnot. It's these meetings I object to, these ... *peace cranks* and their preaching.' She bends down to pick up the poster fragments, opens the stove door and throws them onto the coals. 'Ain't that right, Hannah?'

At lunchtime Daniel comes in and orders a bowl of soup and potatoes. I haven't seen him since before Christmas and I think there's something different about his expression, less melancholy. Dor must be having this effect on him. A thought catches me. Perhaps Dor has invited herself round to his place after all. She'd have told me, though, if things had moved on. She always tells me everything, whether I want to hear it or not.

'Would you like a slice of bread, Mr Blake?' I set the bowl down and he looks up, smiling.

'Call me Daniel, Mrs Loxwood.'

'I mustn't really. Not in the cafe.' I gesture towards the kitchen, where Mrs Stephens is ladling out meals. A waitress has got to be professional with the customers, she says. There's a knack to it, a proper tone to be struck: friendly, not familiar.

'But maybe down the White Horse?' he whispers, as if we're planning some conspiracy.

I can't help blushing when he mentions the pub. I nod quickly, ask him again whether he would like bread.

'Go on, just the one slice. Maybe I'll see you tonight, then. We'll be in a bit later – me and Dor are seeing a picture.'

'Yes, she mentioned.'

'Did she?'

Now he seems embarrassed. Men don't like to be discussed; they think it's disloyal. That's what Mum said, anyway, after she caught me moaning to Dor about a quarrel I'd had with George. I bend down to pick a spent matchstick from under the table, wondering how I can make it right.

'Oh, just in passing,' I say, tossing the matchstick onto the fire. 'Dor does love the pictures. It's a Florence Turner, isn't it?'

'Yes.' He picks up his spoon and tastes the soup. 'That's the one.'

I can sense Mrs Stephens watching us from the counter.

'I'll just get your bread.'

Mrs Stephens decides she'll serve Mr Blake his bread. She stands over him a second longer than she needs to, sizing him up, as if to check for medical complaints. She'll be thinking about the poster, about Pat McCarney. Does she wish Daniel had taken Pat's place? Would she prefer Daniel to have been killed *instead* of Patrick McCarney, or as well as him? It confuses me to think about it, this talk of peace cranks and shirkers. And all along there's still no word from George. Ada hasn't heard from Cole either, not for a fortnight or so. I keep writing my letters to George every Sunday evening, so there's a week's worth of news, such as it is. I've told him about Dor's friends from the factory, how we get together now and again. Does he know Cole Buckley? I asked him in one letter. Because I've got friendly with his wife, Ada. I thought he'd be pleased to hear of the connection, to think of the two of us making new friends – meeting a husband and wife separately like that. No reply. Now I'm wondering if he's got the hump. Maybe Mum's right. If I was a good wife, I would stay

117

inside, waiting for the war to end. Would George prefer that?

In my heart I believe he would.

George would like everything to stay normal; he would prefer me to wait quietly, until such time as he is ready to march back home.

Mrs Stephens nudges me as Daniel leaves the cafe.

'There goes Mr Blake. Perfect figure of a man. Fighting fit, if you ask me.'

I didn't ask you, I think, but I raise my eyebrows and nod.

I'm all set to leave when Mrs Stephens calls me back into the kitchen.

'There's a friend here for you, love.'

Dor is breathless, cheeks pinch-pink with the cold.

'Thank God I've caught you, Hannah. It's about tonight.'

'Are you all right?'

'No, I'm not. All week I've been waiting for this evening and now I've been called in on the late shift.' She flops down at a table and takes off her hat.

'So you can't see the picture?'

'No chance. I was hoping I might catch Daniel here to let him know.'

'He was in earlier. For lunch.'

'Bugger. If only I knew where he lived, I'd drop a note round. The thing is, I'd hate him to think I've stood him up. I don't want to ruin my chances, Hannah. You know how much I like him.'

I take a seat next to her, unbuttoning my coat.

'I'm sure he knows too.'

'Does he? I haven't told him. I was waiting for the right moment. Tonight, I thought. Tonight might be the night when, you know ... I'd go back to his room...' She drums her fingers on the table, thoughtful, and then gives me one of her wheedling looks. 'You might just pop along to the Empire yourself, tell him I have to work? Half past six I said I'd meet him. If you've got nothing better on, that is. I just can't bear to think of him waiting there, cursing me.'

'I can't get out that early in the evening, Dor. I have to put the children to bed.'

'Oh,' she sighs, slumping back in the seat. 'Well, I suppose you might see him in the White Horse later. Tell him I'm sorry, won't you? I'll make sure I'm free next Friday. Brunner's can bleedin' well manage without me.'

'Actual fact, I don't think I'll be going out tonight. 'Specially if you're not there. I've been thinking anyway I ought to be staying in. They reckon this year could be worse for air raids.'

'Oh, leave off, Hannah – you've got to have some sort of life. Cooped up night after night with Jen and Alec? Bombs'll get you wherever you are. Wouldn't you rather die with a gin in your hand and a smile on your face?'

'And how would that look? Blown up in a pub?'

'Why do we always have to worry how it *looks?* Men don't think twice, do they? All them soldiers, queuing up at the French knocking shops, like Ada says. They don't give a monkey's how it looks, so long as they get...' She trails off. 'Sorry, Hannah. Not your George, of course. In the knocking shops, I mean.'

Mrs Stephens arrives with a tray.

'Here you are, girls.' She's brought us a pot of tea and two currant buns.

'Look at that. That's prime, ain't it?' says Dor. 'Sugar on top 'n' all!'

Mrs Stephens smiles. 'Got to keep the workers happy. You're in munitions, am I right in thinking?'

It's not the luckiest guess. You can tell where she works a mile off, with the yellow hair and the matching fingernails. 'Don't I know it,' says Dor.

It's crowded outside the Empire. People huddle in the queue on the steps outside, ignoring the old fiddler swaying around his hat as he plays a ballad. Daniel isn't in the queue. He's leaning against the wall by the side exit, smoking a cigarette. His heavy tweed coat is a little too short in the sleeves. One leg is bent with his foot resting up against the brickwork.

A tram passes, blocking my view for a moment. It's a moonless night, dark and dreary. Perfect night for a Zeppelin. I ought to be at home with the children. Half an hour ago this seemed like the right thing to do, but now... I'm tempted not to cross over to the Empire after all. Daniel will work it out for himself. Does he really need a messenger?

Daniel looks up as the tram passes and I'm sure he's seen me. No getting out of it now. He calls out as I hurry across.

'Hannah!'

'I've come with a message from Dor,' I say.

120

'Righto.' He straightens up from the wall, the cigarette cupped in his hand.

'She ain't coming tonight. Someone was ill at the factory and she has to cover. Only she didn't want you to think...'

'Yes?'

'Well, she didn't want you thinking she'd stood you up.'

'I was starting to wonder.' He slips his hand inside his coat and produces a watch from a silver chain. The Empire doors bang open and the crowd starts to shuffle inside. 'Standing only in the ha'pennies!' the attendant shouts. 'Standing only in the ha'pennies!'

'Good of you to let me know. Shame ... although, tell you the truth, I ain't too keen on Florence Turner. Unless you...' He raises his eyebrows and gestures towards the crowd filtering through the doors.

'Oh no, I need to get home to the children.'

'Course. It's a rotten night. Did you come out special?'

'No, I had ... an errand.' It's a lie, but I don't want him thinking I turned out for him, Dor's obedient messenger.

'I'll see you home. Where you heading?'

'Canning Town, but there's no need.'

'As far as the creek. Come on.'

His raises his right arm and for a moment I think he'll link it in mine, but he is only taking a last drag from his cigarette. He drops the fag end onto the pavement and grinds it with his boot. As we pass the busker, Daniel flicks a copper into his hat. The fiddler lifts his bow in thanks, then drops

121

it back onto the strings, never missing a beat.

We walk in silence for a few yards, past Robin Hood Lane and the looming turrets of the tunnel entrance. Daniel begins to hum the busker's tune, 'Star of the County Down'. There's a peculiar rushing in my head and I know I have to breathe steady, keep looking straight ahead, or the falling will start.

We're passing the Aberfeldy Tavern when I hear a heavy, distant boom and feel a tremor beneath my feet. At first I'm not sure if the sound is real or in my mind. Our pace slows. Another thud and then a red light glows in the sky, just east of Canning Town.

'Fire?' says Daniel. 'It looks like Victoria Dock way – Silvertown.'

'What was the bang? Was it the warning?' People obviously think so: they are hurrying towards the tunnel for shelter.

'Can't have been.' He looks quickly around the street. 'There's no coppers for a start.'

He's right. When it's an air raid, the maroon flares crack and policemen are everywhere, criss-crossing the road on their bicycles, blowing whistles and shouting, 'Lights out!'

'Do you want to go in the tunnel, just in case?' he says.

'No. I want to get home.'

We hurry along unspeaking, until we're almost at the iron bridge, and I stop dead on the pavement.

I grab his arm and we stare towards Silvertown.

The dim glow blisters into a blinding glare and then there is the sound of two more explosions, one quickly after the other, louder this time. The sky is scarlet now, then brighter still, brighter and paler all at once. We're yards from the creek and the weird colours reflect on the water, lighting up the iron bridge so that it looks almost like a fairground ride, an amusement on Brighton Pier. Even the mud is shining on the banks, the reeds waving strange shadows.

'What the... Christ!' Daniel stops and raises his hands, shielding his eyes.

Yellow now, then a white light, as if a new sun has blazed into the sky. Buildings seem to lift up and detach from each other. Arms fling out and pull me close. I'm aware of a scream in my throat. Other people's screams.

The white light flashes away and I know something worse must follow. In less than a second it comes, a thud so powerful I can feel my lungs rattle against my ribs. Next, the sound of glass tinkling, delicate at first, then an ugly shriek as windows from houses and offices and factories smash to the ground.

A soft wind, low and warm, sighs across our skin.

My head presses against Daniel's chest.

I pull away, my mouth so dry it's a struggle to speak. 'I must... The bridge, is it safe?'

'There are people on it, see?'

He's right. Mainly they are racing over to this side. Some have stopped midway, to look back towards Silvertown, where the factory towers and the grain silos are ragged outlines in the orange sky.

'I have to get across ... the children. You go back.

Find somewhere safe.'

He doesn't reply, just takes my hand in his and strides towards the bridge. His hand seems to anchor me, stops me from sinking. We move fast, shouldering our way past the stream of people. 'Brunner's,' they are saying. 'The chemical works. Sky high.'

The munitions factory. Dor.

At the end of the bridge, there's a crush of people and we have to squeeze sideways to get down the steps. Lumps are falling from the sky. Glass, metal. I put my free hand up to protect my head and a sharp stab pierces the top of my wrist.

'It's not far from here,' I shout, as we run past the music hall and the labour exchange. Ambulance bells clang in my ears. Crashes and thuds like the end of the world.

Sabbarton Street is standing, but every window is blown out, and there's a hole in the roof of number eight, twisted metal jutting from the smashed tiles. Mrs Hillier is wandering bewildered along the cobbles, the birdcage tucked into her coat.

'What is it, dear?' she says to me. 'What happened?'

'The munitions factory at Silvertown. An explosion. Have you seen the children?'

'I ain't seen no one much,' she says. 'I was just minding me own business...'

'I must get home...'

I run past her, clutching my wrist, down the side alley and in through the back door. The house is silent.

'Mum!' I shout.

'In here.'

They are squeezed under the table in the parlour: Alice and Teddy, Mum, Jen and Alec. The orange light from the factory fire flashes around the room, reflecting in their eyes, the shattered photograph frames, the daggers of broken glass wedged into the wallpaper. The light dims suddenly and I look up to see a dark shape against the window. Daniel. He touches his cap towards me, then disappears.

I bend to kiss the children. 'Thank God. Stay safe here – I'm going to check on Mrs Hillier. Found her in the street with the birdcage.'

'Your hand?' says Mum.

'Only a cut. I'm fine.'

Outside, Mrs Hillier's gentleman friend has appeared. He takes the birdcage and steers her back through her front door.

Daniel is walking along the pavement, almost at the main road. He turns and stops when I call his name, waits while I catch up. We shelter just inside an alleyway, under a brick arch. The debris has stopped falling, but the air is choked with ash and the stench of burning.

'Dor's at the factory tonight...'

'I'm going there now,' he says.

'To Brunner's? There can't be anything left of it. She must be blown...' A sob clenches my throat.

'No, it might not be so bad. The big explosion came later, remember? They would have evacuated the place, first sign of trouble.'

'Then you'll try to find her? Because, well, you mean the world to Dor and if she could see you tonight...'

'Of course I'll try...' He hesitates, puts his hand over his mouth and then lets the hand drop. 'But, Hannah ... Dor is not ... not somebody I could be close to.'

'What?' I blink up at him, wondering if I heard right. Dor is surely lying somewhere, shocked or injured or worse, and he dares to tell me that he doesn't care for her? 'Why ever are you going out with her, then?'

His eyes shift and then soften, as if he has found the answer to a question he has been asking himself.

'Sometimes she speaks of you.'

A great heat rises in my body, and a surging strength so that when I shove him, he stumbles backwards into the passageway. He steadies himself and then straightens, holding his arm where it knocked against the wall. We face each other. His eyes are black in the shadow of the brick arch. The pulse jumps at the corner of his eye.

'Find her for me,' I tell him. 'Find her or I'll never forgive you.'

The ambulances are less frequent now, but my head still clangs as if there's a bell inside. It's a wonder the children can sleep. Yet somehow they are peaceful beside me, blanketed in all the clothes we could find and their boots still on in case we'd missed some glass. There's no point lying down, so I sit on the edge of the bed, looking out through the shattered window. Dirty air curls in, and although the glow from the fires has dimmed, the midnight city looks odd and bright. Skinned.

I haven't undressed. Haven't even taken off my coat.

Sometimes she speaks of you.

The chain round my neck feels colder than ever, a frozen thread, and my wedding ring is a blister of ice against my throat. I unclasp the chain and drape it on the narrow windowsill.

A commotion starts in a nearby street, two men shouting and a horse rearing. 'Thieving toerag. You want whipping, you fucking...' So much noise that I don't hear him arrive.

The tap on my bedroom door makes me jump. 'Hannah,' Mum calls.

I slip out onto the little square of landing and Mum is standing on the top stair, nightgown and shawl pulled tight around her. From Jen and Alec's room comes the sound of coughing. The bed springs creak.

'Gentleman to see you, Hannah. It's about Dor.' She lowers her voice still further. 'Frightened the life out of me, knocking at this time.'

The lamps are out, so there is only the light from Mum's candle. I can see a corner of him in the doorway, one shoulder rising and falling. He seems out of breath.

Each tread of the stairs leaves me queasy with fear. Fear for Dor. Fear of his eyes on mine.

'You'd better come in,' Mum says to Daniel. He steps into the hall. Even in the candlelight I can see the mess of his face – sweat, soot, traces of blood.

'Dora's at Poplar Hospital,' he says. 'She's got some burns.'

Alive, I think, gripping the bottom banister. Alive?

'How bad?'

'I don't know. They found her a bed. It's mayhem there, people lying on the floors. You can't find a doctor to ask.'

'Did you speak to her?'

'No, she wasn't up to talking. They were bandaging her. Some kind of ointment...' He trails off. 'But it was definitely her. I spoke to someone from Brunner's.'

'Dear God,' says Mum. Then she looks between the two of us, curiosity furrowing her brow. She's asking herself how I know this stranger on the doorstep.

Daniel must sense the same. 'Anyway, sorry to trouble you like this,' he says. 'Dor's... Her family sent me. They knew you'd be wondering.'

'It's kind of you,' says Mum. 'Have a cup of tea?'

His eyes flash to mine, but I look away, through the open door into the night.

'Thank you, I'd better go. They still need volunteers.'

'At Silvertown?'

'What's left of it. Still people under the rubble, they reckon.'

Mum's free hand flies to her mouth. The candle flame shivers in the draught. 'It's terrible. As if things ain't bad enough.' She collects herself, inhales sharply. 'Well, you take care of yourself, Mr...?'

'Blake. Daniel Blake.'

'And thank you for coming, Mr Blake.' Mum

turns to me, quizzical, wondering why I'm dumb-struck.

'Yes, thank you for taking the time,' I say. 'I'll visit Dor tomorrow.'

He touches his cap as he leaves and Mum shuts the door behind him.

'Nice enough feller,' says Mum. 'Dor's fancy man, is it?'

'That's right.'

'He deserves a medal if he goes up Silvertown. Volunteers, they're asking for. Strong men, I sup-pose.' She rolls her eyes to the ceiling. 'Do you think we should wake Alec?'

It's not like Mum to be sarcastic. I've an urge to kiss her goodnight, but she has already turned away.

Dor's face is bandaged, and they've cut off what was left of her hair. One scorched eyelid is visible. She talks with the eye shut.

'Run as fast as I could,' she says. 'Tripped ... a step.' Her cracked lips open only a fraction, just enough to show her front teeth, chipped and blackened.

'You tripped on a step?'

She tries to nod, agitated. I reach out to hold her hand, then pull back. The nurse warned me not to touch.

'Daniel ... don't let him come,' she says. 'Wait till later.'

'Yes. You're not to worry.'

I can't tell her that he's already been. That he ran all the way back to Canning Town to let me know she was here.

Her shoulders relax and she seems calmer. We sit quietly and I wonder if it would be all right to take a sip from the beaker of water on the shelf next to her bed. My mouth is still so dry.

I drink two mouthfuls, but this is a strange kind of thirst, one that water won't cure.

Dor seems to be dozing now. I shut my eyes too and wonder how I can give Daniel this message, that he shouldn't visit. I've no way of finding him. There's only the cafe. But how will I serve him, after what passed between us? Words, I keep telling myself, only words.

Sometimes she speaks of you.

'You still here, Hannah?' Dor murmurs, half asleep. She lifts a bandaged arm and pats the stiff starched sheet. The sheet is raised up like a tent on a frame, must be to stop it from pressing on her skin. The movement of her arm wafts a sharp smell of tar.

'I'm here. And I was dropping off with you. Don't suppose anyone in London slept much last night.'

'Should have been at the pictures with him. Stupid factory.' Her voice grows louder. 'Now it's all gone... A small fire at first. Dr Angel said not to panic.' Her eyelid flies open and she flinches at the sudden movement.

'Shh,' I say. 'You don't need to talk.'

'And Daniel thinks I stood him up. You'll tell him, won't you, Hannah? That I meant to be there. I'll get there when I can. But he ain't to see me ... like this.' She pauses. 'Is it very bad? I keep asking for a mirror, but they won't bring it. The thing is, I can't feel anything...' Her voice tapers

130

off, weaker than ever.

Dora's mum appears with one of the older brothers. Kit is chewing his bottom lip so hard there's a dark red mark.

'We're back, Dor,' says Mrs Flynn, attempting cheeriness. She bends to kiss me on the cheek and rests her hand heavily on my shoulder. 'And that's nice, Hannah is here too. Now listen, Dor, we found the doctor and he tells us you'll be just fine. They've wonderful medicine now, to take away the pain. It's just time, he says. It'll take a while.' Her voice wavers. 'We'll have you on the stage by next Christmas, don't you fret.'

Dor's mouth curls up, almost a smile, and we wait for her to speak again, but there is only a deep sigh, and her head seems to sink back further into the pillow.

'Get the nurse,' Mrs Flynn whispers to me.

A nurse hurries over, her eyes glassy with exhaustion.

'It's Nurse Sands, is it?' says Mrs Flynn. 'You've been so good with her.'

The nurse lifts Dor's arm and feels her wrist through a narrow gap in the bandages.

'She's sleeping, Mother,' she says. 'And if I were you, I'd go home and do the same. Rest is important after a shock like this.' She looks at the three of us and leans in towards Mrs Flynn. 'I must remind you it's two to a bed at visiting time. If Sister finds out, there'll be trouble.'

In the corridor, Mrs Flynn catches my arm.

'Is your place bad?'

'Just the windows smashed, and a few of Jen's wedding plates. We're all right, though. Freezing

131

cold but all right.'

'First off we thought it was Zepps,' says Kit.

'We all did.'

'To think it was one of our own factories.' He lights a cigarette and draws hard. 'We done this to ourselves. Christ almighty.' He shakes his head and gazes through the double doors of the corridor into the ward. It's quiet but for a desperate wail of 'Mummy, Mummy, Mummy': an old woman's voice, delirious.

Nurse Sands passes and frowns to see us still there.

'Rest,' she mouths at me.

Windows are blown out all along Chrisp Street, but the market is trading, busy as ever. Shopkeepers have swept up the glass, hung signs from the door frames saying, BUSINESS AS USUAL. A newspaper boy weaves through the street, shouting, '*Mirror!*' I stop him and he pulls a paper from the sheaf under his arm. 'Ha'penny, miss,' he says, and I drop the coin into his ink-black palm.

There's nothing much about Brunner's in the *Mirror*. Just a couple of sentences halfway down page three: 'The Ministry of Munitions regrets to announce that an explosion occurred at a munitions factory in the Silvertown neighbourhood of London. It is feared that the explosion was attended by considerable loss of life and damage to property.'

The rest is all news of the war, food shortages, a statue of Gladstone unveiled in Edinburgh. I fold the paper neatly and leave it on a stack of crates next to a veg stall. Ahead of me now is St Gabriel's Church. I look towards the row of shops opposite, try to focus on an old man nailing cloth to the inside of an upstairs window. The man doesn't have a hammer. He's using what looks like the sole of a clog. But no matter how hard I stare, the church invades me. I can smell my wedding day, feel it: the wood polish on the pews, the candle grease, the gardenias for purity. I turn to the church, confront it, and a tall, smiling girl appears on the steps with her new husband. She is clutching at him, delighted. The groom is a much older man, dressed in a brown suit that is a shade lighter than the one George wore. Two bridesmaids appear, throwing tiny squares of torn-up newspaper. One square lands on the toe of my boot, then wisps off into the gutter.

I should creep into the church, light a candle and pray for Dor. Try to purge the image of Daniel's face, the sanctuary of his hand in mine as we crossed Bow Creek.

A pulsing begins low down, spreading through my body. A burning ache.

15

He leaves Silvertown as the sun rises, the dawn air dense with smoke and disbelief. His knuckles are crusted with blood and brick dust, and his fingers ache with cold. He cuts through a side street, dodging the swept-up heaps of glass and rubble. In an upstairs room, a baby cries. He remembers the last woman he found, an old lady, who clung on to his bleeding hands as they pulled her out. She was asking for her grandchildren. 'In the back bedroom,' she said, blank-eyed, pointing up at where the back bedroom used to be.

Volunteers are arriving now from across London, their sleeves rolled up. Soldiers, some of them, home on leave. The police are turning people away, setting up cordons to stop the gawpers.

He walks through Canning Town, over the bridge, Bow Creek rising with the unstoppable tide. Church clocks strike the hour as he turns into the dock road. He calls into his room to wash and collect clean clothes. The windows have held in the boarding house, no obvious damage.

His Saturday shift starts in twenty minutes. He should be tired, but he has never felt such strength, such energy, surging through every vein.

Sparks from the spot welder sear blocks of orange-white into his vision. The yard is busy with the smelting and welding and mending of ships. War damage to the merchant fleet is worse than ever with the German U-boats sneaking around the coast. They'll torpedo anything to strangle Britain's supplies.

Daniel's hands throb under his thick leather gloves, but the pain is nothing. To have seen such suffering in Silvertown… He is so sorry for Dora, yet he cannot quell the rising energy, the certainty of this feeling, the blaze in Hannah's eyes when she shoved him in the alleyway. She was angry, certainly. Surprised. But something had passed between them. The crackle and spit of desire.

'Steady there,' the foreman calls.

Daniel straightens up and surveys the wound in the side of the ship that he is attempting to repair. He has overworked the steel. Heavy-footed, the foreman walks to his side.

'Mind on the job, Blake, mind on the job.'

He nods an apology, experiences a rush of relief when the tea whistle sounds.

Walking to the cafe, he notices a soldier in hospital blues standing outside the George pub. He is on crutches, one leg missing from mid-thigh. Daniel takes a folded newspaper from his pocket and reads the headline on page five: 'Gallantry Amid Fire.' In France, it has been a terrible winter. The mud is lethal, he has heard. Healthy lads are drowning in it, choking in slime-filled shell holes. You're not supposed to complain, bad for morale, but there's one old boy at Beaumont's can't keep his trap shut. His nephew is back from the Somme, got pissed one night and told his uncle everything. Corpses liquefy in the mud, seep through the trench walls. 'Hero juice', they call it.

Daniel feels the eyes of the soldier on his back as he passes by, hears him cough and mutter, 'Fucking poltroon.'

The cafe is open as usual, but Mrs Stephens is flustered, not a wink of sleep, she says, and she plonks the mug of coffee in front of him with a sigh.

Later he walks to Lion Street, weaving through the Poplar back roads until he is standing in front of Aunt Winch's low brick terrace, the two ground-floor rooms where she had lived and died, where he had lived too, until he was nineteen years old and could afford a lodging room of his own. He pictures her standing at the window of the front parlour, waiting for his Saturday visit. Through the prism of the rippled glass she would seem tinier each time, hunched, as if the great black shawl was an impossible weight upon her shoulders.

She had seemed in good spirits on that last visit, hobbled across the room and touched him on the arm: an affectionate gesture, the closest she would ever get to a kiss. It was late January, he remembers, a few days before her birthday.

'Off to Greenwich tomorrow?' she had asked. Always the same question.

'As usual.'

'Is Lady Tolland back from Dorset? She didn't say in her letter.'

She had reached up for the Christmas card that was still displayed on the dresser. He knew it wasn't a letter at all, just a picture postcard signed: *Regards of the season, Lady Tolland.* Still, Aunt Winch's face was proud as she reread the card, then propped it back against the picture frame. 'Not yet,' he said. 'She usually comes home February, don't she? March if there's snow.'

'Snow? Her ladyship don't like the cold. And those trains can be terrible draughty.' She captured a wisp of her thinning hair and tucked it back into her bun.

'I believe she gets fetched in a motor car now,'

he said.

'Fancy.' She pulled a handkerchief from her sleeve and dabbed at her watery eyes. Her lips tightened. 'Is she still borrowing you them books?'

'Not so much these days.'

'Just as well, eh? Never done you no good, book learning. It's all very well for those what's born to it.'

There was nothing to be gained from arguing. He would never change her, he knew that. It was what she believed, and after all, perhaps she was right. What good *had* it done him? All those hours sitting in Robbo's shed on the pile of hessian sacks, pages angled towards the cobwebbed window to catch the light. Robbo had given up on him, said he'd turned weird, and if he wanted to sit in his dead dad's shed reading while the rest of them were enjoying themselves round the back of the church hall, that was his lookout.

Sometimes a black cat would be waiting for him at the shed door. Were they lucky, black cats, or unlucky? He never could remember. He loved the cat, loved the feel of her warm purring body, her claws piercing his thighs as she settled on his lap.

Robbo said he was mad, because all the girls were swooning for him – he could take his pick and he'd get further than the other lads ever could. Even Nancy Smith was sweet on him, said Robbo, and she was nearly sixteen. He didn't bother telling Robbo that he'd already had Nancy Smith, had her in the shed, and there were splinters in his palms to prove it. Nancy was a pretty girl all right, but afterwards when they walked around the rec, she had bored him rigid.

He wanted a girl who could attract him like the women in Lady Tolland's novels. Someone with a free spirit: Sue Bridehead before she left Jude; Anna Karenina before Part VI; Elizabeth Bennet, but quirkier. Above all, someone who needed to be loved and who would love him completely. He spent hours in Robbo's shed imagining this perfect woman. It helped him to read his books and to dream because it stopped him thinking about his own lost mother.

Had Esther been a perfect woman? She had read *Anna Karenina*, at least. But after they were married, she became irritated whenever he sat down to read. She admitted she had merely leafed through the Tolstoy. 'Those endless chapters about farming,' she said. 'What do I care about Russian peasants?'

Two children are watching him from the upstairs window of Aunt Winch's old house. They tap on the glass, pull silly faces, and then a woman appears and ushers them away. He smiles and walks on, back towards the dock road.

Perhaps when he gets back to the lodging room, there will be a letter from his sister. She might have enclosed a picture from Sam. Sam can write his name now, with a back-to-front 'S'.

There is no letter waiting on the hall table. He sits on the edge of his bed and instead thinks of Hannah. Blood rushes in his ears. He wonders if he will ever sleep.

16

The bottle of barley water is warm in my pocket. Mum boiled it up this morning, stirred in a little sugar she'd been saving. If Dor can't manage a cup, I'll give it to her with a spoon. Drinking's important when you're suffering from burns – it says so in Jen's first-aid book. I cradle the bottle in my left hand and the warmth of it is a comfort on this cold afternoon.

It's only a few more yards to the hospital. The wide stone steps at the entrance are lined with people waiting for visiting to start. Children lark about on the pavement, buttoned up in their Sunday best, leaping on and off the low wall by the hospital railings. One child has cuts on his face, and his arm is in a sling. He hangs about at the edge of the group, wincing as he tries to join in.

Three o'clock strikes and the visitors shuffle in. The children fall into line, sombre now. The boy with the broken arm is in front of me, clutching at the skirt of an older girl who might be his big sister.

I'm on the third step when a hand touches my shoulder. I know it's him before I turn.

'She don't want you visiting,' I say, quiet as I can because there are faces all around, watching. 'You know how shocking she looks,' I say. 'She don't want you to see.'

He nods and I turn away. I mustn't look at him, his brown eyes so tender. I move forward with the queue. Inside the hospital now, more stairs, up to the first floor. We congregate in the corridor, waiting for a nurse to unlock the doors into the ward. My legs feel terribly shaky, but there's nowhere to sit, just a wall painted shiny green and a picture of two black swans on a river, the varnished frame screwed in at each corner. I lean against the wall and the side of the frame presses against my scalp.

The clock outside Sister's office shows four minutes past three and the crowd in the corridor starts to mutter with impatience. 'Didn't come all this way to be kept waiting,' they say. 'They only gives us a couple of hours as it is.' A large woman with her back to me lets out a long sigh. She has the same hat as Mrs Flynn – green felt and a black ribbon. Mrs Flynn will be on her way, with another of the boys, perhaps. Two visitors to a bed, the nurse said yesterday. I'll have to keep my visit short.

At last a nurse comes. She holds the door wide open, looks us up and down, unsmiling. One man is told to come back when he's cleaned his boots.

In the ward, another nurse is standing in front of Dor, lighting up a cigarette by the look of it. The nurse takes one puff to get it going, then leans down and puts the cigarette between Dor's lips. It cheers me to see it, because if she fancies a fag, that has to mean she's feeling better. The nurse moves away and I catch a proper look at Dor. Except it isn't Dor. It's a different woman: bandaged head, yes, but there are curls of dark brown hair around her temples. Freckles on her hands.

It's happened with Dad over the years – swapping beds or wards or even moving hospitals with not a word of warning. I scan the ward, the two dozen or so patients, but there's no sign of her here. Nurse Sands trots up.

'Who are you visiting?' she asks.

'Dora Flynn. I thought she was here yesterday...' I nod over towards the bed where the woman is dragging on her cigarette. She stares at us, poker-faced, and leans over to tap ash into a small glass bowl.

'Yes, I thought I recognized you,' says Nurse Sands. 'A friend?'

'That's right.'

'Come into Sister's office. I'll send for tea.'

Back down the hospital steps. The taste of strong tea bites at my throat and still there is the thirst that won't be quenched. I stumble down the last step and have to reach out to grab the iron railing. The bottle of undrunk barley water tips from my coat pocket and smashes onto the pavement. I bend to pick up the pieces and curse under my breath. As if I haven't cleared up enough bleedin' glass this past two days. That's all I can focus on: the glass, collecting every last scrap, my gloves wet and sticky with barley water.

White cotton flaps in the corner of my vision.

'Let me help,' says Daniel. He is holding out a handkerchief, gestures for me to put the glass into it, then crouches to pick up the last few pieces.

'How is she?' he asks.

We are both crouching now, heads down, our words directed at the pavement.

'Gone.'

He nods slowly, as if he was expecting the news. It makes me seethe, him taking it so calm like that.

'I'm sorry,' he says.

'The burns were too severe, the sister said.' I take a deep breath. If he can be calm, so can I. 'She was very peaceful at the end. Family with her. Only this dinnertime, by all accounts. I just missed her.' My voice cracks and I tip forward onto my knees. I shut my eyes and there are plumes of light, as if a fire is burning behind my eyelids.

'Here, sit down for a moment.'

He lifts me from the ground and steers me towards the wall, but I shrug him off and steady myself against the railings instead.

'She didn't deserve it.' I meet his gaze then and he has the decency to cast his eyes down.

'No.' He takes off his cap and holds it solemnly in both hands. 'Can I buy you a cup of tea? The shock...'

'I've had a cup of tea.'

'A drink, then, a brandy.' He takes a watch from his pocket and frowns, distracted. 'Pubs are shut, unless...'

His eyes are fixed on me again and this time neither of us looks away. The wind is picking up, rattling the masts and rigging of the ships in the dock. Water laps and sighs. It will be dark by four.

'It's two minutes' walk,' he says. 'My room. I

142

have a bottle of something...'

'Your room?'

'A stone's throw. Hannah... Mrs Loxwood, the colour of you. You're shaking. You can't walk all that way home.'

I touch my face with my damp glove, as if that will put some colour back into my cheeks. A queer weightlessness unbalances my body, and I feel so tired. I should go to Dor's house straight away, give my condolences to the family, but I know my legs won't carry me.

He offers his arm and I take it. He stops me from falling.

We walk along the dock road, past All Saints Church and the gravestones leering in crooked rows. A tram passes, its dimmed front lamps straining at the dusk. I catch my reflection in a pawnshop window: hair fixed neatly at the back, pale face with dark, uncertain eyes. How can I be here, alive, when Dor is gone?

'Just here,' he says, reaching into his pocket. I stand close by him as he bends to put the key in the lock.

He steps back to let me in. 'After you.'

The hallway floor is spread with strips of lino, and red wallpaper peels from the walls. The lamps are not yet lit. Near the stairs is an occasional table with a waste bin pushed underneath. Daniel places the tied-up handkerchief inside the bin. He looks awkward as I follow him up the stairs, his shoulders tense, and as his left hand moves along the wooden stair rail, I realize that he is trembling too.

Daniel's room is small, dark and square, just

one tiny window, which faces out onto the road, and sloping eaves on the left side.

'I wasn't expecting a visitor,' he says, picking up a cloth from the washstand and refolding it over the edge of the bowl.

Under the eaves is a single bed. I think the linen may be unmade, but I can't bring myself to look directly at it. I take off my damp gloves and stuff them into my pocket. I leave my hat on.

'Let me light this. Brighten things up.' He stoops to light a candle, and with the same taper he lights the paraffin stove. It can't have been on for weeks, because at first there's the smell of burning dust, masking the paraffin.

'It'll soon warm up. I'm sorry, there's just one chair. Please...'

I follow his eyes to the armchair on the other side of the window. There is a cushion of worn green velvet and a fancy antimacassar. A pair of muddy boots lie carelessly in front of the chair. It's the sight of those unlaced boots, the intimacy of them, that brings me to my senses.

'I won't sit down, thank you. I really should be going.' My mouth is so dry now it hurts to speak. 'Coming here... I wasn't thinking straight. It was the shock, as you say. My mind isn't right–'

'Please. Stay five minutes. Just a talk. A drink.' He turns his back, quickly produces a bottle and a mug from a small cupboard and brandishes them in the air.

'No, I shouldn't be here. I should have gone straight round to Dor's house, pay my respects. How they'll get over this I don't know. Those kids, they idolize her.'

The thought of Kit without his big sister sends my head spinning again. Every scrap of strength drains from me and my legs fold and sink until I am down on the floorboards, sobbing. When Daniel sits beside me, I know I should move away, but instead I let him take my hand. My coat sleeve slips and he turns my arm to look at the cut on my wrist, strokes the skin around it. The touch of him is so beautiful and gentle it seems to steady my blood, help me breathe.

'You've had a terrible shock.' He stands and takes a clean handkerchief from the drawer in his washstand. 'Here, have this. I'll be back in a moment.'

I dry my face, get up and sit in the chair. He appears with a glass. It's sparkling clean, with a thin gold line round the rim.

'A small drink,' he says. 'Just before you go.'

He pours a measure of what looks like port wine and it's only then that I notice his hands: the cuts on his knuckles, his fingernails split and ragged. He offers me the glass and splashes his own drink into the mug. From under the washstand he pulls a small wooden box, places it in front of the chair and sits down facing me.

There is only the sigh of the stove to break the silence.

'Did you rescue anyone at Silvertown?' I ask finally.

'It was a long night. I did what I could.' He drains his wine and tops up my glass before pouring himself another. 'They reckon sixty-odd dead.'

'And now Dor.'

'Yes.'

He sounds quite calm again, almost matter-of-fact. And then it strikes me. It suits him, doesn't it, to have her out of the way? Dor off the scene and me up in his room? Waiting for me at the hospital like that. He thought I'd be a soft touch and he was bloody well right.

'Still, you couldn't care less, Daniel, could you? Dor was nothing to you, like you said.'

He straightens his spine, rests his mug on the trunk.

'That's not right,' he says. 'I liked her very much. Just not...'

'But you weren't even shocked when I told you she was gone. As if you were expecting it. Wishing her dead, were you, to get her off your back?'

'I *was* expecting it, that's the truth. I knew she couldn't survive. But I didn't wish it. Never.'

'How did you know?'

'I've seen people burned. There was a fire once, in a neighbour's house. Well, you can last a day or two, maybe a week, but there's nothing anyone can do. Not with burns that bad.'

Silence again, and my face is flaming. It's too warm now, with my coat still on and the stove hissing away. Perhaps I should apologize, but he speaks first.

'Friday night, I'm sorry if I offended you. I–'

'Please don't ever speak of it. It's time I was going.'

We both stand. He is so tall, his broad frame between me and the door. I think he might reach out to me, block my way.

'I must see Dor's people. Pay my respects.'

'Of course.'

He stands aside, then follows me down the stairs, several steps behind. I have to wait for him to unlock the front door. We are both breathing heavily. He opens the door wide. I thank him and brush past. He holds out his hand for me to shake, but I hurry off, tears clouding my eyes.

I said I'd be back by five, but in fact it's nearer seven. Jen is in the scullery when I let myself in the back door, busy as ever, sorting the washing ready for tomorrow. Everything's filthy, with all the ash and soot that has blown in over the weekend. I thought she'd have the hump, stuck inside with all the chores, but she's humming a tune and her face is softer than usual.

'Kids are in the parlour with Mum,' she says. 'We saved you some bread.' She nods at a plate with a tea towel over it, a scraping of marg still in the dish.

'How's Dor, then?' she asks. 'They let you stay long enough.'

She doesn't believe me when I tell her. The pillowcase in her hand flaps onto the flagstones, wafting up a chill from the floor. It's colder in the scullery than it is outside.

'Dead from a few burns?' says Jen.

'It was worse than we thought.'

'You been to the house?'

I nod. Yes, I went to the house. I'm not sure Mrs Flynn even registered I was there. She was sitting on the piano stool with Dora's feather boa, winding it round and round her wrist. Every so often she'd stop and press the feathers to her face.

'House is packed. All the family, the whole crowd from Ellesmere Street – you can imagine it.'

'Oh, Hannah.'

To my surprise Jen starts to cry. I don't think I've seen her crying since she was a little girl. It's peculiar to witness. For one thing, she didn't even like Dor.

'You'll miss her terrible,' says Jen. 'To have a friend like that, you don't know how lucky you've been. All this bad news, it's too much. It's not good for me.' She places a hand on her stomach and her apron flattens against the broad curve of her belly. She must be four months gone. To think I hadn't noticed.

17

The funeral mass is on Thursday. From the rustling and the coughs and the closeness of the air, I can tell the pews have filled up behind us. I don't like to feel so many eyes watching me, especially here, with the strange rituals: the bells tinkling and the prayers that I can't recite.

The priest thinks we should be pleased that Dor is being raised up to heaven. He looks so satisfied, so untroubled, as he sprinkles holy water on her coffin. Dor's voice rings in my head then, clear as if she's standing next to me. 'Forgive me, Father.' And I can see her smile, a wicked light in her eyes.

I don't notice Ada until after the service, leaning against a pillar at the back of the church. She beckons me over. It's strange to see her in a proper coat instead of rolled-up shirt sleeves, her hair brushed and almost neat. No gloves, though. Her hands are raw: cracked and scabbed so that you wince just to look at them.

She touches my arm. 'You all right?'

I nod. 'Sort of. What about the others?'

'Edie's injured. Her face is a mess, but she's up and about. It's just Dor from our shift.' She looks around, lowers her voice. 'Listen, we're not going back to the house. The Steamship tomorrow night. We'll give Dor a proper sendoff.'

I glance over to Mum and Jen. They're watching me from the aisle, the two of them hanging back from the crowd shuffling towards the priest. Jen has a hankie pressed to her nose; the smell of incense has set off her sickness.

Ada takes a toffee from her pocket and lodges it in the side of her mouth.

'You'll come, then?' she says.

'I'll try.'

They don't mention Ada until we're halfway down Ellesmere Street. I walk slightly ahead of them on the narrow pavement, slowing every few hundred yards while Jen blows her nose. We don't say anything when we pass our old house, but I know we're all thinking of Dad – Dad how he used to be, whistling on a ladder as he cleared out the guttering or polished up the windows.

Mum offers occasional remarks on the funeral – how dignified Mrs Flynn was, how smart the boys looked, didn't the priest go on?

'No sign of Dor's fellow, though,' she says. 'Did

149

you see him, Hannah?'

I shake my head. No, I didn't see him: I made sure not to look.

'Who?' asks Jen.

'Dor's fellow. Daniel, wasn't it? The one who called by Friday night.'

'You'd think *he'd* turn up,' sniffs Jenn, as if she'd known about him all along.

'You would really. And who was that woman you were chatting to, Hannah, in the church? Scruffy sort. Sucking on a sweet like she hadn't a care.'

'Ada? She works with Dora in the factory. There's a group of them thick as thieves. They're having a get-together tomorrow, to remember Dor. Asked me along.'

'You'll go?'

'If you'll mind the children.'

'It's at this Ada's place, is it?'

'Just round the corner. The Steamship.'

I don't have to turn round to know that Jen will be raising her eyebrows, and Mum's lips will be thin and pinched.

Plates of paste sandwiches and bottles of stout are crammed onto an oval table. The air is dim and sticky, people squashed elbow to elbow, drinks held close. I can feel myself breaking into a sweat, the chemise clinging to my skin, the cotton of my dyed black blouse prickling at the cuffs and neck. One of Dor's uncles leans against the keys of the piano. When he moves, the high notes squash out like mangled birdsong through the chatter.

Mum and I weave our way across the room to

speak to Dor's mum. She's standing at the front window, half an eye on the street outside.

'It was a lovely service, Meena,' Mum says.

'The Mass? Yes.' Mrs Flynn has an odd, hopeful look in her eyes. Her lips are very red, as if she's been at Dor's petals. 'Tell you the truth, I can't take it all in. Keep thinking I'm going to wake up. I didn't know half the crowd in the church. People from the factory, I suppose.' She glances at Mum and me, then quickly turns her eyes back to the window.

'No doubt,' says Mum.

'Counting their lucky stars, that factory lot. Why her? That's what I can't fathom. My lovely girl. Just when she was so happy, too. This Daniel she'd taken up with...'

'He seemed ever so nice,' says Mum.

Mrs Flynn looks surprised. 'You know him, Susan? Did you see him in the church today?'

'No, it was just last Friday I met him, when you sent him round. It was kind of you. Hannah was so worried.'

'Not me, dear. I never met the man.'

Mum turns to me, starts to speak and then hesitates.

'But... Oh, I'm mixing myself up,' she says. 'I'll get us some more tea.'

The uncle has turned towards the piano now and he's picking out a tune with his right hand. Mrs Flynn sweeps over and tips the lid down. He jerks his hands away just in time. The room is silent for a second; then the conversation starts up again, hushed and faltering.

Slowly people start to disappear. Dor's house

151

has never been so quiet.

That evening I've a peculiar feeling that I'm expected somewhere. The date nags at me – Thursday, 25th January – until I remember the girl in the cornflower-blue gloves and the peace meeting poster. Railway Street, tonight. Dora and I might have been there. Will they go on with it, after Brunner's? Of course. It will only make them more determined. They'll be there now, the peace brigade, striking a blow for freedom and right, just like they promised. I wish I was with them.

I unbutton my funeral blouse and drape it on the edge of the bed. On my wrists and under my arms there are dark blotches where the clothes dye has run. The facecloth is still damp from this morning, damp and freezing, but I rub at the dye until my skin smarts and the cut on my wrist starts to weep. How long before I wear the black blouse again? I imagine the army letter pushed through the front door, George's name in the newspaper casualty lists. It occurs to me that George could have been killed a hundred times over while Dor was being laid to rest. I have no idea if my husband is alive or dead. It's as if I'm caught in the centre of an unending bridge. On one side lies my old life; on the other side ... what?

The bell rings over the cafe door. It's six-thirty and there'll soon be a queue of men wanting their breakfast. Mrs Stephens drapes pastry over a pie dish, then wipes her hands on the damp tea towel.

'I'll go,' she says, picking up the pad from the counter. 'Because you do look peaky this morn-

152

ing, Hannah. I can send for Mr Stephens if you need a sit-down. He's only up there doing the order books.'

'I'll be fine. Just tired. The funeral yesterday...'

'Terrible business.' She shakes her head and lifts the counter lid, turns sideways to fit through the gap.

I scrape dried mud from a potato with the sharpest knife. A picture of Daniel's unlaced boots edges into my mind. I scrape harder, replace the image with something safe: Alice in her hand-me-down shoes, jumping in hopscotch squares, her dusty knees with their scars and scabs.

The day drags. Regulars come and go: Mr Travers, Mr Stooks, Vernon Cridge. Everyone but Mr Blake.

Laughter echoes from the pubs on Hallsville Road, but the streets are quiet for a Friday. This time last week the sky over London blazed orange: I should be grateful for the black.

An old boy and his wife walk ahead of me. They are slow, but I hold back so as not to overtake them. Arm in arm they negotiate the dark pavement, the man carrying a lamp in his right hand to pick out the uneven stones.

It's after eight. Ada and the girls will be wondering whether I'm coming. Just the creek to cross now, then a few hundred yards to the Steamship. The old couple turns off towards Plaistow and I am alone. Bedraggled grasses rise from the bank next to the iron bridge. I pick up a stone and throw it down the bank. Rats rustle and scurry. There's a splash into the water: rat splash, a large one. My right foot on the bridge, both feet, and the walkway seems to sway and shift, dragging downwards, as if the bridge is falling. I grip the handrail, try to breathe. It's you that's falling, I tell myself, not the bridge. *Daft old Hannah-Lou, daft old Hannah.* Dad tickling my waist as he lifts me onto his shoulders.

Why should I cross over? Why should I meet these women I hardly know? I don't want Ada looking at me, holding up her latest letter, asking about George. The snide glances, making out like I'm lah-di-dah. It's not a send-off for Dora. It's Ada's excuse for a drink-up. *Mine's a barley wine.* What does she want me there for? They hadn't known Dora two minutes. If only Dora had stuck with her job at the laundry, there wouldn't be any of this. Everything is because of the war. Everything.

The river stinks worse than ever. Might be a dead cat down there, rotting in the oil-slimed grass. There are footsteps approaching from the other side. I make a decision: run across fast as I can, so we don't have to pass in the middle. Could be unlucky to meet in the middle, like crossing on the stairs. The man touches his hat – 'Evening' – but I dash by and don't slow down until I reach the pub. Through the window I can see Ada laughing and there is Daisy too, a painted comb dangling from her hair.

Icy raindrops strike my face. I look up to the murky sky, but there are no stars, only the blank heavens. I shouldn't be here. I turn back towards the bridge. I should stay at home tonight. Every night. A respectable wife and mother.

18

Something invades my dream: a hand pressed to my forehead, then fingers tugging gently at my braided hair. My eyes flick open and there is Alec, bending over me with a smile. His night-shirt hangs lopsided over his thin shoulders.

'Sleeping Beauty,' says Alec. He whispers so as not to wake the children. 'You'll be late for work. It's gone five.'

Usually he wakes me with a tap on the bed-room door. What is he doing in here? I pull the blanket up to my chin and Alec takes a step back, runs his finger along the windowsill as if he's checking for dust.

'Not like you to sleep so heavy,' he says, looking at his finger, then wiping it on his sleeve. 'Up all night, were you, busy practising your letters?'

My head feels muzzy, and my limbs are dead weights. I can't have had more than two hours' sleep.

'Don't know. Just a rotten night.'

'I'll leave you to it, then. It's icy this morning. Tap's frozen.'

The only way is to jump straight out of bed, get moving and try not to think about the cold, but I can't do it. My head is pounding, and when I try to move, every muscle aches. At six Jen comes in.

'You're not going to work, then?' she says. 'You've been peculiar all weekend.'

155

'I can't get up.'

'What is it, a cold? Well, you won't mind if I steer clear.' She turns towards the door. 'I'll send Mum in.'

I doze again, dream of an omnibus journey and a schoolhouse in a field, a bell ringing, children running down a hill in the sunshine. I leave the other children and run to the shade of an oak tree where a dead mole hangs over a high branch. I want to reach up to the mole, stroke its beautiful fur, but the tree is too big to climb, and when I look around, I realize the field has disappeared and I am surrounded by the high walls of the workhouse. The workhouse children are laughing, holding their thin bellies.

'Up you get, Alice, else you'll miss the whistle.' Mum is leaning over the bed. 'Get your things on and leave Mummy in peace.' She walks round to my side of the bed and puts a cup down on the floor.

'Nice cup of tea for you. So you're not going in? What your Mrs Stephens is going to think I don't know. Alec will call in with a note. He's down that way this morning.'

I try to thank her, but I can't manage more than a groan. Mum tucks the blanket back around Teddy, then shepherds Alice from the room. Teddy breathes in with a delicate snore and pushes his toes into the backs of my knees. If only I could be alone for a moment. Just an hour or two. A proper sleep to clear my head.

On Wednesday I drag myself to the cafe. The walk feels twice as long and it must be after six

156

when I push open the side door, because I can already smell the stock boiling. I unbutton my coat and reach for the first hook on the wall, where I usually hang it. But on my hook is a hat I've not seen before, green felt with a spray of red fabric flowers, and underneath it a grey coat trimmed with ribbon.

Mrs Stephens comes out into the hall. 'Oh, you're here, then,' she says, almost as if she's disappointed. 'Thought I heard the door.' She lowers her voice. 'Now listen, there's a Miss Wilton come to help out. A sweet girl, very dependable by all accounts.'

So Mum was right. One day sick and now I'm for the chop.

'I'm sorry about Monday, Mrs Stephens. I'm right as rain now. Won't happen again. Just a silly fever, something and nothing...'

She waves her hand as if to shut me up.

'So you says now, but I had no way of knowing, Mrs Loxwood. The note didn't say when you'd be back. And the chap what brought it, he dashed off before I could ask.'

'He was supposed to tell you – Alec, my sister's husband – he was going to say I'd be in Wednesday unless you heard otherwise.'

'Like I said, he just left the note.'

I start to put my coat back on, and it's as much as I can do not to cry. Mrs Stephens looks me up and down and narrows her little eyes so that they're nothing but piggy specks.

'Don't get the wrong idea, Mrs Loxwood – it's not the sack, for heaven's sake. I ain't that cruel. Come on, hang up your coat. Fact is, I need a bit of extra help. There's my aunt going doolally in Hackney and I ought to visit her more often. Poor dear's got no one but the next-door neighbour, and she's after the money, such as it is. Miss Wilton could be a godsend. You'll get on fine, I know.'

In the kitchen, Miss Wilton is slicing onions. She stops briefly when I walk in, looks up and says hello. Her eyes are swimming, but she's managing not to cry. I recognize her face, and her voice is familiar too, high-pitched but husky, like a little girl with a sore throat.

'Ices at the Queen's,' she smiles.

'Sorry?'

'You won't place me without the uniform; no one does. You know – "Ices, toffee, sherbet lemonade."' She calls it out just like in the interval and yes, I can see her in the red and gold uniform, smiling over a tray of ices.

'The Queen's, that's it. You still work there? I've not been in a long time.'

'Most weekends. It's not so busy now, of course.'

Mrs Stephens interrupts, and from the look on her face she's blaming me for the chit-chat. 'Mrs Loxwood, if you can write up the new prices before the rush.' She hands me a list and a piece of chalk. 'They'll huff and puff, but you can tell them straight if I don't increase my prices, I might as well give the whole thing up. Milk will be dear as port wine at this rate. Any troublemakers, you refer them to me.'

I collect the boards from around the cafe: two displayed in the window and two up on the walls, wipe them clean and lay them out on the counter. I feel dizzy leaning over to write, trying to concentrate on the words, the fancy strokes from *Barter's*. BUNS ¾d. Dor stood at this counter not two weeks ago. 'Sugar on top 'n' all!' Is that right, less than a fortnight ago she was in here, chatting away, stirring sugar in her tea?

'Lovely handwriting, I'll say that for you,' says Mrs Stephens, leaning over to inspect my progress. It's as if that's all she can say for me. I look at the piece of chalk and imagine it stuck up her snouty nose.

'Shall I make a start on the potatoes, Mrs Stephens?' calls Miss Wilton, so polite and willing with her little girl's voice. Butter wouldn't melt.

The customers love a new face, of course. You can hear the cash tips jangling in her apron pocket. Smug isn't the word. They'll soon tire of her, so let her get on with it and enjoy the glory. Not that I'd swap places. Fair game, that's how some customers see Miss Wilton. A pretty girl, and a single girl. Vernon Cridge doesn't waste any time – snakes his hand towards her arse as she clears his plate, but she twists sideways and he gets an elbow in the lughole for his trouble. Seems she can look after herself. That's good.

At lunchtime I stay in the kitchen stacking dishes. Mrs Stephens is ladling out soup.

'Pea and ham for Mr Blake,' she calls.

The shock of his name, like a maroon crack through the silence.

She places the bowl on the counter and Miss Wilton hurries to collect it.

'Tall man facing the window,' says Mrs

Stephens. 'He wants two slices with it.'

Miss Wilton carries the soup carefully to Daniel's table. I hover near the counter. She sets the bowl down and they exchange some words. He looks up at her and smiles. He doesn't even turn to see if I'm there, just picks up his spoon and starts to eat. He hasn't asked for me, then. I keep busy in the kitchen, washing pots and pans in scalding water straight from the copper. The cut on my wrist is healing, but the hot water seeps under the scab and the wound begins to sting.

'Leave the pots for now,' says Mrs Stephens. 'Table of four just come in.'

I have to walk past Daniel's table, but he doesn't look up. He has finished his soup and he's writing something, scribbling with a pencil on a scrap of brown paper. A note for me? He'll press it into my hand when I clear his table. I'll need to be quick to get there before Miss Wilton.

A whiskery old boy dithers over his order. Shall it be the liver or the pie? he asks me. Which would I recommend? And it's all looking a bit pricey, sweetheart. He'll have to dig deep... Finally he decides. As I take down the order, Daniel gets up and leaves.

I'm at the table first. I pick up his bowl and plate. There's no sign of a note. Nothing tucked under the salt cellar, nothing under his mug.

It's what I wanted, isn't it? I told him not to speak of what passed between us. I brushed him off, refused to shake his hand. I can't blame him for respecting my wishes. I should be grateful.

At the end of the shift Miss Wilton asks where I'm heading.

'Canning Town.'

'I'm Stepney.'

I suppose she'll want to walk up the road together. She straightens her hat and her brown hair squashes around her ears. We step out into the damp afternoon. In her basket is a bag of leftover buns; all I got from Mrs Stephens was half a loaf of yesterday's bread.

'I'm Nettie, by the way,' she says. 'You know, when Mrs Stephens isn't listening. You don't have to worry about "Miss Wilton".'

'Righto.'

'Listen, I hope I'm not stepping on your toes.'

The poor girl looks worried and now I feel guilty for being so sour.

'It was a surprise to find you there, that's all. I never knew Mrs Stephens was hiring. And to tell you the truth, I ain't feeling too good. Got a cracking headache.'

'Oh. I hope you feel better soon.'

'Thanks. See you Friday.'

I should have told her my name, I realize, as I turn onto Manchester Road.

There's a fog settling and it's colder than ever. The Thames could freeze at this rate; there might already be ice in the water. I shove my hands into my coat pockets and my glove catches on a piece of paper. A note.

19

At the base of the apple tree, the earth is rimed with frost. He almost slips on the icy ground and the pruning saw jabs into the bark, lodging itself in the trunk. There is a gash in the bark and he curses his carelessness. With a deep breath he kicks his heel at the earth to roughen the icy surface. Now he works methodically around the tree, cutting out any dead wood with the saw, then trimming back the side shoots with the sharpest secateurs. The shoots are green and fleshy inside, satisfying to slice through. He stands back to admire the shape of the tree, its branches curving upwards like the smooth sides of a wine glass.

Next the smaller pippin, then the Conference pear. When he has finished, he stacks the brash in the covered woodpile at the side of the house. Woodlice scurry in the crevices between the flagstone path and the wall.

The ground is too hard for digging. He surveys the flowerbeds, the snowdrops fading now, and the hellebores with their muted pink flowers, nodding down as if they daren't admit their beauty. He bends to pick a hellebore, drops it into his jacket pocket on top of his tobacco tin. If he's careful, the petals won't crush.

In the church nearby, the first hymn starts. He pulls the watch from his waistcoat. It's still too soon.

He cleans the pruning tools with a rag, pad-
locks the shed and walks up the garden towards
the house. Lady Tolland is sure to be away for at
least another fortnight, with the weather so bitter
and the threat of more snow. But he won't risk
the library today. All the outstanding books are
returned, in any case. Everything is in perfect
order.

Two men are setting up a refreshment kiosk just
outside St Mary's Gate. Daniel looks at his watch
again. Half past ten. A cup of tea would calm him,
but he decides not to stand around until the kiosk
opens. He'll climb the hill now and wait.

Greenwich Park is almost empty. He takes the
hill at a steady pace, scanning the pathway ahead
and the frosty swards that slope up to the observatory buildings at the top. When he reaches the
observatory, it is still only a quarter to eleven. He
wanders towards a bench, but it is wet with thawing frost, and anyway, he would prefer to stand. He
takes off his gloves and lights a cigarette.

The sky is overcast but curiously bright. To the
north, the city is laid bare: he can see the dome
of St Paul's, milky in the winter haze; Tower
Bridge; the cranes and the chimneys rising from
the Isle of Dogs. To the east, there are the factories, the crumbling tower of a burnt-out silo.
And everywhere the rows and rows of dreary
houses, their Sunday-morning rituals, the peeling
of a million potatoes. He can almost smell the
wet starch, the mouldering eyes flicked carelessly
into the bucket.

A nanny passes with a large perambulator, two
babies sleeping inside. He touches his cap, but

the nanny looks away. Three stray dogs appear and bound down the avenue towards the bandstand. They look thin, hunted; one of them has a bald patch on its flank. A park keeper tries to chase the dogs off, but he has a limp and cannot run. The keeper abandons the chase a hundred yards from the observatory and leans against the trunk of a chestnut tree as he catches his breath. When he notices Daniel watching, he straightens up from the tree trunk, rights his braided cap and walks towards him, grimacing with every tread of his right foot.

'Can I 'elp you, sir?' says the park keeper.

'No, thank you.'

'I see.' He raises his eyebrows. 'Loitering outside the Royal Observatory like the world owes him a living.' The park keeper addresses this comment as if to a colleague who may be standing nearby. 'I know your sort. Other side of the gates, if you don't mind. Why, the king himself sometimes drives out on a Sunday.'

Daniel takes a last drag of his cigarette but decides not to drop it on the path. Got to keep on the right side of these people, he thinks; they reckon they're higher than the law. He keeps hold of the cigarette, though it is burning close to his fingers, and starts to walk back down the hill. When the park keeper is out of sight, he flicks the cigarette across the grass.

'We're both early, then.' The voice comes from behind him. He spins round and she is there, not quite smiling. She must have approached from another path, the one that strikes off to the west.

'Hannah.'

164

'I got your note.'

'I gather...'

'A talk, you said?' She is wearing a straw hat with a black ribbon, and in her hands she twists a white handkerchief. She seems hesitant, defensive. But she is here.

'I just thought, well, wondered how you were.'

She shrugs. 'I'm fine, really.'

'You've been to Greenwich Park before?'

'No, never.'

'It's better in the spring.' He gestures to the avenue of leafless chestnut trees. His limbs feel awkward, something stiff and artificial about every movement, every word. 'The chestnuts are a grand sight – you can imagine.'

'I didn't know it was such a big place.'

'There's a flower garden, and the Wilderness,' he says. 'What about the Queen's Oak? Would you like to see that?'

She nods. 'But I can't be long. My sister's cooking.'

They take a narrow path eastwards towards Queen Elizabeth's Oak. A sparrowhawk shrieks in the sky above. Daniel wants to offer his arm, but Hannah's body seems so closed in, so clamped together, that he is sure she will not take it.

When they reach the oak, she stares up and he notices the white skin taut around her throat. The oak is immense – fifty, perhaps sixty feet tall – its lifeless black boughs held up by a mass of clinging ivy.

'They say Henry VIII and Anne Boleyn danced round it, and Queen Elizabeth used to picnic here.'

She swallows, still gazing upwards, and he is transfixed by the delicate movement of her throat, the way the light seems to soak into her skin.

'But it's dead,' she says. She grasps the tops of the iron railings that enclose the tree, peering up still further so that her hat clings precariously to her head. Ivy curls through the railings, skimming her coat, her long black skirt. 'Funny to think it's been around so much longer than we have.'

'And it'll be here long after.'

'Will it?'

'"*Had we but world enough, and time, this–*"'

'I know the poem, thank you.' She loosens her grip on the railings. With her ungloved hand she pulls at an ivy leaf until the stem breaks.

She knows the poem. He feels breathless. It was a little forward of him, perhaps. Too direct. But something has to alter the mood, snap them out of this wretched polite conversation: the Sunday dinner and the chestnuts and the fascinating history of the ancient bloody oak. She is examining the ivy leaf in minute detail. Watery sunlight filters through the cloud-bleached sky and her dark hair glows a reddish shade, light as amber. Why has she bothered to come? He watches the back of her head, the gold chain at the nape of her neck, the hairpins pushed neatly into plaited coils. It occurs to him that this is the first time he has seen her in sunlight. No ... there was a day last year, when they crossed on the swing bridge. He had been reading a newspaper, pretended he hadn't noticed her, though of course he had. He had noticed everything about her.

'Hannah, listen.'

She turns to face him and her eyes offer a silent challenge. Beautiful, but inscrutable. *Listen*, he had said. Listen to what? He cannot think of anything to say. A dull panic presses upon his chest.

He takes a step towards her. 'I am sorry about Dor. Truly.'

'Don't speak about her. It's bad enough I'm here.'

He feels the pressure again, a pain around his heart. It is the saddest thing. They are the same, wreathed in loneliness. 'I'm glad you came,' he says.

She edges back so that her spine is hard against the railings and her hands are low down, gripping the iron. He steps closer. His body is a fraction from hers. He lowers his head and brushes his lips against her ear. The contact with her skin is shocking, intense. She breathes in sharply, lifts her face upwards and suddenly she is kissing him, their mouths colliding, rough and frantic, until a small cry sounds in her throat. She pulls away, turns her face again towards the towering dead oak.

'Hannah?' He puts one hand on her shoulder.

'We shouldn't. Not here.'

'Of course.' His heart thunders, every fibre in his body burning. He looks across the park towards the river, attempts to calm himself. 'Shall we walk?' he asks.

He takes her arm and they wander through the flower garden and into the Wilderness, where yews and rhododendrons form a low evergreen canopy. Somehow it is enough to feel the press of her arm, the warmth of covered skin through the fabric of their winter clothes. He suggests a drink and they leave the park through the south gate, crossing Shooters Hill Road, past mournful horses and the frozen pond, until they reach Blackheath and the pub with its warm air drawing them through the open door.

They sit in a private booth. There is too much to say, so they say nothing. For the first time he is able to look at her properly, study her face and her eyes. Disbelief is what he sees, and something else: joy, is it, or fear?

'I'd like to see you again,' he says.

She nods but does not speak.

'Come to my room, Hannah. You remember the address?' She wants to come, he's sure of it. He mustn't give her an opportunity to say no. 'Tell me when.'

She looks around the pub and lowers her voice. 'Perhaps on Friday. Friday at seven?'

'I'll be waiting.' He reaches into his pocket and takes out the hellebore. 'Something for you.'

She holds the stem between her thumb and forefinger, strokes each petal and the long stamens, dusty with pollen.

'I do love flowers.' She tucks the bloom into the buttonhole of her coat.

'When spring comes, I'll buy you violets.'

She smiles and with her free hand she touches the side of his face.

Part Two

Leman Street Police Station

21st day of July 1918

Statement of George Alfred Loxwood
Rifleman

I married Hannah Louise Loxwood in February 1912 at St Gabriel's Church, Poplar. We lived together at Alton Street, Poplar, with our two children, Alice and Edward. My wife was a respectable, sober and hard-working woman, and our married life was a very happy one.

On joining the army in 1915, my wife and our children went to live with her married sister in Sabbarton Street, Canning Town. I remained in England in training for about seven months. We corresponded regularly, and her letters to me were very affectionate. I saw her twice during that time, the last occasion being about four days before I embarked for France. We parted on the best of terms. I was afterwards removed from France to Salonika. During the whole of that period I wrote to her as often as my duties permitted, and she regularly replied. Her letters continued to be of an affectionate nature.

20

Colney Hatch is set in green parkland with a driveway running down the middle. There are domes and bell towers and a flag flying. For a moment I'm almost proud to think my dad is living here, surrounded by green fields and fresh air, miles from the city. It's more like a mansion than a madhouse.

A man in a top hat walks up to the gates ahead of me, silver-tipped cane in one hand and leather briefcase in the other. We reach the lodge house and he is waved through a side gate. 'Morning, Dr Hetherington,' says the chap on the gate, touching his cap as the doctor strides through.

I follow behind, but the gatekeeper holds up a hand to stop me.

'Your business?' he says.

'Visiting.'

'Visiting ends midday on Thursday, and the time now is–' he takes a pocket watch from his waist-coat '–eight minutes to.'

'Oh.' I look down at the bunch of catkins I bought from a flower-seller outside the railway station. The pollen has brushed onto my coat like smears of mustard powder. My eyes prick.

'You can always wait till three,' he says. 'After they've had their sleep.'

173

I shake my head. 'Sorry, I can't stay. My children...' The gatekeeper sighs and walks over to a little office in the lodge house. He brings out a ledger. 'Ward?'

'I don't know. It's my dad I'm visiting. I've not been before.'

'Name?'

'Hannah Loxwood.'

'Not your name, yer dad's.' His grey moustache twitches in amusement.

'Edward White.'

The man goes back into the office and chooses another ledger from a shelf. Through the window I can see him running a finger down pages of names.

'Edward White of Poplar?'

'That's him.'

'"Low Grade... Ward D1." You'd better hurry. Through this gate, then at the main entrance to the hospital turn left, stay on the path, keep going for five hundred yards or so. You'll see the signs.'

I half run down the driveway, the catkins jiggling like proper lamb's tails and my breath catching in the icy air. *Low grade.* The words sing in my head, so trifling, so hopeful. Low grade can't be serious, can it?

Skirting the front of the main building, I can smell meat roasting. Knives are being sharpened in the hospital kitchen, the scrape, scrape, scrape of metal on metal. The asylum is vast, a never-ending wall of yellow bricks and arched windows. I glance through one of the windows. Two women in neat white pinafores sit side by side on straight-backed chairs, their hands clasped in

174

their laps. They are smiling.

Finally a sign: WARDS A–D. LAUNDRY. ORCHARD. It must be after midday by now. I dash through an open archway and into a dark courtyard where clipped boxed hedges surround a frost-pinched lawn.

Wheeled chairs are lined up along one side of the courtyard. There's a scrap of grey material on the wicker seat of one of the chairs. When I pass, I look closer: it's a tiny rag doll, the hair fashioned from twines of white cotton, apple pips for eyes.

The ward marked 'D' is at the far end of the courtyard. As I approach, the door is opened by a nurse and three women file out. The women walk in detached silence; only one nods a greeting to me as she passes. I quicken my pace and reach the door just as the nurse is drawing it shut.

'Excuse me, Nurse!'

She stops in surprise and looks up.

'Yes?'

'I'm visiting my dad, Mr White. Ward D1.'

'Visiting's finished.'

'Please, just for a couple of minutes. To give him these?' I hold out the bunch of catkins and she jerks her head back as if I'm presenting her with a pail of pigswill.

'Just a moment.'

Eyes are watching me as I wait, I'm sure of it. I scan the courtyard, but the visitors have all left and there is only the queer rag doll, slumped in the wicker chair. In a nearby building, cutlery clatters and voices drift: calm voices, none of the jabbering or wailing you'd expect in a place like this.

The nurse reappears. 'You may visit for five minutes. Just on this occasion.'

I follow her into the hallway where a desk is covered in tidy stacks of paperwork.

'Sign here, please.'

I write my name and address in the visitors' book. She nods, then takes a wooden box from a drawer and places it on the desk. The white label on the lid is upside down, but I can read it easily: 'Low Grade Mental Defectives. Male D.' There are hooks inside the lid of the box, a large key hanging on each one. She takes a key, shuts the box and locks it back into the drawer.

'Follow me.'

Inside the ward, the walls are bare – not even any plaster to cover the bricks. There's no ceiling either, just the wooden beams and an echoing space up to the rafters. The room is like a barn; there may as well be straw on the floor. Dad's bed is at the far end, near the fireplace at least, though the heat is blocked by a heavy iron guard.

Dad is sitting on a chair next to the bed. He hasn't shaved and his stubble is grey. Around his mouth, there are deep creases, straight down his jowls like someone has scored ink into his skin. Four months he has been here. Four months and he has become an old man.

His face lifts into a smile when he sees me. 'Beatrice!' he says. 'Look at you, beautiful as ever.'

I shouldn't be surprised. He was always getting names mixed up, even when he was well, and this isn't the first time he's called me Beatrice.

'It's Hannah, Dad.'

'That's right. Well, sit down, then.'

I'm not sure where to sit. There's only the chair that Dad's in and I don't want to borrow one from another patient. I brush down the blanket and perch on the edge of the bed.

'How are you, Dad?'

He stares at me with dull eyes. 'I've been worse,' he says. 'It's the flames you have to watch out for.' His voice is strong enough, but somehow it doesn't belong to him. It's slower, more careful.

'I brought you these.'

He doesn't take the catkins, just stares intently.

'There you go again, Beatrice, suiting yourself,' he says. 'It's not right. This has to stop!' He bunches his hands into fists and bangs them on his thighs.

'Dad? Some flowers for you!'

But he doesn't take the catkins, just keeps thumping himself and shouting, 'This has to stop!' I leap up from the bed and look for the nurse. She's here already, must have been watching, and she takes me by the shoulders and ushers me away. Two orderlies stride down the ward, big men, both of them.

'Visitors can agitate the patient,' the nurse says as we reach the double doors that lead into the hallway. 'He's perfectly calm most of the time.'

'But ... low grade, isn't he? Surely that means not too serious? You'll be letting him home soon?'

'I'm not at liberty to discuss the patient. Perhaps – your mother is it, who generally comes?

– perhaps your mother would like to make an appointment with the doctor next time she visits.'

I turn back to Dad and I wish I hadn't. He is out of the chair now, weeping. 'Beatrice! Beatrice!' he sobs. One of the orderlies takes a screen from the corner of the room and unfolds it around Dad's bed.

Back in the courtyard, I hurry past the line of wheeled chairs. The little rag doll has disappeared. A gong sounds and the smell of gravy makes my stomach heave. Again, I have the sensation that someone is watching. Crows caw, closer now.

Why did I come? I wanted to see Dad, of course I did, but I wanted something more: his forgiveness. Forgiveness for Daniel, for what is to come. When I was a girl, he'd forgive me anything. Used to eat Jen up with jealousy. I can hear her taunting me now. *Rotten creep. Rotten daddy's girl.*

So much for forgiveness. Perhaps, in his illness, Dad recognizes me as I truly am. A wicked wife? Wicked as Auntie Bea.

I drop the catkins in the wheeled chair where the rag doll used to sit. A gift for the watching eyes.

Guilt laps at me like a rising tide, but I won't let it seep in. Wicked or not, I can't be sorry. How can I be sorry when I feel like this, as if my life has started up brand new, sharp and colourful, a swirl of terror and bliss like I'm lost in a fairground, blinded by naphtha flares? Friday at seven, the lights flash out. Friday at seven.

The London-bound train is just pulling in as I arrive, breathless, at Colney Hatch Station. I find

178

a seat in an empty carriage and I give in to my wickedness, push away the other faces: Dad and George, Mum and Jen with their disapproving eyes. I won't even think of Dor. No ... I'm with Daniel under the blackened oak. I feel his lips on mine, and his breath warm on my skin.

Friday at seven.

21

'You up there, Hannah?'

Can't get a minute's peace.

'Just coming.' I take the stairs slowly, folding George's letter into my apron pocket. He sounds glum, says he's missing me and the kids. He wants me to go down Whiffin's, get some family photos taken. *The children must be growing fast. Give them a kiss from their old dad.*

In the parlour, Mum is dozing, and Jen is knitting a shawl from an unpicked pullover. Teddy is trying to make a house from his cigarette cards, balancing them against one another to build the walls. His sock puppet is inside the cigarette-card house, squashed into a ball.

'Don't forget Alice needs fetching,' says Jen.

'As if I would.'

'Just saying. And why don't you take Teddy along? He hasn't been out all day. He likes to see them coming out of school, don't you, Teddy? You'll be one of them before we know it.'

'Want to stay here,' Teddy says, and his arm

179

jerks a little so that the house collapses on top of his Ducky. He doesn't cry, though; he picks up the cards and starts again. A glob of dribble forms at the side of his mouth.

'Do you want to come and collect Alice?' I ask him, impatient.

'Too cold.'

'I'll be off, then.'

Alice skips ahead of me, her grey school socks sagging round her bony ankles. She stops when we turn onto Sabbarton Street and points at the dilapidated baby carriage parked outside the house. The sight of it catches my breath. I'd recognize that carriage anywhere, with the coloured ribbons looped round the iron frame and the crooked wheel that always sent it weaving towards the gutter.

'What's that?' asks Alice.

'Dor's mum must be here. That's their old baby carriage. We spent hours pushing the little ones round in that.'

'What, you and Auntie Dor?'

'Yes, when we were your age. And if we kept the babies out long enough, Mrs Flynn would give us a toffee apple with a farthing stuck in the top.'

'Can I have a toffee apple with a farthing?'

'When you start being a bit more helpful, p'r'aps.'

As we pass the carriage, Alice tugs at one of the ribbons. My nerves are terrible: I can't cope with her fiddling. 'Leave off and get inside.'

'I didn't do nothing!'

'Just don't start. If Dor's family are here, the

last thing they need is your whinging. Show some respect, can't you?'

Alice flounces in the back door and I follow her into the parlour. Mrs Flynn is in the armchair, her face red and puffy from crying. At her feet is a pile of folded clothes, and on her lap is one of Dor's new hats. There's no sign of Jen. She'll be upstairs: she doesn't like any upset, not in her condition. Mrs Flynn turns to me and I bend to give her a peck on the cheek.

'Hannah, love,' she says, then wells up, pulling a handkerchief from her sleeve.

'Meena has been having a sort-out,' says Mum. 'She's brought some of Dor's clothes round in the pram.'

'Thought you might like them,' says Mrs Flynn. 'She'd splashed out on a few bits recently, with her money from the factory. They paid her well, you know.' Her voice rises, shaky.

At the top of the pile is the cream striped blouse, the one she wore for Daniel.

'Oh, I don't know. I couldn't...'

'Why not?' she snaps. 'I'm too fat for them. They'll only waste. And this hat, it's too modern, with that peculiar brim. Here.' She spins the hat towards me; it stirs up the air and there's the smell of drink from Mrs Flynn, strong drink, probably whisky. I catch the hat and hold it at my side.

'Put it on, Mummy,' says Alice.

'Not now. I'll look after everything for you, Mrs Flynn.' I scoop the clothes into my arms along with the hat. 'It's kind, thank you.'

'Wear them, why don't you? You'll look a pic-

181

ture.' She starts to cry again. Mum takes the almost-boiled kettle off the stove and warms the pot.

'Have a cup of tea, Meena,' she says. 'It's a terrible time for you. The worst.'

'And now Kit going off,' says Mrs Flynn.

'What?' Mum looks shocked, but it's no surprise to me.

'Kit. He's eighteen now, isn't he? Dear God...' She raises her eyes to the ceiling. 'I can't stop him. And my little boys will be next. Where will it end, Susan?'

Mum hands her a cup of tea and I carry Dor's clothes up to the bedroom. Each stair creaks under my feet. I take the steps one at a time, both feet on each tread, trying to breathe deeply, shake off the giddiness, the guilt, the thought of Dor in the cream striped blouse.

I squash the clothes into the wooden trunk with the kids' old baby things. The hat won't fit, so it has to slide under the bed. Tangles of dust gather around the brim. I've not cleaned in here for days – weeks, probably. Not since I swept up the glass the night of the explosion.

Back downstairs, the children are playing in the corner near the stove – Teddy still with his cigarette cards, and Alice doing her best to finish a line of knitting. She grips the large needles like her life depends on it. I sit beside her and watch as she loops the blue wool under and over the right needle. She's determined to make a pair of socks to send to her daddy. Bless her, this first sock looks as if it's turning into a tea cosy. When she drops a stitch, I place my hands over hers and help her to put it right. Her little hands feel so warm under mine, so vulnerable.

Mrs Flynn drains her teacup. She has stopped crying. 'I've not heard from Dor's other friends – you know, this Daniel she was seeing, or the girls from the factory.' She blows her nose into the handkerchief. 'Well, there was a letter from the management, very nice and all, but they didn't really know her. I'd like to meet the other crowd sometime. I couldn't chat after the Mass. Just couldn't do it.'

'Hannah is seeing them tomorrow night, aren't you?'

'Oh?' Mrs Flynn is looking at me, but I keep my eyes on Alice's knitting.

'Yes, you were saying this morning, weren't you, Hannah? You're getting together with the factory girls again.'

'That's right.'

Friday at seven.

'Where you meeting them?'

'Oh, I'm not sure...' Ridiculous to pretend I don't know. Does that sound more suspicious? 'The Steamship, I think. Yes, the Steamship at seven.'

'You could go along, Meena. Hannah could introduce you.'

Mrs Flynn taps a teaspoon against the cup, weighing up the suggestion. *Shall I? Shan't I?* with every tap. 'Perhaps another time,' she says. 'When I'm more myself. They meet every week, do they? Dor used to look forward to her Friday nights. And Saturday nights.'

'Queer going-on, isn't it, young women out in

the pubs? And some of them with husbands abroad,' says Mum.

Heat prickles on my cheeks, but still it's the knitting I focus on, Alice pulling the stitches tight as she reaches the end of the line.

'I don't think there's any harm in it,' I say. Then I clap my hands as if there's work to be done. 'Kids, come and have a wash before your tea.' They don't even look up. 'Come and have a wash, you two. Pair of ragamuffins.'

They drag themselves from the floor and follow me into the scullery. I take the lid from the copper and ladle some lukewarm water into the wash bowl. Teddy picks up the copper lid and holds it across his tummy as if it's a shield. Alice grabs the ladle for a sword, starts bashing the lid and shouting, 'You're dead! You're dead!' I let them screech and yell. Can't even be bothered to scold them. I wring out the flannel, watch the drips of water settle into the blue china bowl. I feel it must be a punishment, this visit from Dor's mum. A warning. How can I lie to the people who are so dear to me – my mum, Mrs Flynn? I could shrivel with the shame of it. Yet I can't give up the thought of Daniel, this need to feel his kiss again, the warmth of his skin.

Friday at seven.

It's a clear night and the moon is already rising. The iron bridge spans the creek like the hunched back of a giant. I hurry over, glancing up at the dark sky, a habit I can't shake, though it's months since a Zeppelin flew over London. They say we've got the Zepps beaten, but a part of me still

184

jumps every time a cloud shifts across the moon.

On the dock road, I keep my head down, past the bottom of Chrisp Street with its crowded evening market, the costers calling and the smell of hot rum.

My nerve breaks as I reach Daniel's lodging house and I think that perhaps I will double back and go to the Steamship after all. I hesitate outside the door, raise my hand and then the door opens before I have even had a chance to knock.

'Been watching from the window,' says Daniel.

'I'm late. Sorry. The children...'

'But you managed to get away.'

'They think I'm out with the factory girls.'

He shuts the door very quietly and turns the key in the lock. I follow him up the stairs. When we reach the landing, a woman appears in a thin print dress, her large feet bare and red with cold and her hair loose around her shoulders. She twines a leg round the stair post and the dress clings so that you can see the shape of her thin body clear as anything. She can't be wearing a slip. Can't be wearing any drawers, for that matter. She must be freezing.

'Well, well, Daniel,' she says. 'And who's this pretty girl?' She's about my age, but she looks at me as if I'm a child.

'Evening, Sonia. This is ... a friend.'

She smiles at Daniel and squeezes one eye shut in an exaggerated wink, her mouth half open so that you can see her spit-shiny teeth. 'Well, that's very nice, lovey.' She laughs and her small breasts shiver under her dress. 'You enjoy yourselves. Friends is all we got, at the end of the day. Ain't that right?'

'If you'll excuse us. We don't want Mrs Browne up here poking her nose in.'

'I'm going out shortly. Won't disturb you.' Sonia uncurls her leg from the post and pushes up against the banister as we pass along the narrow landing. From her opened door drifts the scent of lavender water.

'She don't mean no harm,' whispers Daniel. He tilts his hand towards his mouth as if he's holding a glass. 'Been on the booze.'

Daniel's room is neat and warm. He has found another chair from somewhere, a small wooden chair, with flecks of paint on the seat. It's placed near to the armchair, a respectable distance apart.

He gestures towards the armchair. 'Sit down. A drink?' He lifts the bottle of port wine that stands on the floorboards next to a pile of books.

After one drink the awkwardness lifts and for the first time we talk properly. We talk for an hour, about anything and everything – where we grew up, the jobs we have had, books and poems, music-hall turns. He mimics Wilkie Bard and I nearly choke on my port wine for laughing. Of course, the conversation comes down to the war in the end, how everything is so dreary now. So little to laugh about.

'You're not joining up, then?' I ask him. 'You're exempted?'

'They count it as war work. Ship repair at Beaumont's.'

I think of Ada with her teeth curled round her lips. *A feather man more like.*

'I ain't afraid of the war,' he says. 'I ain't afraid to die. It's the living I can't stand. Cheek by jowl with the other lads, the banter, the boredom of it, a living hell. I'd be first out of the trench when the whistle sounds. Just to get it over with. I'm more use here – I truly believe that.'

'But the whispering. You know what people say.'

'I don't care what others say.' He looks directly in my eyes and I meet his gaze. 'I've never cared.'

My heart thuds against my ribs. Daniel stands and steps towards the window, unhooks the string of the blind. Rough calico tumbles down over the glass panes. There is no moonlight now, just the candle burning steadily on the wash-stand. He unfolds my hands from my lap and pulls me up so that we are facing each other. Tenderly he lifts the hat from my head and removes one pin from my hair. I reach out to him, unknot his neckerchief and drop it on the floor. We kiss slowly and the pleasure of it is almost too much to bear. I unbutton his shirt. His chest is broad and smooth. There is a pale scar on his collarbone, like a bird, with both wings outstretched. Our skin presses together, our every breath a shudder.

This is what I was born for. This is why I exist.

22

Good Friday. A skipping rope thwacks on the cobbles. The whole street has turned out, everyone wrapped in scarves and overcoats because it's cold for Easter. Even Mrs Hillier is having a turn, her gentleman friend holding one end of the rope and Fat Eddie the other. At first they sway the rope gently from side to side.

'That's it, Winnie,' says the gentleman friend, and Mrs Hillier manages a few jumps before he speeds up suddenly, catching the rope on her ankles.

'Leave off,' she laughs. 'I'll lose me drawers!'

'Not for the first time,' someone shouts, and she thrusts a hand to her hip, pretending to be cross.

Alice notices me watching behind the upstairs window. Her hair is a tangle of ringlets tied with yellow ribbons. 'Come down,' she shouts up from the street. I shake my head and shush her with a finger on my lips. I daren't call out for fear of waking Jen.

The baby is sleeping too, on his own pillow next to Jen. His fists are tight under his chin, and there is a milky blister on his top lip. He loves his food; in that respect he takes after Jen, but it's Alec I see in this child's face: the high forehead and the wisps of fair hair. Alec to a tee.

I move over to the fireplace and warm the backs

of my legs. Jen likes to keep the fire lit up here, night and day. She's frightened the baby will catch cold; Alice and Teddy aren't allowed near unless they've washed their hands. I wonder how long it will take before she stops all that nonsense. There's no use mollycoddling him, I've told her, but she won't listen. 'It's just her instinct,' Mum says, as if I've got no instinct myself.

If I stand here any longer, my skirt will scorch. I ought to go back downstairs, finish the dusting and put the baby's muslins in to soak. I tiptoe across the room, but the door opens wide and Alec appears.

I put a finger to my lips again and point over to the bed, but Alec doesn't step back out to the landing. He creeps closer towards me. I can smell fresh sweat on his shirt.

'Just checking up on my little family,' he whispers.

'All fine. They're resting.'

'I could do with a lie-down myself.' He winks and puts his hand on my waist. 'I'm getting too old for these Easter games. Can't skip for toffee.'

I turn sharply, shaking off his hand, and walk out onto the landing. Alec follows. He's been more of a nuisance since the baby was born. He'll be feeling lonely. Jen won't be letting him near her for a long while yet.

'Heard from George?' asks Alec, as he shadows me down the stairs.

'I'll let you know when I do.'

'Are you coping all right? No husband, all this time?'

My pulse quickens. Is it just a smutty remark,

or does he know something? Surely he can't have seen me with Daniel? I've not been out in the street with him, not since that day in Greenwich Park.

'We all manage, don't we? We have to.'

'Not even a week's leave.' He shakes his head.

He follows me into the parlour now, standing close by as I stir the pot on the stove.

'If you ever need anything, you will let me know, Hannah?' His hand is on the small of my back.

Alec...' I begin, and at the same time there is Jen, standing in the doorway wearing only her nightie. Milk from her breasts has soaked through the white cotton.

'Hannah? Weren't you going to come up with some tea?'

'You were asleep.'

'And now I'm awake.'

As Alec scurries to her side, she throws me a scowl. Anyone would think I'd lured him into the parlour and tempted him to touch me. Surely she doesn't trust Alec over me? I watch him stroke her arm and I know the answer.

'You get some rest, Jenny,' he says. 'I'll be right up with your tea.'

Friday nights, I visit. Sometimes I call into the Steamship on the way, just to have a drink with Ada and the girls so I can give an honest answer when Mum asks how the evening went. I don't like to lie, but it's curious how quickly the habit takes you, how your mind snakes ahead, keeping your story straight. I find myself adding little flourishes of detail, even on nights when I haven't set foot in the Steamship. 'Oh, Ada, she was dressed up posh for a change. She's actually gone out and bought a dress.' Or, 'Remember Daisy, the one with the sweetheart in the navy? He sent her a beautiful necklace, all the way from Malta.'

But tonight there's no need for lies. I won't see Daniel and there's no getting round it. His children have come to stay for Easter and he has promised to take them up Chrisp Street for hot cross buns. I can write to him, at least, post a letter to his boarding house. Mrs Browne isn't happy, says Daniel. 'No children or pets' – it's written in the rules pasted up in her hall. But she's made an exception for his children, so long as they're quiet and don't go treading muck up the stairs.

We're eating our fish stew at the table, mopping up the juice with thick chunks of bread. Jen is having her stew in the bedroom. Give it five minutes and she'll be banging on the floor for seconds.

'Is it Friday today?' asks Alice. 'Are you going to see your friends, Mum?'

'Not tonight. It's Good Friday. That's why Nana cooked this lovely stew.' Alice makes a face. Mum is sitting next to her, but I don't think she notices. 'She went up Billingsgate special,' I say. 'Come on, eat nicely.'

Alice puts her spoon down and fiddles with the fish bones on the side of her bowl. 'Can we go over Victoria Park tomorrow?' she asks. 'Violet says there's a fair.'

'Maybe, if you're good. You were going to draw

one of your lovely pictures for Daddy, remember? Show him how you can write your letters? Do that nicely and we'll go to the fair.'

'What about Teddy? Don't he 'ave to do nothing?'

'Teddy is only three. He can't write, can he? You're almost five.'

Alec smiles and gives Alice a pretend cuff round the ear.

'Enough verbal from you, madam,' he says. 'You're wearing your poor mum out. I'll take you all to the fair tomorrow. I'll treat you to the ghost show. Woo-ooo!'

He sways his hands as if he's a ghost and Teddy squeals, covers his eyes with his grubby puppet.

'We'll have a fine time, won't we, Hannah?' says Alec.

'No doubt.' I can't meet his eyes, though I know he is staring. 'Perhaps Jen will feel up to the trip?'

Mum frowns. 'Oh, I don't think so. A quiet house is what she needs. You all go and enjoy yourselves. I'll stay and help with the baby.'

There's a recruiting stand at the entrance to the funfair, a large banner draped across the top that reads: YOUR CHUMS ARE FIGHTING. WHY AREN'T YOU?

'Now's your chance, Alec,' I say, nodding over towards the stand and the grey-haired sergeant in khaki who's stationed under the banner. I expect they'd accept Alec now, however much he may cough and wheeze. Alec knows it too, but he pretends not to hear me, veers off in the opposite direction, over to the right where there's an organ playing a waltz in front of the bioscope show. A girl in a frilly Bo Peep dress sits on a swing that hangs above a narrow platform at the front of the show. Her plaited hair is draped over one shoulder, and she's smiling at the drib-drabby crowd waiting to file in. Faded advertising boards are propped against the side of the stage. THE BIOSCOPE – LIVING PICTURES! LOVERS ON THE SOFA. BATHING AT BRIGHTON. A REALLY WONDERFUL SIGHT.

Alice and Teddy run to the little stage and wave at the Bo Peep girl. She smiles wider than ever, swings a little higher. The paper flowers tied along the ropes flutter in the damp afternoon.

'Fancy the bioscope, Hannah?' says Alec. He's standing too close to me. I step to the side, but he puts his arm around my shoulder and draws me back in, so that anyone would think we were husband and wife, out with the children for an Easter treat.

'I'll give it a miss if it's all the same.'

'Spoilsport.'

'The bioscope's old hat now, ain't it?'

Alec shrugs and drops his arm. 'S'pose. Kids!' he calls to Alice and Teddy. 'Last one to the ghost show's a rotten tomato.'

He runs past the bioscope and the children chase after him, laughing and stumbling, their boots gathering mud and sawdust with every step. I follow behind, clocking the stalls and wondering how much I'll be able to afford. Two sideshows and a bag of nuts, that's my limit. I don't want Alec to treat them, don't want to owe him anything, but I don't suppose I'll get much choice.

The fairground seems busier now, the music from a hurdy-gurdy clashing with the stop-start jangle of the carousel. Everything looks tired and run-down, so different to before the war. At the animal show, an old man is trying to drum up business. The whites of his eyes are yellow, and when he smiles at me, his front teeth slip sideways. 'Step inside,' he says, bowing and sweeping his arm towards the shadowy flaps of the tent. I scan the painted boards. A SURPRISING LARGE FISH, AFFIRMED TO HAVE IN HER BELLY, WHEN FOUND, ONE THOUSAND, SEVEN HUNDRED AND NINETEEN LIVE MACKEREL. That fish can't still be alive? I remember seeing it when I was Alice's age, its great sucking mouth and giant eyes like squishy marbles.

I've lost the children now, lost Alec. Teddy will be frightened in the ghost show; he'll want to sit on my lap. 'Maybe later,' I say to the yellow-eyed man, and he sucks his top teeth right off, letting the dentures drop onto his poked-out tongue. It's the most horrible sight I ever saw. I rush from the stall, shoulder my way through the crowds until I find the ghost show: the black wooden gravestones nailed to the facade, white paint promising spine-chilling apparitions. There's no queue, which means the show must have just started. Maybe they'll let me slip in.

'Hannah!'

The shock causes me to drop the shilling I'd just taken from my purse.

Daniel smiles as he picks the coin from the sawdust and presents it to me on an upturned palm. I take it and without thinking rise onto my tiptoes and kiss him on the cheek.

'You never said...' My words come out as a gasp. It's knocked the breath right out of me to see him unexpected like this.

'Neither did you.'

'Alice only mentioned it last night.'

'The children?'

'In the ghost show. Yours are here?'

'The gallopers.' He looks down at my hands, which are holding tight on to his. Quickly I drop them and step away, a decent distance apart. He turns to the gallopers and waves at a boy and a girl as they lurch past. I catch sight of a swinging blonde ponytail, the patched elbow of a corduroy jacket.

'I was just going into the show.' I glance towards the entrance, a hundred yards to my right, and suddenly there is Alec with Alice and Teddy, sucking on toffee apples. The children haven't noticed me, but Alec has. Alec is staring. He raises his cap and Daniel tips his hat back.

'You know him?' asks Daniel.

The gallopers seem to be whirling nearer, closing in on me. I put my hand to my face, to shield my eyes from the lights. 'My sister's husband, and my children. I ... I thought they were in the ghost show.'

'Don't look so worried, Hannah. We're only talking.'

'But...' Surely anyone can tell that I care for him. The way I'm blushing and stammering, I may as well have a fairground sign above my head.

'A peck on the cheek, that's all it was. Say I'm

someone you knew from school. Haven't bumped into me in years.'

'Yes, that's it.' I step away from him. 'Bye, then. Nice seeing you.'

I try my best to seem careless as I walk towards Alec and the children. Muddy sawdust clags around my boots. The fifty yards feel more like a mile.

Alec's thin jaw juts forward, and his eyes are sly with delight. 'Who's yer gentleman friend?' he asks.

'Someone I knew at school... Matthew, I think he's called.'

'Funny, thought I recognized him. He come knocking at Sabbarton Street, didn't he, night Brunner's went up?'

'Did he?'

'A friend of Dor's, weren't it?'

'Oh, maybe you're right.'

'I saw him plain as anything, from up in the bedroom window. No glass in the windows that night, remember. Well, if it's not him, it must be his double.' He hawks some phlegm from his throat and spits into the sawdust. 'You look as if you've seen a ghost, Hannah. And the show ain't even started yet.'

That night Jen's baby finds his lungs. Each time I drop off, his crying starts and drags me from sleep. I dream it's one of my babies crying, Alice as a newborn, driving me spare with her wailing, up and down like a hurdy-gurdy. I jolt awake again to find Alice and Teddy sleeping soundly. They don't even twitch.

I try to think sensibly about Daniel, about how I must end it. If we stop now, there's no harm done, only my conscience to think of, and somehow I'll live with that. Alec might have an inkling, but he's got no proof. He won't leave it alone, though; I know that for sure. He'll be watching me closer than ever.

Perhaps it wouldn't be so bad to finish it now. I could survive on thoughts of Daniel, just the memory of our times together: Greenwich Park, the evenings in his room.

But then ... perhaps it needn't be as final. Perhaps we could break off for a while. Six months, or three. So much could change in that time. I can't stop myself picturing the scene: the army letter dropping through the postbox. On His Majesty's Service. I imagine opening the envelope, can actually see the words: *It is my painful duty to inform you...*

Well then, if I'm sinful as all that, sinful enough to wish George dead, I may as well run off with Daniel and finish what I've started.

On the landing, floorboards creak. Jen is pacing around, singing to the baby under her breath, patting his back until the crying dies away. 'Baby Alec,' she murmurs. 'Baby Alec.'

My skin prickles under the blanket. Even when the house is silent, I hear the echo of the baby's cry and I wonder if sleep will ever come. Easter Sunday dawns, and a pigeon coos from a rooftop. The sound is so soft, so comforting. Calm blankets me and I find myself walking along a white chalk path. There are no waves on the sea, only bobbing gulls and a distant pier winking under a

197

blue sky. When I wake from this dream, the calm sea seems to lap at me still.

I think I have the answer.

I will write to Daniel now, before the children wake.

23

At the end of his Friday shift he walks to Cubitt Town, past the cafe and into the George. He avoids the cafe now, even on days when Hannah will not be working. He tried going in last month, on a Tuesday, when he knew she wouldn't be there. It was an experiment, he had reasoned; it may help him, somehow, to take the edge off the pain. He had managed a bright greeting for Miss Wilton and a polite conversation with Mrs Stephens. 'Why, Mr Blake,' she'd said. 'We thought you must've gone to the front.'

'No, I'm still here. Still at Beaumont's.'

She had looked him up and down, smiled thinly, then turned away.

Miss Wilton had fussed around him, asking if he wanted more bread or a sprinkle of pepper. That maddening voice of hers, it put him in mind of paper tearing. No, he didn't want more bread; it was a struggle to swallow what he had.

He regretted the experiment, of course. It was torture, no question of healing. The smell of egg-brushed pastry, Hannah's handwriting on the chalkboards, the cold, clean teaspoon between his thumb and forefinger – a teaspoon she may have washed and dried – he was deluded to think he could stand it, to think it might actually help.

The pub is busy with Friday drinkers and he has to wait to be served. On the bar is a copy of the *Mirror*, the front page damp and crinkled with spilt beer. He looks at the date, 1st June 1917. A new month and he hadn't even registered. The talk is of daylight bombing raids. The Germans have given up on the Zeppelins. It's all about aeroplanes now, great sodding aeroplanes, any time of the day or night. The papers are sketchy on the details, but stories have filtered in from Folkestone – a hundred dead, hundreds more injured. Families were out shopping for the Whitsun weekend, queuing for potatoes, when the aeroplanes swooped from nowhere and blew the high street to kingdom come.

People are muttering. It feels subversive to be a young man dressed in civilian clothing. Doubtless there are customers in this pub passing judgement on him right now. Well, the warmongers can mutter all they like. He has his exemption: he is needed at the docks. How will the war be won if all the ships lie broken?

He buys a pint and takes a seat near the window. He can see the cafe from here, the windows obscured with chalkboards and posters, adverts for Bovril and cocoa, American cream soda. In the spaces between the posters, a shadowy figure moves, wiping down the tables.

From his jacket pocket he takes a small volume and opens the book where a thin red ribbon marks the place. It is a collection by Ezra Pound,

Lustra, lent by Lady Tolland last Sunday. 'Avant-garde,' she had said, handing it to him with a deadpan expression. 'Such a bore.'

He reads the words and manages, almost, to concentrate. There is a wildness to the poems, beautiful but unsettling. He thinks of the rhododendron bushes in Greenwich Park that cold Sunday, their twisted branches and the tightly wrapped buds waiting to flower. The blooms will be dying now, brown petals falling onto a bed of leaves.

He hasn't seen his children since Easter. His sister wrote and said they oughtn't to stay with him at the boarding house again. They acted up terrible after the Easter visit. No wonder, complained Ellen – they were exhausted, sleeping all together in one room like that, and the sanitary conditions leaving so much to be desired. *I'm sorry, Daniel, but it's not hygienic,* Ellen had written. *We've moved on from those days.* And he couldn't argue with that: they had a new semi-detached house in Maidstone, whole place to themselves with a bathroom upstairs. White enamel and the taps plumbed in. Ellen could afford to be sniffy. He was welcome in Kent at any time, she said. *But send us plenty of warning because it does unsettle them when they see their dad.*

Without Hannah, he is fading.

He tries, again, to see the sense of her letter. Hannah was right to break it off. It was all too dangerous. He'd be lynched if word got out at Beaumont's, and she'd lose her job at the cafe, guaranteed.

All the single girls in London and he has to fall

for a soldier's wife. He can't help that finally he'd met her, the woman he'd dreamed of in Robbo's shed, standing before him at the Glengall cafe: beautiful, odd, vulnerable. She was his salvation, and he was hers, and they both knew it as surely as they knew their own names. How sentimental it sounds. How impossible to explain.

Saturday lunchtime and the weather has turned warm. Heat shimmers from the pavements as he turns onto Poplar High Street. He could find someone new, surely, if he tried. Christ knows the girls are willing.

It's true. Sonia would give herself any night of the week: no charge for Mr Blake; she's made that perfectly clear. He is tempted to knock, of course he is, but the thought of her bare pink legs repulses him, her cheap scent, the melodrama as she comes to her pleasure. Just as likely an act she puts on, all that moaning: nothing but a show.

Immy in the bivouac, she was willing. He had found the perfect hiding place, not ten yards away, in a clump of tall ferns behind a young lime tree. He would catch flashes of Immy's white skin between the bivouac branches, Ralph's pale arse, rising and falling.

Poor old Dora. She couldn't have been more willing. He had liked her, she was a character, but the brash humour soon began to grate. It would have been wrong to take her to bed. She was Hannah's friend; that was the attraction. If he had slept with Dora, Hannah would have drifted beyond his reach.

He pushes open the pub door. Half a dozen men are dotted along the bar, a couple in khaki, the rest of them older men in shirt sleeves and waistcoats. Tobacco smoke has settled above the drinkers in flat clouds. At a table near the back room, two women are chatting. One of them is shelling peas, a basin clamped between her knees.

He buys a pint and chooses a seat near the door, but the voices of the two women carry from the back of the pub, some drama over a bailiff. 'I told 'im straight, I'll give you a shilling a week, but you don't put your 'ands on our 'ome...'

Daniel pictures Hannah in the Sabbarton Street house, sitting on the front step, perhaps, watching the children play fourstones in the road, the sun warming her face. The brother-in-law, the little fellow, would he be hanging around too? Daniel didn't like the look of him, the way he stared at them from the ghost show, his sharp sallow cheeks, like a rat. And it was that very night she changed her mind, wasn't it? It gave her a fright, being seen together at the funfair; she said so in the letter. Even the remembrance of her handwriting is enough to pain him, those pen strokes so elegant and strong.

Please forgive me – it's for the best, she'd written. *Cheating isn't my nature, although I hope you know I only did it out of the strongest love.* Daniel does know that, but the fact she loves him only makes it worse. He drains the pint, though the beer is on the turn and he's certain it will give him belly-ache. The Eagle might be a better bet.

Outside, a queue for vanilla ices straggles along

the pavement. Two young women stand aside to allow Daniel through. One of them reminds him of Dor: blonde hair and a striped blouse, a cheap brooch pinned above her bosom. She blinks slowly up at him, her lips parted, whispers something to her friend as he passes. The two women giggle, but he does not turn.

After the Eagle he moves on to the Gun at Coldharbour. Anything to keep away from the boarding house, from Sonia and her stained blue gown, and the small room that has never felt so lonely.

24

'Hannah!' Ada bursts into the cafe and marches up to the counter. Flypapers sway in the warm draught from the open door, already black with corpses.

'What you doing here?' It tumbles out of my mouth without thinking. *What a surprise!* I should have said, or, *How lovely to see you, Ada.*

'Tracked you down, haven't I? Not that it was any trouble. Cafe in Cubitt Town – you'd told us that much – and this one leaped out at me.' She looks around the dining room, nods to Vernon Cridge, who's staring at her with his mouth hanging open.

'Are you all right, Ada?' The rash has spread from her arms to her face. It's scalding red with crusts of yellow skin around the edges. Hard to tell if the yellow is chemicals from the factory or some kind of ointment she's rubbed in.

'Oh, this, you mean?' She pats her cheeks as if she couldn't care less, like a man who's just had a tidy shave. 'I'm working in Woolwich now. Don't think the new factory agrees with me. Still, got to do my duty, eh? King and country. Anyway, where've you been? Haven't seen you in weeks.'

'I haven't been out. Don't want to chance it with the air raids.'

'Can't blame you, girl. But the way I see it, if one of them bombs has got my name on it, there's nothing I can do.' Ada scratches the skin on her left hand. 'But look, the reason I've come is that my Cole's got leave. His old man's dying, thank Christ, and they're letting him home on compassionate. What he'll make of me Lord knows, but then, he never married me for my looks.' She winks and I can't help smiling. 'I thought you might want to give Cole something to take back for your other half – George, ain't it?'

'Take back?'

'You know, a little gift parcel, a token of your affection?'

'Yes. Yes, thanks, I will.'

'Drop it round at the weekend if you like.' She picks up my pad and pencil from the counter and scribbles her address. 'I'll be home Saturday morning.'

I spend the rest of my shift wondering what to send George. Some cigarettes, toffees if I can find them and a couple of handkerchiefs from the stall at Chrisp Street. It occurs to me that what he really wants is a photograph: he asked for it months ago. I make up my mind to take the children to Whiffin's after school tomorrow. I might be able to pick up the photos Saturday; then I could call straight round to Ada's with the parcel.

Nettie comes out from the kitchen, her face sweaty from the washing-up.

'That's me finished,' she says, untying the knot at the back of her apron. 'I'm ready to drop.'

'Go careful.'

'I'll take the long way home. Gives me the willies to walk near North Street, just thinking about those poor children.'

'Is it a terrible mess up there?'

'You can't imagine unless you see for yourself. Scraps of desk and blackboard swept up in a pile. I crossed to the other side and there was some charred paper crumpled in the gutter, tiny flowers drawn on in pencil. It was one of them paper lanterns they'd been gluing. My cousin's friend's little girl goes to North Street – did I tell you? A fireman carried her home on his shoulder. She wouldn't let go of her lantern the whole way. "Clare and me was doing it," she said, and of course Clare was her little chum. She got killed.'

'Horrible. I can't think about it.'

'Must be worse if you have your own little ones?'

'If we'd stayed in Alton Street, Alice might have gone to that school.'

'Don't. But you're all safe and that's that. Life goes on...'

She's doing her best to sound brave, but her

voice is shaky nonetheless.

Something has changed since the raid last Wednesday. The weather is dry and hot, and everyone's nerves are boiling. It's hard to believe the Germans can just turn up like that on a warm summer morning, a whole fleet of shining silver aeroplanes dropping bombs.

Nettie is scared stiff. She sleeps every night in Stepney Green Tube. No wonder she looks so tired.

There are no more dinners to cook, and the tables are all wiped down. I refill the salt cellars and clean out the cutlery drawer. If he was going to come in, he would have by now. Nine weeks it's been. Nine weeks and four days without setting eyes on him.

Once or twice I've been tempted to tell Nettie about Daniel, in a sideways fashion, perhaps, a friend-of-a-friend-type story. We've become quite pally, me and Nettie: took a walk once, around the Island Gardens, when she was upset about losing her weekend job at the Queen's. They'd told her it was because of the war, audiences down, et cetera, et cetera, but she knew the real reason: the boss had found a new girl, a seventeen-year-old with a look of Theda Bara.

Fancy being on the scrapheap at nineteen, she'd said as we walked into the gardens. There was a warm wind blowing off the Thames. Almost pleasant if you didn't breathe in too deep.

'Try being twenty-five.'

'Oh, you're all right. You've got your children, and a good husband. Bet you miss him something rotten, though, don't you, Hannah?'

'I didn't want him to go, but it's done now and you have to make do.'

Nettie was quiet for a moment. 'Shall I tell you a secret?' she said.

'If you like.'

'I'm married meself.'

'You're never!'

'October last year. I had to ... you know.' She patted her stomach. 'So he takes me up St Anne's – he was a trumpet player at the Queen's – says, "I do," and then a month later he disappears. Last I heard he was working up west. I'm back at me mum's and there's nothing I can do but wait.'

'The baby?'

'Lost it, a week after the wedding. All that fuss for nothing.'

I ached to tell Nettie my secret. I even opened my mouth to speak, but the words didn't come out. *Daniel*. How I wanted to say his name aloud. As if speaking of him would conjure some of the happiness. But I couldn't risk it.

We stopped at the river wall and Nettie leaned over, looked down into the surging Thames. A barge hooted and she waved at the watermen, the top half of her body lurching forward.

'Careful!' I grabbed at her coat.

Nettie turned to me, amused. 'I ain't ready to chuck myself in just yet,' she said. 'Ain't letting the bastard off that easily.' She linked her arm in mine and we carried on walking. 'We girls have to stick together, eh?' she said. 'You can cope with anything if you've got friends.'

It's after three. I go out the back to collect my coat. Too warm for a coat really, but I slip it on anyway, shove my hands into the pockets. Empty pockets: scratchy black lining against my skin.

Jen is sitting in the armchair feeding the baby. The top of her blouse rests on the baby's head, and his wispy hair looks damp with sweat. Jen is clutching at him with hunched shoulders. She has been crying.

'Jen?'

Mum stands up from the chair by the window. 'She's had a shock.'

'What is it?'

'Alec. They're taking him.'

'The army?'

Mum nods, and now Jen speaks. 'They've re-examined him and by some miracle he's fit for service.'

'With his chest?' I try to sound upset for her. 'Can't he appeal ... the tribunal?'

'This was the tribunal. Final decision.'

'You never said it was coming up.'

'Didn't want to talk about it. Wouldn't have made no difference.' The baby breaks off and starts to fuss. 'Shush, shush,' says Jen. She drapes him over her shoulder and pats his back to burp him. The silly thing is that she burps first. I almost laugh, but somehow I turn it into a cough.

'Well, you've got little Alec now. That's a blessing,' says Mum.

'Yes.' Jen lifts the other side of her blouse and the baby latches on. Her shoulders relax.

Outside in the street, a tin can rattles. The children are throwing stones.

'You'll miss Alec too, won't you, Hannah?' says

Jen. She has that strange slant to her eyes.

I manage a nod. 'So will the children.'

'He's fond of your two. You might want to call Teddy in, by the way. He's looking a bit pink from the sun. Didn't you notice?'

'I'll get him a cap. When does Alec go?'

'A fortnight, he thinks.'

'I'm sorry.' I put my hand on her shoulder, but she looks out of the window.

'Don't be,' she says. 'We'll manage.'

That evening I try to make an effort with Alec, chat to him over our supper, look him in the eye. He's putting a brave face on it, says he's hoping for the eastern front, might even be fighting alongside George. If he gets the eastern front, the warmer winter might do his chest good. He might come back a new man.

I'm feeling almost kindly towards him. That is until he corners me in the scullery when I'm putting away the dishes.

He sidles up so close my back is pressed against the wall. 'Suits you, don't it, Hannah, to have me out of the way?'

'Don't be daft.'

'I'm not daft – that's the point. You're a pretty little thing, ain't you? Some men might find you hard to resist.'

'I don't know what you're talking about.'

He puts his hand up to my face, cradles my chin. 'It's not just me who's watching you,' he says. 'I've got friends everywhere. You mind how you go. I don't want nothing upsetting Jen while I'm away.'

He's bluffing, trying to provoke me. I won't rise

to it. Even if he has been watching me since the funfair, there hasn't been anything for him to see. 'I'm sure Jen can look after herself,' I say. 'Just as well as I can.'

Whiffin's is on the dock road, not far from Daniel's boarding house. I mustn't think of him. The trick is not to look around, not to give in to memory. Keep hold of the children's hands, march along eyes straight ahead, take no notice of the hospital steps where I dropped Dor's barley water, try not to breathe in when I pass the florist's and the scent of violets that reminds me of the flowers he never had the chance to give.

Whiffin's Photographic Studio, 237 East India Dock Road. Six postcards for two shillings. It's a fair price – cheapest you'll get. Not that I need six postcards. One for George, one for Mum ... maybe one for Dad?

'Frock's itchy,' says Alice. 'When are we there?'

'We're here. This is it.'

I push open the door and a woman behind a desk looks up. 'Can I help you?' She has round tortoiseshell spectacles and neat wavy hair tied back in a bun. A little girl is sitting behind the desk next to her, writing out sums in an exercise book.

'I'd like a photograph, please.'

'A special occasion?' she asks.

'Not really, just something to send out to my husband. He's been asking.'

'Of course. The children grow up so quickly. He's at the front?'

Alice and Teddy must be staring at the little girl

because she pokes out her tongue and shuts the book.

'Eastern front.'

'Salonika? Oh, that's something. They say it's not too bad. Building roads, growing tomatoes, I've heard. He's drawn the long straw there.'

She shows me into the waiting area. It's a queer-shaped room, the furthest wall veering off at an angle. There are no windows, only two mirrors: a large one on the angled wall and a smaller one opposite. Alice stands in front of the large mirror, plucking at the tight collar of her dress. Teddy and I sit on a bench that has green cushions tied to the seat.

'Magic!' shouts Alice suddenly. She hops up and down in front of the mirror. 'Hundreds of me. Look.'

I stand next to her. It's a curious sight, the two mirrors working together so that our reflections go on and on. There I am: my face, the back of my head, two sides disappearing off into some unknown place. I can't understand it, can't fathom where I must be going.

Strangest of all, the person in the mirror doesn't look like me at all. I've not stopped to look at myself in the glass at home, haven't seen my reflection in weeks. There are shadows under my cheekbones, and my eyes seem small and creased. I can see my mum's eyes. My face as I'll look in twenty-five years.

'Mrs Loxwood?' an old man with a greying moustache peers round a second door in the corner of the room. 'I'm Mr Whiffin. Do come through.'

Alice skips ahead, but Teddy is unsure and holds my hand. He has never had his photo taken before. George and me once took Alice to a studio in Bow, not that she'll remember it; she can't have been more than six months old. Whiffin's is much smarter than the Bow place. It smells very clean, of wax polish and fresh paint. On one wall is a backdrop done up like a park, the canvas decorated with pictures of trees, white flowers and green grass. In front of the canvas is a pile of huge grey stones, stacked up to form a kind of seat, and an old stone pillar that looks like it could have come from the ruin of a posh house or a castle.

Teddy lets go of my hand now and rushes over to the stones, which Alice is already attempting to climb. I follow them with my comb, raking it through Teddy's hair and tidying Alice's ringlets now she's perched on the top.

'That's it, children,' says old Mr Whiffin. His jowls wobble as he speaks. 'You make yourselves comfortable. You're King George–' he points at Teddy with his sunburned face – 'and, little lady, you're a fairy princess.' They both laugh, but Mr Whiffin puts a finger to his lips. 'Got to keep a straight face for the photograph, children. Show your daddy how grown-up you are. Like this...' He strikes a pose, his hands clasped together over his waistcoat, chin raised a little and his lips pressed together. 'Smile with your eyes,' he says. 'Only your eyes.' The children giggle and then quieten down. He must have something magical about him, this Mr Whiffin, because even Alice stays calm, her eyes wide as she practises how to smile

212

without moving her lips.

'Now, Mrs Loxwood, if you'd like to stand next to the column.'

I remember my reflection: the hollow cheeks and the tired eyes. I shake my head at Mr Whiffin. 'It was just the children I was thinking of. He's got one of me.'

'Are you sure? I know how much it means to the men, something new...'

'I haven't dressed for it.'

'You have, Mum!' pipes up Alice. She turns to Mr Whiffin. 'She's put on her locket special.'

I can't explain it to Alice, this sudden feeling that to have my photograph taken for George would be wrong. It's too intimate. Better to keep the distance between us.

'Shush, Alice. Daddy knows what I look like. It's you two what's changed. All grown up now – he won't believe it.'

Mr Whiffin nods and positions himself behind the camera.

'Remember, children,' he says, his voice low and grave under the heavy black hood, 'smile with your eyes.'

The camera shutter clunks and the room glares with light.

When we leave Whiffin's, the sun is still hot, though it must be after five. There's a ripe old reek coming off the docks, and the horse dung in the gutter is alive with flies. A white nag clops past, pulling a brewer's van, great big old thing he is, temperamental, and the driver is in a sweat trying to keep him in a straight line.

213

'When's tea?' asks Alice.

'Now, if you like. Thought we'd go up Chrisp Street for fish and chips.'

They grin at each other and then up at me.

Alice squeezes my hand. 'Can I do me own vinegar?' she asks.

'I should think–' I stop mid-sentence and listen. A whistle is sounding from somewhere ahead. Not a ship's whistle, a policeman's whistle. Then the clanging of bells, warning flares exploding in the sky, and suddenly everyone is running.

The policeman shoots past on his bicycle. 'Take cover!' he calls, between blows of the whistle. Crowds bolt in the same direction: the few hundred yards to the Blackwall Tunnel. We can hear the aeroplane engines now, and when I look up, they are right above us, wings gleaming.

If I was on my own, I'd run into a shop and ask to hide under a counter, but we're only two seconds from the tunnel now, and the crowd is surging towards the entrance, a mass of people swirling like water down a plughole. If I try to pull away, I might lose hold of Alice or Teddy. There's no choice but to stay in the swirl, file down the spiral stairs and press ahead into the shadows. It has to be the tunnel.

We keep walking for a few hundred yards, and then the movement stops.

'Keep moving!' someone shouts.

'Can't,' comes a yell. 'It's full from the Greenwich side!' We stand for ten minutes or so, crammed tight, and then somehow the crush relaxes and we have a little space to breathe.

People sit on the ground, laying out jackets if they have them, or just settling on the grime, brushing aside the dust and the debris: the top of a broken bicycle bell, a mouldering carrot stalk, scraps of wood from a smashed crate. A woman starts playing a mouth organ, 'Oh! Oh! Antonio', and her friends all sing along.

'Shut that row,' someone shouts, but the singers laugh and carry on.

Anywhere but the tunnel – I'd rather be anywhere but here. If a bomb fell on the river, could it crash right through the water, crack open the ceiling? I daren't look up. Alice and Teddy don't seem frightened; their eyes glitter with excitement. When Alice says she's hungry, a woman delves in her shopping basket and produces a bag of monkey nuts. 'Here, take these,' she says. 'My treat.' The children eat them greedily, splitting open the soft shells and pushing the nuts into their mouths.

Sound is peculiar in this tunnel; it's hard to decipher. Is it gunfire I can hear, or the tap of a walking stick? Then a loud boom, not gunfire this time. The ground shakes and the mouth organ stops. A bomb for sure.

Is Daniel at work? Is he sheltering in the dock vaults, or is he at home, sitting it out with Sonia and Mrs Browne? Is he thinking of me?

I lean against the cool tunnel wall, tilt my head back and shut my eyes. For a few moments I allow myself to think. And what I think is this: I can never make it right with George; the betrayal can't be erased. What's done is done. So why shouldn't I go to Daniel again? Once, twelve times, eight hundred times ... what is the difference?

Two more bombs and then the rattle of gunfire. I feel more certain with the crack of each bullet.

25

It is the last day of August. The sun has set, but the heat of the afternoon still pulses in the air. Ten weeks now since she came back to him. Ten Fridays.

Tonight they are meeting away from his lodging room: they are risking a trip to Greenwich instead, while the evenings are still warm. He waits for her by the park railings at the top of King William Street. A jackdaw struts in the gutter, pecks up a squashed crust and then flies to the eaves of a butcher's shop. Three pale black fledglings demand their share of the crust, squatting and screeching until the mother abandons them for a nearby chimney.

When Hannah arrives, they greet each other with a guarded nod. The pavements are busy and they don't want to be noticed. He falls into step with her and they walk along Stockwell Street, up the hill towards Lady Tolland's house. He is wearing his gardening clothes, the heavy boots and the brown jacket with one button missing. She follows him silently down the dark passageway at the side of the house, and he unlocks the gate that leads through to the garden. In the passageway – alone, finally – he kisses her against

216

the cool brick wall.

Trees and shrubs edge the garden boundaries, but still they must be quiet. Sound floats on a night like this, high on Greenwich Hill. The casement windows of neighbouring terraces are open to the evening breeze; from a nearby house there is the chink of fine glass. Laughter.

They walk to the end of the passageway and down the garden until they reach the shed by the raspberry canes. Pushed against the side of the shed is a broken bench, the wooden slats weathered and rough. He sits on the bench and pats the space next to him, but she remains standing.

'She won't come back?'

'I told you. She's in Dorset for the duration.'

Their whispers hang in the half-light of the London dusk. She looks towards Lady Tolland's house, the white paint peeling from the brickwork.

'Imagine, all this … one old lady. Imagine if we lived here, Daniel. You and me, and all our children.'

'They'd have a bedroom each.'

'And we'd have our own bathroom. A white enamel bath. Rose oil in the water.'

'One day, Hannah.' He looks around the garden, the hidden strip of overgrown lawn between the two beds of raspberries. Summer raspberries, autumn raspberries, both heavy with fruit. One crop is almost finished, the other just beginning. The canes are leaning towards each other like a guard of honour, green leaf epaulettes, ripe red medals.

He takes a key from under a water trough near the shed. The padlock has been recently oiled and the catch jumps open with one quick turn of the key.

'I bought in some supplies.' He reaches into the shed and pulls out a small bottle of port wine and a penknife. 'We'll have to drink from the bottle, I'm afraid.'

'Fine way to treat a lady,' she smiles.

They sit together on the bench. One of the slats is missing from the seat. Lady Tolland has asked him to repair it, but she has not given him any money for the timber.

He flicks a corkscrew from the penknife and uncorks the bottle. 'Ladies first,' he says, handing the wine to Hannah. She drinks a mouthful, then passes it back to him. Tiny flies close in on the neck of the bottle. Daniel swats them away, but they are persistent.

Shouts drift up from the pubs at the bottom of the hill. They have not been to a pub together since that February day in Blackheath. They've not been anywhere, other than his room, until this evening.

'Alec has gone now?'

'Finally. Left for the training camp on Wednesday. Jen's taken it bad.'

He passes her the bottle again. She drinks a few more mouthfuls, stands the bottle on the uneven brick path and looks up at the quiet sky. Stars are beginning to flare. They seem brighter, from up here.

'I feel like I'm in another country,' she says. 'The air smells different. Sweet. Not Tate and Lyle sweet. Proper sweet.'

'It's the jasmine,' he says, standing to pick a

sprig from the climbing bush that twines round the lower branches of the apple tree. 'Here.' He puts the jasmine to her nose; she breathes in and then sighs. 'Heaven.' He tucks the sprig into her hair and kisses the lobe of her ear, her cheek, her neck. She slips off his waistcoat, unbuttons his shirt and spreads her hands across his chest, traces the bird-shaped scar.

Daniel leads her to the raspberry canes, to the strip of lawn under the canopy. The ground is soft after the wet August weather. They sit together on the unmown grass. He picks a fat raspberry and she opens her mouth to eat it. He unfastens her blouse, then takes another raspberry, crushes it against her throat and licks the juice as it runs between her breasts, onto the lace of her chemise.

From the bottom of the hill comes the sound of singing: a music-hall tune.

She removes her clothes slowly, until she is wearing only her chemise. He lies back on the grass, his arms around her back, and she lowers herself onto him. They sigh together. He looks at her beautiful skin, white as apple flesh, and he cannot help himself.

Afterwards she kneels by his side and there is panic in her eyes. The sprig of jasmine from her hair is crushed under her knee. He wonders if kneeling will be enough, a question of gravity, nothing more. If only. She rinses herself with rainwater from the trough, the movement of her cupped hand terse and quick.

'I'm sorry,' he says, but she doesn't reply, just carries on cupping water from the trough. It trickles down her thighs, forms a lazy puddle on the path.

Of course she is angry with him: he has broken a promise. She knows all about the bus ride. He promised her he would always jump off one stop early. They had joked about it. 'Take me up the Mile End Road', or 'A return to Cockfosters, please.'

She puts on her drawers and fastens her stays, buttons up her blouse and skirt. He dresses too and sits back on the bench. He wants to light a cigarette but decides to wait.

'I'm sorry,' he whispers again. 'What are the ... the...?'

'The chances? I couldn't say.' She picks another sprig of jasmine and inhales the scent. Her shoulders soften. 'Let's not talk about it, not tonight.'

'No, you're right.'

She sits down next to him, and as he puts his arm around her, she shivers a little. Night has fallen now, and on the breeze comes the lightest chill of autumn. The seasons seem to be passing so quickly.

'I'll call into the house before we go. Need to borrow something.'

'Borrow?'

'Just a book. We have an arrangement, a mutual agreement. Lady Tolland lets me use her library and I look after her garden. She gives me books, sometimes, if they don't take her fancy.'

'She don't pay you a penny, then?'

'A tin of shortbread at Christmas.'

'Why can't you go to the lending library? There's one near the cafe.'

'I do go, occasionally, but they're wall to wall

with those terrible old novels: Mrs Henry Wood, Ouida. Lady Tolland's tastes are more ... varied.'

They sit for half an hour, talking in hushed voices, dreaming about the life they could have together. A cottage in Dorset, that's what he wishes for them, a cottage in the Marshwood Vale. He describes the house, its yellow stone walls and slate roof, a stream flowing nearby, the water so clean you can bottle it. They would have their own garden: chickens, a pig, sunflowers soaring from the flowerbeds.

'My dad used to grow sunflowers,' she says. It's not often she mentions her father. 'I used to watch them from my bedroom window. I thought that if I watched long enough, I'd see them grow.'

'And did you?'

'I suppose I must have.'

He wishes it could always be like this. Out in the fresh air together, no cause to hide. But all they can do is make the most of this evening. He strokes her dark hair, which still hangs loose around her shoulders, brings her hand to his mouth and kisses her fingers.

26

After one week the copper taste comes, so strong there might be a penny lodged under my tongue. A little girl, then. I had the copper taste with Alice, not with Teddy. With Teddy it was just the sickness.

After two weeks my monthly is due. I carry my rags to work, hoping I might be mistaken and it is just the thought of a baby that has upset my dates: my mind playing tricks.

After one month I cannot stand to drink tea. I take my rags from my handbag and stuff them back in the sack under the bed. Next day I take them out again, rinse a few, hang them out in the yard for appearance's sake.

I'm queasy all the time, though I've not yet been sick.

Daniel is wondering, I'm certain, but we haven't spoken of it. I'll wait a couple of weeks longer, just to be sure. We have such little time together – just a few short hours on a Friday night. I can't bear to ruin an evening. Daniel says I mean everything to him; he loves me more than his life. He's telling the truth, I know he is, but who's to say his feelings won't change when he finds out there's a baby?

At work I muddle through, do my best to be cheerful. Mrs Stephens doesn't seem to notice, but she's not in the cafe with us much these days. She sits upstairs with a magazine and cabbage leaves under her stockings to ease the pain in her knees. It's a damp autumn and damp weather plays havoc with her rheumatism. We take her cups of tea when Mr Stephens is out. 'Lovely as you like,' she says, 'but what I wouldn't give for some sugar.'

Nettie asks would I fancy a walk down to the Island Gardens after work. 'Promised I'd get some conkers for my little cousin,' she says. 'There's a particular tree always full of them.'

We wander down Stebondale Street, our coats unbuttoned because the sun has come out and it's ever so mild. We pass a factory where labourers are repairing a roof. 'Aye aye,' shouts a man from the top of the scaffolding. And then a chorus of whistles, until Nettie turns round, flaps open her coat and bobs a little curtsey. The men cheer and bang the wooden boards of the scaffolding. Nettie grabs on to my arm, laughing. I'm blushing even if she's not.

'You've got some nerve, Nettie.'

She squeezes my hand. 'Just a bit of fun. You have to make your own these days.'

She's right about the conker tree. There are schoolboys throwing sticks into the high branches, but there's no need – there are tons of conkers just lying on the ground, fresh-fallen from their prickly cases, staring up all glossy amid the crumbling yellow leaves. I collect a dozen for Alice and Teddy, and stuff them in my pockets. Nettie chats away, but I don't say much. I'm thinking things through, wondering if it's worth the risk.

We walk back the long way, to avoid the building site. My idea, not Nettie's. Nettie dilly-dallies, jiggling conkers in her pockets as we follow the curve of the Thames round the edge of Cubitt Town. A motor bus rumbles by, the driver peering up as he passes under the bow of a ship that overhangs the street. A rigger is working at the very end of the bowsprit, thirty feet up, maybe forty. It makes me nervous to see him there, nothing but the hard cobbles below.

Nettie is quiet suddenly. She sighs and tells me it's her wedding anniversary coming up. One year ago, a warm autumn day just like this, she says.

'Any word from him?'

'Not a dicky bird. I might as well forget him, Mum says. It's all very well, but where do I go from here? I can't afford to divorce him. And meanwhile he's free to swan around, sweet-talking the next poor cow who falls under his spell.'

'It's always the women that suffer, ain't it, Nettie?'

'Oh, we can't do right for doing wrong. My mum as good as said it: if I can't keep a man at my age, there must be something wrong with me. Nothing wrong with *him*, of course. Men can't help themselves – that's what she thinks. Shut up and put up is all a woman's good for. If we get into trouble, it's our own fault.'

Would she help me, if I tell her now? There might not be a better chance. 'Actual fact, Nettie, I'm in a spot of trouble myself.'

'Really?'

'The thing is, well ... I'm carrying.'

Her face is blank and for a moment I wonder if I have to spell it out. Then she cottons on, stares at me in surprise. 'I didn't know your George... Did he get home leave?' And there was me thinking she was so broad-minded.

'No. The baby...'

'It ain't George's?' Her hand flies to her mouth and a conker falls from her pocket, bouncing into the path of a bicycle. 'Blimey, Hannah, sorry. I just didn't... I never thought...'

'What? You never thought I was a tart?'

'Oh, not that. It's just a surprise, that's all. Whose is it, then?'

'Chap I was at school with,' I say, the lie coming easily. 'We were sweethearts years ago. I happened to run into him one evening and we got carried away, too much to drink, you know. He was ... on leave from the navy. It was only that one night. He don't know nothing about it and he ain't going to.'

'How far gone, Hannah?' She looks down at my stomach, but she won't find any clues there. If anything, the worry has made me thinner.

'Not long, two months. And, well, I thought you might be able to do me a favour.'

She nods, a little wary. 'If I can.'

'I'm going to send for some pills, to bring it off. Dr Patterson's.'

'Yes, I know them. I've a friend who swears by Dr Patterson's.'

'I can't have them sent to my sister's, so I was wondering... Can I put down your address?'

She fiddles with her earring. 'I don't know. If my mum gets hold of the post...'

What was it she said that time? *We girls have to stick together.* 'Forget about it, Nettie. I shouldn't have asked.'

'No, go on I'll do it. I'll think of something. It's 71 Ernest Street, Stepney East – shall I write it down?'

'I'll remember. Thank you,' I say, but I feel rotten all the same, dirty somehow, knowing I've confided my troubles and it's made her so uncomfortable.

'It's all right. Now hurry up or we'll catch a bridger.'

A steamer is heading towards the lock, a goat

bleating from a wooden cage on the ship's deck. Nettie takes my arm and we belt across. I'm queasier than ever when I reach the other side, the shock of running over like that. Nettie stops and turns to me with a smile. 'I'll be seeing you, then. Don't you worry. You'll sort it out. And I promise I won't tell a soul. We've both got our secrets now, haven't we?'

I smile and wave, watch her walk off towards Stepney. She's a decent enough girl, but how I miss Dora. How I ache to share my secret with my only true friend.

The river laps at the lock gates, licking and gurgling like a chuckling babe. Of course, if Dor was here, I might not have any secrets to share. If she had lived, I might be respectable still.

Alice is skipping around in front of the house, waving something above her head.

'Mum,' she says, running up the road towards me. 'A letter from Daddy!'

'Give it here. It's for Mummy, Alice. You shouldn't have opened it.' I try to take it, but she snatches her hand away.

'It's a letter for me,' she says. 'It says my name on the front, look!' She displays the envelope as proof, takes out the letter and starts to read. '*My … dear … little … Alice… I … was … very … ple…*" You read it, Mum. Too hard.'

She presses the letter into my hand and I squint down at the notepaper. George has tried to make his writing bigger for Alice, but it's still an effort to read.

My dear little Alice,

I was very pleased to get the lovely photograph from Mummy. Don't you look grown-up in that pretty dress. Is it a new one? And Teddy too is a proper little lad sitting up on that wall. I was only sorry not to see Mummy in the picture. She said she was feeling poorly that day. I hope she is all better now and you are both being good to her. What is your new cousin like? I hope he is not keeping you awake with his crying in the night. Fancy Uncle Alec being a soldier! Now Teddy will be the man of the house. Do you think he is strong enough to shovel coal?

I am quite safe here, Alice, and do you know that some days you wouldn't even know there was a war on.

Well, I'll close now and hope that I will be back with you all soon. It might be a while yet, but don't forget that I am thinking of you day and night.

Please thank Mummy for the package and her letters, and tell her that I will write again soon.

Daddy xxxx

'A letter all for yourself, Alice. Ain't you lucky?'

He took his time, mind you. I sent the package off with Ada's husband back in June. This is the first we've heard from him in four months. Perhaps Cole took a while to get back to the regiment. Perhaps he was injured on the journey. I make up my mind to pop into the Steamship this Friday. About time I made an appearance.

'I've got another surprise for you,' I tell Alice. 'Put your hands in my pockets.'

She delves in and pulls out the conkers. 'All for me?'

'You can share them with your brother.'

She nods slowly as she eyes up the conkers. She'll be working out which are the biggest, the firmest, the most likely to smash the opposition. She's no fool, this girl. Quickly she divides them into two uneven piles on the pavement. 'Teddy,' she shouts, 'look what Mum's got us!'

Teddy runs out from the yard.

'Conkers!' says Alice. 'There's yours.' She points to his share with her foot.

Teddy scoops up his pile, delighted. He's happy with what he's given, little Teddy. Such a trusting boy, I feel I could cry.

Ada's not in the Steamship, so I try the White Horse. I don't want to be long. Every minute in the pub is one less minute with Daniel. Sure enough Ada is huddled round a table with a few of the girls: Daisy and Fran and a couple of others I don't recognize. It's the table Daniel once sat at with Dor, the night she wore her cream striped blouse.

When Ada turns round, I can't hide the shock.

'Well, look who it isn't,' she says, screwing her cigarette into the ashtray. Both her hands are bandaged, and her face is swollen and raw. There are scabs everywhere, even on her ears. I don't know how she can step outside the house, let alone drink in a pub.

She smiles wide and a sore on her cheek cracks open. 'How are you, Hannah? Honoured, we are, I'm sure. And if you're asking, mine's a barley wine.'

Same Ada. No point giving her any sympathy.

She'll just shrug her shoulders and trot out her line about duty.

'I'm not staying, actually, just wanted to call in as I was passing.'

'Got time for a quickie?'

I make a show of checking the clock above the landlord's bell.

'No. I was just buying a few bits from the market. Have to get back. But I wanted to thank you, Ada, for getting Cole to pass on the package. Finally had a letter from George this week.'

'Not one for putting pen to paper, is he, your George? Cole must have given it him months ago.'

'He's all right, then? It crossed my mind that he might have been delayed. Torpedoed or something, on the way back?'

'Oh, he's all right. They've left Greece, though. You know that much?'

'No, I didn't hear.'

'Moved to Egypt. They're fighting the Turks now, in the desert.'

'George plays it down when he writes. He says some days you wouldn't know there's a war on.'

'Does he, now?' She swigs a mouthful of her drink. 'Well, they have to keep it sweet, don't they, or the censors will have a field day. Anyway, how've you been, Hannah? You look peaky.'

She's got a cheek, talking about how *I* look.

'I'm fine.'

'That's good, then. So long as you're fine.' Ada stares up at me as she drains her glass, so that all I see are her small brown eyes above the disappearing liquid. She places the glass on a wet

229

mat and winks. 'You mind how you go, then, Hannah. We'll have a drink another night, eh? When you can spare the time.'

I know she's staring at my back as I leave the bar. And I know she'll have something to say about me to the other girls. Is it just the usual – 'Lah-di-dah, thinks she's a cut above' – or does she know something more?

The door opens the instant I tap on it and I slip into the dark hall. We don't speak until we are in his room, the door locked behind us.

'Could've sworn I heard the warning,' he says. 'I didn't know if you'd come.'

'I never heard anything.'

'Turned out to be a fire engine, Limehouse way.'

I tell him about Ada in the pub. He puts a little finger to the edge of his mouth and chews at the nail. It's a peculiar habit he's started. He never bites the other fingernails, just this one.

'There was something strange about her, Daniel. Like she knew.'

'She always seemed strange to me. It's just her manner. How can she know?' He takes out a flask of beer and holds it over the gold-rimmed glass. 'Drink?'

'No.'

'I can pop out, get something else?'

'No, I don't want anything. Tell you the truth, I'm feeling queasy.'

He sits on the edge of the bed and stares across the room at me. I'm in the armchair, still wearing my coat. 'Don't suppose we can keep ignoring it,' he says.

I look down into my lap, my hands clasped and the knuckles white as ice.

I shiver. Wish he'd light the heater.

'I'm getting some pills. Very reliable, by all accounts.'

'And if they don't...?'

'I'll have to take care of it somehow.'

He gets up from the bed and stands behind the armchair with his hands heavy on my shoulders. The grip of his fingers is so strong I can sense his worry pressing down.

'Take care of it?' he says. 'No, nothing like that. You know what happened to Esther.'

'A natural miss, you said. She lost a baby, but...'

'She tried to bring it off herself. Sam was only two, and Maddie was tiny – she didn't see how we'd manage, three babies so close together. I didn't talk her out of it as I should have done. I ignored the whole thing. Left her to it, Esther and her know-it-all friend – they said it was safe...'

I'm sorry for Esther, but this is a different situation, a different baby. 'If the pills don't work, I'll have to do something, Daniel. If only George would come home on leave now.'

'You want him home?' He skits round the armchair, crouches in front of me and takes my hands in his.

'Well, why do you think? It could be his baby then. I'd just have to say it was early. Pray for a small one.'

'But it's *my* baby,' he says. 'I'm the father.'

'How can we bring up a child?'

231

His face lifts in hope. 'We could move out of London. To Dorset, like we talked about.'

'Don't be daft. It's only the ship work keeping you from the war.'

He sighs, but the hopeful expression is still there. 'All right, then, we'll find rooms, move in together.'

'What about my work? Minute Mrs Stephens finds out, I'll get the sack.'

'You'll find another job.'

'With a baby and no one but me to look after it? And I can kiss goodbye to the army allowance. That's twenty-eight shillings a week. We couldn't do it, not with three kids to feed. And there's your two to think about. What do you give them?'

'Six shillings a week, thereabouts.'

'Well, then. It don't add up.'

'There must be a way.'

'Oh, there's a way all right.'

He draws me to him and kisses my forehead. It is a solemn sort of kiss, like a promise, or an unspoken vow.

Nettie brings the pills to work on Wednesday. She slips the plain brown packet into my coat pocket as we're leaving. 'Take care of yourself,' she says. She holds up both hands, fingers crossed for luck. 'I'll see you on Friday.'

I lock myself inside the privy as soon as I get home, tear open the packet quiet as I can in case Jen has come into the yard. Inside is a small brown bottle and a folded leaflet. 'Dr Patterson's Famous Pills,' it says. 'A boon to womankind. Guaranteed to remove all female obstructions, irregularities and ailments. Two to be taken three times a day after meals.'

I hold the bottle to the shaft of light at the top of the privy door. There can't be more than three dozen pills in there – enough for a week or so. When I take out the cork stopper, a mustard smell wafts up. I swallow one dry; it sticks in my throat and it's as much as I can do not to cough it up. I'll take the other with a cup of tea. Mum'll have a pot brewing inside, though the taste will make me gag. I stick the second pill under my tongue and stuff the bottle back into my pocket.

27

Last Christmas he spent the holiday at Ellen and Alf's. It was only a year since Esther had died and Ellen said of course he must come to Kent to be with the children, mustn't sit around moping in his lodgings. This year there was no invitation. Ellen had sent a card, saying they were all going to Alf's family in Broadstairs. He could come in the new year, Ellen said, if he was able to get the time off work.

All day he has been walking. It was important to get out of the boarding house, in case Mrs Browne invited him down. He couldn't face her chit-chat, the paper hats and the silly jokes. If he cannot be with his own children, or with Hannah, he would rather be alone.

He thinks of her sitting down to Christmas

dinner at Sabbarton Street, chair pulled up close to the table to keep her belly out of sight. The pills were a waste of money, as he'd known they would be. She tried other methods: tinctures of pennyroyal washed down with gin; a scalding-hot soak at Poplar Baths. Last Friday she mentioned the surgical shop again, but, for now, he thinks he has talked her out of it. How would she pay for an operation, in any case, without his help? She can't ask her family, and she has precious little to pawn.

No, their baby is determined, and he is glad. His baby, growing inside her. He feels choked with emotion just to think of it. Why must Hannah always think of the child as the problem, when it could be the answer? He has promised to face the trouble with her. What is the baby after all but a chance of being together?

As twilight falls, he walks back to the boarding house through deserted streets. Lamps are lit in warm front rooms, and there is the sound of singing and laughter, upright pianos clanking off-key carols. The docks are quiet, only a whisper of wind in the rigging.

Mrs Browne's front parlour is dark, but when he lets himself into the hallway, he hears talking from the middle sitting room, and music from a gramophone. Is the gramophone a Christmas present? He has never heard music playing in the house before. He pauses to listen to a woman's voice droning along to the tune, one he doesn't recognize, the words in French. The voice sounds too young for Mrs Browne – her married daughter, perhaps, or a niece he has never met.

He climbs the stairs. On the landing, Sonia's door is wide open, but she is not inside her room. Of course, it was Sonia singing with the gramophone. Mrs Browne must have asked her down.

His own room is stiff with cold. He puts a match to the candle and sits down to read, but it's impossible to concentrate with the noise from downstairs. The music seems to be getting louder; now it is a dance tune, something American, and the women are clattering and stomping so that in the end he wonders whether he might go out into the night again and see if there isn't a lock-in at the Eagle. He pulls on his gloves.

Footsteps fly up the stairs and his door rattles with three fierce knocks. 'Daniel?' calls Sonia. 'I know you're in there. Come down and say happy Christmas!'

He can hardly pretend to be asleep.

Sonia is wearing a red dress with a low neckline, pleats in the calf-length skirt. Around her neck is a sequinned black scarf. One of her gold hooped earrings has caught in her hair and it hangs sideways, pulling at the lobe. She sways in his doorway with hands splayed on her hips.

'Merry Christmas, Sonia,' he says. 'Mrs Browne has guests?'

'Just me. And now you. Come on, get yerself downstairs. I've never seen the old cow so cheerful. She's come into a little legacy and splashed out on the gramophone. Plus there's a bowl of punch and a bottle of sherry waiting to be drunk.'

She puts her hand on his arm and tries to pull him towards her. He fixes his feet to the floor.

235

'I'll come for ten minutes. I have to work tomorrow.'

'Boxing Day, Daniel?'

'Double time, Sonia.'

She laughs and pouts up at him. 'I'll give you double time, Mr Blake.'

In the event he stays an hour. He drinks two glasses of punch, dances with Mrs Browne and with Sonia, pecks them both on the cheek, then backs out of the doorway. Sonia calls him a spoilsport and blows him a kiss. Mrs Browne lifts her skirt and twirls her ankle to Al Jolson.

Daniel is pleased with himself as he treads the stairs to his room. A year ago he might have given in, allowed Sonia to tempt him to her bedroom. At the very least he might have removed the hanging from the wall to watch her undress. But his desire is mastered now, more focused. With Hannah, he has become a better person, a better man.

He cannot sleep, and by the early hours he is shivering with cold. He gets up, takes his coat from the back of the chair and drapes it on the top blanket. He imagines Hannah in bed next to him, her smooth blood-warm body, and the way she lifts his hair from his eyes, strokes his eyebrows and kisses them, then moves down to kiss the tip of his nose, his mouth. He thought he had loved Esther, but now he knows it was something more flimsy than love; it lacked the intensity and the ... *wholeness* of his feelings for Hannah. He fell in love with Esther because she wasn't interested, not at first in any case. She was friendly, but there was that hint of superiority, her office job at the GPO, and him a welder at the docks. He found the challenge exciting. Perhaps it's because Hannah is married, then: the thrill of wanting what isn't his. No, he is sure that's not right. He would love her even more if she was truly his.

She writes to him at Mrs Browne's, brief letters on smooth blue paper, such beautiful hand-writing, and the words so affecting. *When I am with you, it's as if I am flying.* He feels the same way. They soar together.

Sometimes they play a game, working out when they might have met, growing up in Poplar. Their paths must have crossed twelve dozen times, at the Queen's, the dance halls, the Boer victory parades. So why on earth did fate lead her to George? Daniel envies George and he pities him. He wishes he would die. A painless death, he'll give him that. A bullet in the head, or a stab of shrapnel through the heart.

George's division is in Palestine now, and there's plenty of fighting: Beersheba has been captured and they're moving into Jerusalem. He is desperate for leave, Hannah says, but none is being granted.

Is George much of a fighter? Would he fight for his wife? Hannah says he is placid, a decent man with an honest heart. He has never hit her, never even hit the children. A good man, then.

Daniel is sorry for what is to come.

28

I wake from the strangest dream. On a dinner plate were two raw eggs, cracked from their shells. Instead of flattening out, the eggs had kept their oval shape and the transparent whites quivered around the yolks like oversized fish eggs. 'Eat up,' my mum was saying. I poked at the eggs with a fork, but still they didn't spread; they kept their shape and the yolks stared back at me.

I sit up in bed, queasy to the pit of my stomach, convinced the eggs must be waiting for me downstairs. I can hear the kettle whistling on the stovetop. The back door shuts and from the quick footsteps I know it's Mum, dashing inside after her morning visit to the privy. She takes the kettle off the boil. I dress quickly, pull one of George's knitted jumpers over my blouse and tie my shawl loosely round my middle. I'm thankful it's such a cold January: no excuse needed for extra layers.

Snow is melting outside and the streets are black with icy slush. The snow never settled in Canning Town, but you could see it over the river, up on Shooters Hill and the slopes of Greenwich Park.

The children haven't woken yet and I can't hear Jen or the baby. I creep downstairs and find Mum in the parlour, sitting in the armchair with her cup of tea.

'Just brewed,' she says, nodding at the pot.

'Sleep all right?'

'Not really. Peculiar dream.'

'What was it this time?'

'Nothing. It's too daft to say. Are you going to see Dad?'

'I think I'll risk it, now the weather's thawing.'

'Shall I come with you?'

'It's Saturday, love. You stay here with the kids. Jen needs a break.'

Perhaps Mum meant it as a dig, but I refuse to feel guilty. Jen plays the martyr, but she enjoys having the children around. Teddy is a help with the baby, dangling rattles and pulling daft faces so that she can get on with the dinner. The kids love their little cousin, especially now he's started to talk. 'Dee-dee' the baby calls Teddy, and Teddy puffs up with delight every time.

'I'd like to visit Dad soon. Is he well enough, do you think?'

'I'll see how he is. You know it upset him when you turned up that time. The nurses said he was agitated for days.' She breaks off and sips her tea. 'Don't look so down-hearted. It's not your fault. He's still not himself.'

Are any of us ourselves?

I don't think Mum has guessed. I'm not so sure about Jen. I caught her looking at me yesterday as I was stretching to hang my wet coat over the dryer. She was feeding little Alec a piece of bread, breaking off tiny chunks rather than give him the whole crust. She stared at me, then all of a sudden scooped Alec up and disappeared into the scullery.

I pour tea into a cup and warm my fingers

around the china, sit on the edge of the wooden chair, forwards so that the cup is resting on my knees. There is a sudden movement deep in my belly.

One flicker, and then another.

Dear Christ, the baby is alive.

I've watched my waist thicken, my breasts swell, yet all this time I've been hoping, hoping that it might be a phantom, or that even if it was real, the pills or the gin would do their work. My hands begin to shake.

'Hannah?' says Mum.

I can't speak for the rush of tears and the sickness in my throat.

'What is it, love?'

'It's ... it's just Dad. I don't like to think of him in the hospital.'

Mum leans over and pats my knee. 'We'll get him home, see if we can't. They're doing more tests, might finally come up with some answers. Got to keep hoping, haven't we?'

I nod and reach for the hankie inside my sleeve. I try to take some deep breaths to stop the hysteria bubbling through me. The baby kicks again. Jen walks in and speaks to Mum as if I'm not even in the room.

'What's up with 'er?' she says.

'She wanted to come with me to the hospital. I've told her Dad's not up to it.'

'Sit down and drink your tea, Mum. You know what Hannah's like – she'd squeeze tears from a glass eye.'

Funny how two seconds in a room with Jen brings me to my senses. My tears dry instantly, just as they did when I was a child, trying to be brave so my big sister wouldn't tease.

'Cheer up,' says Jen, bustling over to the teapot. 'I don't want to be stuck indoors with that glum face all day.'

In the afternoon Jen puts little Alec down for a nap and I send Alice and Teddy to call for their friends on the street. A blast of cold air will do them good. Mrs Hillier has a granddaughter staying. With any luck she'll ask them in for their tea. I've got no patience with the children today.

Jen is in the armchair reading the *Pictorial*, a plate of shrivelled apple rings balanced at her elbow. When I come in, she tucks the magazine down the side of the cushion and stretches her legs towards the stove.

'Put a few more coals on, would you?' she asks.

I can feel Jen's eyes on me as I squat down to shovel coals from the scuttle. The hinge creaks as I open the stove door.

'Why were you so upset before?' she asks.

'Just thinking of Dad. Sometimes it catches me.'

'Only, you've got a lot on your mind, haven't you? Did you enjoy yourself at the Steamship last night?'

'It was nice enough. Same as usual.'

'Funny that. The Steamship is closed for a few days, I heard. Burst pipes, after the snow.'

She's staring at me, watching my reaction.

'That's right – I was forgetting. The White Horse we went to. They're all much of a muchness, aren't they, these pubs?'

241

'I wouldn't know.'

My only thought is to get out of the room. I start walking towards the door, but she lifts up one leg to block me. 'Who's the feller, then?'

'Sorry?'

'The feller. You're not getting fat on bacon, that's for sure. You was with him last night, wasn't you?'

Panic shrieks through my brain, twists my tongue. I mustn't get angry with Jen, got to play it carefully. An idea has been chasing round my mind for a couple of weeks now: a possible escape route. If only I had more time to choose my words, had a chance to calm myself... But if this is the moment, then I have to take it. I grab the chair and set it down closer to Jen.

She's staring at me and somehow I meet her eyes. 'I've got into trouble, Jen.'

'I knew it.' She spits out the words. Her top lip curls in disgust. 'How could you? How could you do it to George?'

'He don't deserve it, I know. I tried to end it, I swear, but ... we picked up again and that was shameful.'

'So what are you going to do? You're after money, I suppose, for an operation?'

'No.'

I take a deep breath. The shrieking gets louder, a shrill pitch, stabbing at my mind. There's no dressing it up. I'll have to ask her straight.

'What about you, Jen? Would you have the baby? Alec didn't go till September, did he? The dates work out – it could be his baby. You're so good with them, and ... I know how much you'd

242

like another.'

As I'm speaking the words, I'm aware how ridiculous they sound, what a perfect bloody idiot I am. What possessed me to think this was a good idea?

Blotches blaze like fresh burns on Jen's cheeks. Her mouth opens and closes. Seems I've knocked the wind clean out of her. Finally she speaks.

'Your baby? You want me to have it ... bring it up as my own?'

She doesn't sound as angry as I'd expected. Perhaps Jen is considering it, after all. Dear Christ, Jen *is* considering it.

'Alec wouldn't need to know,' I say. 'We can cover it up somehow. Think of Clare, from Flint Street. She got away with it.'

Her face clouds and the lip curls up again, a look of sheer loathing. 'Clare didn't do what you've done. What you've done ... it's hateful. George away fighting. And if you think I'm going to lay a finger on your little bastard... I don't think I can stand the sight of *you*, let alone–' she jabs a finger towards my stomach '–*it*.'

In my heart, this is what I expected. And I know what's coming next.

She speaks quietly now, looking down at her hands and picking at some dirt under a finger-nail. 'I thought it was Alec you were after, but he said don't be silly, he'd seen you with someone else, big tall feller, kissing in Victoria Park. And he was right all along. Assuming that's the only fancy man. P'r'aps there are others...'

'No!'

She stares up at me. 'You'll have to leave, of

course. Leave and take the children with you.'

'But, Jen, I don't know how I'll manage. I won't be able to work. Daniel–'

She thumps a fist on the arm of the chair. 'Don't. I don't want to hear his name or nothing about him. I want to be able to look George in the face when he comes home. I've a good mind to write to him now.'

'You wouldn't. He doesn't have to know yet. I'll find a way to tell him.'

'What about Mum? Will you tell her the news, or shall I?'

'I will. But please, Jen, please don't make us leave now. Give me a month, at least. A month to find somewhere and get sorted. Spring will be here soon. I'll be able to think straight.'

'All right.' She sighs now, as if she is actually bored and I am nothing but the silly little sister who needed putting in her place. 'But, Hannah, if you believe this feller's going to stick with you, you must be more stupid than I thought.'

I want to fly at her, tear out her hair, slap her smug mouth, but I stay in my seat, gripping the sides of the chair. My voice is low now, cracking with anger. 'Don't you dare pretend to know about me and Daniel. Don't you dare. You don't know nothing about love.'

She stands up and her elbow sends the plate of apple rings crashing to the floor. The china cracks and a piece of apple rolls into the ashy hearth. She leans in close so that her face is an inch from mine, words spitting from her lips. '*Love*, is it? We'll see.'

I listen to Jen's footsteps pounding up the stairs

and I hate the sound of her, the heft of her, every bloody thing about her. She has never liked me, not really. We rubbed along as kids, we had to, but it's as if she has been waiting for this moment – the chance to stamp on me and watch me squirm. *Oh, Hannah, she may be clever, but she's got no sense.* I've heard her say it more than once. When Dad got ill and I had to leave school, start earning, she made no secret of the fact she was cock-a-hoop. *All those spelling tests… Ten out of ten ain't going to do you much good when you're skivvying up west.* Well, now she has the biggest stick to beat me with. I hope she enjoys every minute.

The back door bangs and Alice runs into the parlour. Mrs Hillier's granddaughter trails after her with Teddy, their noses red and their lips blue-tinged with cold.

'Can Kathleen come in to play?' asks Alice. 'Mrs Hillier's got a headache.'

I wipe my eyes with the end of my apron and try to force a smile. 'Do what you like,' I say. 'But don't disturb Jen. She's upstairs with the baby.' The children flop down onto the rug and Kathleen takes a little knitted doll from her pocket. Teddy edges closer to Kathleen, inching his Ducky across the rug towards the doll.

I untie my apron and drape it over the back of the armchair. 'I'm popping out for a while,' I tell the children. 'There's bread if you're hungry.'

A raw easterly is blowing down Victoria Dock Road. The force of it makes me gasp, but I like the cold, the creeping numbness. At the station, a train has just pulled in and passengers begin to file along the street. I hurry past, keeping my head down in case Mum is among them, on her way back from the hospital. A huddle of Indian sailors emerge from the seamen's hostel, thin cotton trousers flapping around their bony legs.

Left towards the creek. The tide is in. Ice splinters the murky grey water. In the sky, rain clouds mingle with drifts of black chimney smoke. Wooden hulls of small boats knock against the redbrick piers that hold up the bridge. *Knock, knock, knock*, as if looking for an answer.

The parapets are shoulder-high, solid metal with fancy panels inlaid. The rivets on the panels are big enough to give a foothold. I reach out and run my hand along the ridges. How long would it take to go up and over? Is this how Auntie Bea did it? Up and over without stopping to think, or pacing the dockside, taking her time, reasoning it out? I imagine the water surging into my lungs, the feeling that there is no solid ground beneath me, and I know then that I have left it too late. I shouldn't have stopped to think.

Nettie is sitting at the kitchen table with a cup of tea when I get to the cafe on Monday morning. A pile of carrots is criss-crossed in front of her, and a scrubbing brush floats in a bowl of water. She smiles and asks if there is any news.

I look around for Mrs Stephens, but there's no sign. Nettie points towards the storeroom. 'Unpacking an order,' she says.

'The pills still haven't worked, if that's what you mean,' I whisper.

'You heard from your George?'

'Not since Christmas.'

'What you gonna do?'

Mrs Stephens bustles in. 'Morning, Hannah!' she says. 'You're looking well, dear. A bit of colour in your cheeks for a change.'

'I think it's just chapped skin. All this cold weather.'

'And you don't seem so skinny, thank goodness. There's the rest of us, fading away on these blessed rations.'

'Too much custard at Christmas, Mrs Stephens. I'll be watching my weight before you know it.'

'Don't go doing that. Nothing wrong with a few womanly curves.' She pats her hips and turns back towards the storeroom. I don't think she knows yet. If she had guessed, she wouldn't chat so casually about womanly curves. She would be watching, silently, until she was sure. And then she would take me to one side.

Nettie raises her eyebrows, but I don't want to talk anymore. It would have been better if I'd never confided in her. It's not as if the pills worked anyway. She's forever asking questions – have I run into the father again? Is he married too? – and I know she's dying to hear the full story. I stick to my lie about an old flame, someone from school I happened to bump into.

Daniel comes in at lunchtime. He sits down and Nettie rushes over to serve him as usual. I let her get on with it, the batting eyelashes and the little-girl laugh, trying to get him to put down his book and take notice of her. I haven't any need to feel jealous. It's enough for Daniel and me to be in the same room together. There is a comfort in it, a promise.

When Daniel leaves, Nettie says goodbye with a soppy wide smile. She thinks she looks like a film star, but the truth is, her mouth is crooked when she smiles, and you can see a gap at the back where she's had a bad tooth pulled out.

When Daniel is out of view, Nettie turns to me with a cheeky look. 'What I wouldn't give...' She winks and disappears out into the kitchen.

I clear his table, but today I can't catch the scent of him, the metal and the peppermint that sometimes lingers. I take the bowl and plate through to the kitchen. Nettie's not there, but I can hear her voice shrill and startled out the back. 'What you doing?' she says, and next thing she's rushing into the kitchen with her mouth hanging open.

'I just saw Mr Blake putting something into your coat. A piece of paper.'

'Shh.'

'That's just what he said. Put his fingers to his lips like I was a stupid child and dashed out the door...' It dawns on her then why Mr Blake might be passing me a note. She looks down at my belly. 'It's him!'

'It's him, yes.' The bell on the cafe door rings. 'I'll see to the customer. We can have a walk later if you like. I'll explain.'

'If you're sure,' she says, and her little-girl voice turns icy. 'Don't feel obliged.'

Damn, is all I can think as I take down the customer's lunch order. It was always a risk, Daniel creeping up the side of the cafe like that, opening the back door, just so he could leave me a message. He had a plan in place if anyone should see him. *I was chasing a rat off, Mrs Stephens*, he was going to say. *Horrible big brute, disappeared under your door.*

A great wave of tiredness washes over me. What does it matter if Nettie knows about Daniel? Soon Mrs Stephens will know too and I'll be sent packing. This is the journey I am taking now. The future is rushing to meet me, fast as a spring tide.

Nettie is angry, says I should have told her the whole story and she feels a proper fool being lied to like that. We loop round the side streets near Glengall Road: Launch Street, Galbraith Street, past the library on Strattondale Street and then up Galbraith again.

I tell her I'm sorry and she seems to soften.

'So what are you going to do? You'll have the baby adopted?'

Adopted by the workhouse, she means. Who else would take it?

'Daniel wants the child. He has a notion we can face it out.' We're on Manchester Road now, coming up to the swing bridge. I shake my head. 'I had an aunt who threw herself into the lock. They fished her out just here.' I stretch out my hand and run it along the filthy bricks of the dock wall. 'I found out recently that she jumped in. Always thought she'd fallen. Happens all the time, don't it? Funny how things get hushed up. Have you ever seen a drowned body?'

'Don't, Hannah. You're giving me creeps.'

'The skin swells up; eyes pop out like a fish. Peculiar colour, your hands go. Sort of dark purple, like rotten cherries.'

We're on the bridge and my heart is beating so hard I can feel it thick in my throat. How long did it take Auntie Bea to drown? Did she welcome the water as it filled her lungs, or did she wish, after all, that she had learned to swim?

Nettie pats me on the arm. It's a sort of dismissal. She's heard enough.

'Can't miss my bus,' she says. 'Good luck with it all. I'll see you Wednesday.'

I wave and smile, try to look normal, but in my head a voice is shrieking.

I dig my thumbnail into the side of the pencil, squeeze my eyes shut to try and think of some words, but I can't get further than '*Dear George*'. I know I can't confess. It would be downright cruel for him to learn the truth while he is out there in Alexandria or Jerusalem or wherever he is now. Imagine. He rips open the letter in his grubby tent; he's looking forward to our news. He holds the letter in his hands and reads that I am in love with another man, that I am having this man's baby, that I don't love him, and I realize now that I never have. Oh, and just to finish, I am setting up home with my lover, and I'm taking our two children. *That's all for now, George. Take care of yourself...*

What if George should be killed the next day, knowing that I had betrayed him?

No, better to wait. Wait and see.

I scribble out the usual:

We are fine here, apart from a fall of snow last Friday. Sugar is rationed now, and they're bringing in tickets for meat and butter. Can you believe Mum queued four hours for a pound of mince last week? Teddy's chest has been good this winter; perhaps he's grown out of his weakness. Alice is still keen on her knitting and sewing. Did you ever wear those funny socks?

I read through the letter and I'm surprised at how light-hearted it sounds. Hard to think of myself as a good liar, but I suppose that's what I am now. I fold the notepaper in half, run my nail along the edge of the fold. A sharp pain jags in my wrist, deep under the scar from the Silvertown explosion.

Part Three

Part Three

Leman Street Police Station

22nd day of July 1918

Statement of Annette Wilton
Waitress

About January this year, I am not certain of the date, Mrs Loxwood told me that she had been about with Blake and that she was in trouble by him. In March I met her outside the Black Lion public house, Whitechapel, and she asked me to help her during her confinement. I at first told her that I didn't think I could do so. She then said: 'I haven't got a friend in the world.' I then promised her that I would. She asked me not to say anything about it at the café.

29

The tram is busy, but there is very little chatter. Each passenger concentrates on ignoring the soldier, who mutters to himself and pulls again and again at the cuffs of his greatcoat, examining the seams and blowing on them as if he is trying to get a fire going.

When we boarded the tram at Limehouse there was a woman I recognized, but she left at Stepney and now we're alone with strangers. Daniel takes my hand and the touch of his skin strikes some warmth in me, a sense of calm. There is something simple and complete about this feeling: taking a tram with Daniel, past unfamiliar shops on White-chapel Road: Italo's Eel & Pie House; Paikin & Co., watchmakers; Lissack Pianofortes; Joseph Mauerberger & Son, draper. Outside the draper's is a trestle table piled with offcuts, and a woman is picking through them. She holds a piece of flowery fabric up to the weak sunlight. Suddenly the warmth leaves my body and I feel a chill of envy for this woman with her neat waist and nothing more to do on a Thursday lunchtime than choose a piece of fancy cloth to pretty up a sofa cushion.

The tram stops next to a Salvation Army shelter.

'This is us,' says Daniel.

He gets off first, holds out his arm as I step down. On the pavement, I gulp a breath of the Whitechapel air – damp February air, but there is a spiciness to it, richer and more complicated than the factory fumes that blow across Canning Town.

Daniel laces his fingers into mine. It's strange to be so free with each other. The soldier in his greatcoat shuffles past, still fussing at his cuff, and turns into the Salvation Army.

With his free hand Daniel pulls a piece of paper from the breast pocket of his jacket and shakes out the folds.

"'*Mr Specterman*,'" he reads. "'*Number 9 Union Buildings, Adler Street. Look for St Mary's Church on Whitechapel High Street – big clock on the side. Adler Street is next to St Mary's.*'"

The church is only a hundred yards ahead, its huge steeple rising from a square brick tower. We walk towards it, weaving through the crowded pavements, past a saddler's and a toolshop, the sharp sound of metal spinning against metal. There are smells I don't recognize here, cooking smells drifting from the alleys, heavy aromas of onion, over-ripe fruit and ... nutmeg, could it be? My mouth waters and I realize that I am hungry.

We turn into Adler Street and the first thing I see is another church – ST BONIFACE ROMAN CATHOLIC, the sign says, and then some writing in a foreign language. Daniel is looking too. 'A German church,' he says. We stand in front of the sign, and I know we are thinking the same thing. If that church was in Poplar, it would've been smashed and boarded up by now.

'Are there lots of Germans here?'

'All sorts in Whitechapel, ain't there? People are more accepting.'

'Just as well.'

He smiles and clutches my hand tighter. 'Anyway, this is it... Union Buildings.'

The block is directly opposite the German church. On the ground floor of Union Buildings are four little shops, their windows dusty except for a bootmaker's, which has a display of children's shoes and a higher shelf stacked with workmen's boots. On one side of the building is a stairwell and a small carved sign screwed to the wall saying, OFFICE, NUMBER 9, 3RD FLOOR.

'How many floors d'you think there are, Daniel?' I gaze up. Washing flaps from the balconies. One filthy sheet looks as if it must have been hanging for weeks.

'Five?'

'And the rooms will be in this block?'

'The agent weren't too clear on the details.'

We climb up to the first floor, Daniel in front of me because there isn't enough room to walk side by side. The narrow staircase spirals round, then runs straight for a few steps before spiralling again onto a narrow stone landing. There are three doors on the landing. Behind one of them a woman shouts. 'And if that weren't cheek enough, she wanted ten sets a bedclothes fetched to the laundry! I coulda frottled 'er.'

At the second passageway, I pause for a rest. My legs ache and I'm stupidly breathless. I lean against the wall. The iron balcony looks wobbly, rust bubbling through the black paint. Daniel has already gone on ahead. He hasn't noticed I've stopped.

'Hannah?' he calls down from the third floor.

'Coming. Just needed a breather.'

He rushes down the stairs and takes my hands. 'It's too much for you, ain't it?'

'Don't be daft. I'm jittery, that's all.'

I follow him up to the third flight and he kisses my hand before knocking on the door to number nine. I smile up at him, try not to look nervous.

'He-llo!'

'Hello?' says Daniel. We both hesitate, unsure whether to walk in or wait for the door to be opened.

'Come!' says the voice.

Daniel turns the handle and we step inside. A man looks up from behind a desk. The window-less room is small and sparsely furnished. It takes a moment for my eyes to adjust to the dim light. On the desk are two shallow boxes containing piles of papers, and a wooden bowl filled with pears. Behind the desk, there are several shelves lined with more boxes, each marked with in-decipherable words. A gas lamp is burning, casting shadows onto the man's lined face.

'Mr Specterman?' says Daniel.

'I am. And you would be?'

'Mr Blake. We're looking for rooms. Two rooms ideally, with a kitchen. We have two children and...' Daniel gestures towards me. I make a show of cradling my stomach, though it embarrasses me to act so forward.

'Another on the way! *Mazel tov!*' He jumps up

from his chair and shakes Daniel's hand so hard that the glasses fall off his nose and clatter onto the desk. 'You've chosen the right day to come. Perfect day. Number twelve has just been vacated. I will show you now, if you have time?'

We climb one more flight to the fourth floor. When we reach the landing, I glance over the balcony. We're so high now, level with the bell tower of the German church. Beyond the church are rows and rows of terraces, lining the cramped roads behind Whitechapel High Street. I look down at the houses, squinting into the sunlight, and I wonder if this is where the woman outside the draper's lives. She'll be unpacking her shopping at this moment, holding up the offcut to see if it matches her curtains.

This landing is identical to the lower floors. There are three doors – number eleven in the centre, facing the balcony, numbers ten and twelve on opposite sides, facing each other.

Mr Specterman takes a single key from a pocket inside his jacket. He opens the door and stands back. 'After you, Mrs Blake.'

The front door leads straight into a small, dark kitchen. On the back wall, there is an enamelled sink with one tap, a geyser and a gas oven, the ceiling blackened above it. There is just room for a tiny table and four chairs.

I risk a deep breath through my nose and to my surprise the smell isn't bad at all. There is the scent of onion and nutmeg again.

Mr Specterman taps his fingernails on a metal box high on the wall by the front door. 'Penny-in-the-slot meter,' he says. 'This provides all your gas. Light and cooking. Hot water.'

'How much do you get for a penny?' I ask.

'A day or two. Depends how often you cook. Summer is coming, eh?'

Daniel walks over to the sink and pulls back the thin curtain that hangs across the cupboard below it. Tiny flashes of light shimmer in the crevices. Silverfish.

Mr Specterman ushers us through the door to the left of the kitchen. In this room, there is one lace-curtained window, a fireplace with a mantelpiece over, three candlesticks of different sizes on the mantel shelf. A two-seater sofa is covered in a dark purple fabric, the cushions dimpled where the springs have gone. The wallpaper is patterned with bunches of pink hyacinths. It's torn in places, but I've seen worse. 'This is the living room-cum-second bedroom,' says Mr Specterman. 'Very cosy in the winter. And now, please...' We follow him back through the kitchen and he stands at the double oak doors that must lead into the main bedroom. He opens the two doors with a flourish and stands back, beaming.

This bedroom is large and bright, with a window straight ahead, looking out onto the German church. There is a circular table of polished mahogany, a chest of drawers and an iron bedstead. In one corner is a carved mahogany chair, the seat upholstered in red velvet. A cupboard is nailed lopsidedly to the wall over the bedstead. That would have to come down.

'Very spacious, eh? The furniture is available to rent also,' says Mr Specterman. 'Top quality. Bring your own mattress.'

Daniel nods and I can feel myself blushing.

'And the rent?' asks Daniel.

'Ten shillings a week, with the furniture.'

'If we can have a moment to talk it over...?' says Daniel.

'Certainly you may.' He adjusts his spectacles and smiles. 'Come and find me in my office as soon as you're ready.'

I stand at the bedroom window while Daniel paces around, tapping walls, rattling things. Beyond Whitechapel, beyond Stepney, lie Poplar and Canning Town. I cannot see the Thames from here, the creek. There are no bridges to cross. This is our only choice, isn't it, a new start where no one will know our business? But the fact is, this could be a foreign land.

'Will it suit, Hannah?' He's standing next to me now, and his arm is around my shoulder.

'It's very high up, ain't it? We'd cop it if a bomb dropped.' There was another raid only a few days ago, thirty-odd killed. The Germans' aeroplanes are bigger now; deafening giants with scores of bombs on board.

'We can shelter in the Tube station. Aldgate East is only two minutes away.'

'And the gas oven. I ain't used to gas...'

'You'll soon catch on. It will do, won't it? For now, anyway. Till we get ourselves straight.'

I lower my voice. 'We don't know that he'll have us yet.'

'He's very understanding, the agent said. Won't ask too many questions. Look, I know it ain't much, but it's the best we can manage right now.'

Daniel pulls me close, puts his hand on my

swollen belly and then kisses me. For all the fear there is excitement too. I can't stop the ache, the need to have him near. He strokes the nape of my neck. 'We better go down,' he whispers, 'or I might not be accountable for my actions.'

In the office, Mr Specterman is peeling a pear with a knife. 'Spitalfields Market,' he says, lifting up the pear for us to inspect. The juice glistens in the gaslight. 'Finest fruit in London. You like the rooms?'

'Yes,' says Daniel. 'We'd like to take them, but we can't move until March. First week in March.'

'Let me see. That's–' his brow furrows as he turns to look at a calendar '–two weeks away.' He taps the end of the knife on the desk. 'As I like you, I'll keep number twelve until March.'

'Thank you,' smiles Daniel.

I smile too, but the mention of 'two weeks' has stirred up a heap of dread. I can't breathe for thinking of all the things I must do before March. Somehow I'll have to explain it to the children, tell my mum I'm moving out, leave the cafe. But... I'm running away with myself. There's still one more hurdle to overcome.

'I'll need details for your rent book,' says Mr Specterman. 'You have identification?'

Daniel pulls an envelope from his jacket and takes out his registration card and an insurance booklet. Mr Specterman opens up the registration card and nods.

'Dry-dock worker, I see.'

'Ship repairer,' I say. 'He ain't a feather man.'

'No, no, I'm sure. Keep away as long as you can, Mr Blake. The war is a terrible thing. I've lost two sons myself, one of them an officer.' He takes a handkerchief from his pocket and blows his nose. 'My wife will never get over it.'

Daniel and I speak at the same time, the hushed 'I'm sorry' that never sounds right, no matter how often you say the words.

'But!' Mr Specterman rallies, looks directly at me. 'The business at hand. Mrs Blake, your documents, please?'

I open up my bag and push my hand inside, pat around as if I'm certain they're in there somewhere. 'Sorry, I don't seem to have brought anything. Kids must have been in my bag...' How I hate myself for the lie. For blaming the children.

'I understand,' he says, casting his eyes down and scribbling in a rent book. 'We'll manage without.'

30

On Sunday he walks the foot tunnel to Greenwich. He can see that Lady Tolland's house is occupied as soon as he turns into the street. Bluish smoke drifts from the main chimney, and the upstairs curtains are pulled open.

He lets himself into the side gate as usual, walks up to the garden shed and feels in his pocket for the padlock key.

'Daniel!'

Lady Tolland is waving at him from the terrace. A plain knitted shawl is wrapped around her shoulders, and she looks thinner, less fussy. It's over a year since she left for Dorset, vowing to stay out of London until the end of the war. He wonders what has brought her back.

'Daniel! A word, please.'

He strides up the garden path, touching his cap as he steps onto the terrace.

'Lady Tolland. I hope you're well?'

'Yes, yes. And you?' Her hand moves to her throat, a habit she has of fingering her gold brooch. But the brooch is not there and instead she twists a jet button.

'Very well. The garden is ticking over. We had snow in January. You'll see the box hedge...'

'It looks sorry for itself, indeed. But the daffodils will bloom soon – they'll cheer everything up. Come into the house, would you, Daniel. It's so damp out here.'

He leaves his boots in the lean-to and follows her through the kitchen and into the drawing room at the front of the house. Lady Tolland picks up a letter from the writing table under the window.

'A neighbour wrote to me in Dorset, touching on your ... conduct. I may as well read this.' She peers down at the letter and clears her throat. *"Your man Blake has been busy as ever in the garden. Although, I hope you won't mind me mentioning, I have a strong suspicion that he may have brought a companion into the garden: a woman. Perhaps this is something you have sanctioned, but, if not, I thought it might be wise to bring this to your attention. In addition, last Sunday I happened to notice Blake gaining entry to your property from the*

266

lean-to, via a kitchen window.'"

She looks up from the letter, eyebrows raised.

There's no choice. He'll have to confess, and face the consequences. He opens his mouth to speak, but Lady Tolland cuts in.

'Naturally I have checked the house thoroughly and everything seems to be in order. It was just the library where I sensed ... activity. Disturbance of the dust on the bookshelves, nothing more.' She pauses, twists the button at her throat, then takes a deep breath. 'Daniel, what were you thinking?'

'Our agreement, ma'am. Gardening in return for books? I borrow one or two now and again. I should have asked permission. I'm very sorry.'

'And today? Which of my books did you intend to return today?'

He takes an Arnold volume from his jacket pocket and places it into her outstretched hand. He notices that her hands are trembling. His own hands are steady as ice.

'It was only once, ma'am, that I brought the lady here. It was wrong of me, I know.'

'And who is this woman?'

'A friend, Lady Tolland. She's fond of flowers. I wanted to show her the roses.'

'Indeed?' She looks towards the hallway where the telephone is fixed to the wall. Is she thinking of calling the police? His heartbeat quickens.

But then she turns to him, the frown lifting from her forehead. 'You may continue in the garden, Daniel, but you must promise me, faithfully, that you will never bring anyone here again, or enter the house, without my permission.

Really, after all these years, I thought we had such a good understanding.'

She stands, straight and satisfied, awaiting his grateful response.

'It's very good of you, Lady Tolland.' He takes a deep breath, remembers how Esther had resented his Sunday trips to Greenwich, and never a shilling to show for it. He can't do the same to Hannah. Perhaps, finally, it is time to leave. 'But I'm afraid I shall have to move on in any case. My situation is changing. I'm needed at ... at home.'

Her face flushes as she folds the letter back into the envelope.

'I'm disappointed in you, Daniel. I thought perhaps you might show more loyalty. Especially in the circumstances.'

Is this a threat? he wonders. *If you desert me, I will go to the police* – is that what she's saying?

'Shall I finish the digging, or would you like me to leave now?'

Her skirts swish and she turns towards the window so that he cannot see her face. 'That will be all,' she says. 'Goodbye.'

In the lean-to, he laces his boots and steps out onto the garden path. He pauses, wonders whether he should be more humble, grovel a little to make sure she doesn't report him. But he decides not to turn back, to keep walking, and as he unlatches the side gate, he feels light-headed with a sense of liberation. Hannah is right. What's wrong with the public library? They had passed a library in Whitechapel – spitting distance from Adler Street – a fine-looking building next to an art gallery. This time next Sunday they will have

268

moved. Their own rooms, at last. And what of Lady Tolland's garden? He'll miss it, of course he will, but there are other gardens. They can take summer trips to Hyde Park. They can grow sunflowers on the landing.

31

This is my last day at the cafe. When Nettie leaves at three, I hang back and ask Mrs Stephens if I can have a word.

'What is it, dear?'

We stand facing each other across the kitchen table.

'I have to leave. Sorry it's so sudden, but today's my last day.'

'Your last day? Working here, you mean?'

So she hasn't guessed. Her eyesight must be worse than I thought. I hold my bag across my buttoned-up coat, hiding the bump. If I can get away with it, so much the better.

'I'm moving to Whitechapel, you see. I've not been getting on so well with my sister. Been offered a job there ... in a draper's shop. It came up just yesterday and I had to make a decision.'

'Whitechapel? Of all places... Have you taken leave of your senses? What's your old man say?'

'He don't know yet.'

'Fine surprise for him when he gets home. Lovely, I'm sure. Why can't you find somewhere more local? Seems an awful long way to go for a quarrel with your sister.'

'The rent is cheap. Anyway, I like it. I've got a ... good friend nearby.'

Mrs Stephens lets out a long breath between pursed lips, somewhere between a sigh and a whistle. She walks over to the till, opens the drawer and starts counting out coins.

'I can't pretend to understand you, really I can't. Uprooting them kiddies too.'

My nerve is wavering. It's more than I can stand, trying to sound so matter-of-fact when it breaks my heart to leave this place.

Mrs Stephens puts my wages on the table. 'A bit more notice would've been nice,' she says. 'You'll be wanting a reference, I suppose?'

'Thank you.'

She tuts to herself – '*Whitechapel!*' – as she reaches under the counter for notepaper. I stand at the table watching her scribble the reference, my bag held close.

I put the children to bed early that night. Jen goes up soon after, leaving me and Mum in the parlour. She's in the armchair with her knitting on her lap. Her eyes are beginning to close, but she's fighting sleep, jerking her head and grasping the knitting needles again.

'You're tired, Mum. I'll help you make up the bed.'

'What time is it?'

The clock on the mantelpiece hasn't worked for months. Alec was the one who kept it ticking. I stare at the clock face anyway. The hands are still stuck at twenty-five to eight. The wedding photos on the wall nudge into the corner of my vision. George staring down at me.

'Must be ten-ish.'

'I'm not sleeping,' says Mum. 'All this worry.'

I put my mug of tea on the ground, rock forwards on the chair and press my hands between my knees.

'Worry?'

'I've tried to ignore it. Thought perhaps you'd get it sorted ... but that frightens me too. Whatever's going to happen, Hannah? You and this baby.'

So she knows. Of course she knows. The pressure in my head builds, a thin whine at first, and then the shriek, the sense of falling.

'Mum–'

'No excuses. No nothing. The whole thing makes me feel ill. I just want to know what you're going to do.'

'I'm going to have the baby.'

'But you'll give it up? George needn't know if we're careful.'

'No. The father ... he wants the baby too. We want to be together.'

Mum covers her hands with her face and hisses into her fingers: 'Give me strength.' I've never heard a sound like it before. Such pain in her voice, unbearable pain, and I'm the cause. 'How can you be together? You're *married*, Hannah. You're a soldier's wife. Why do you think George is over there fighting? He hasn't done it for himself; he's done it for you and the kids. To make you proud. And this is what he gets for his sacrifice.'

What? He never did it for me. He did it for Pandora Pavelle, for his own pride, for appearance's sake.

'I didn't want him to join up. I begged him not to go. And if he hadn't gone...'

'So it's his fault, then? Oh, I've heard everything now. Talk about twisting it.' She gathers her knitting and winds the loose wool strangle-tight round the ball.

'I've told Jen I'll be out by the end of the month.'

'Jen knows?'

I nod. 'I've got a van coming Saturday. I'm sorry, Mum. If you met him...'

'I've met him all right. It's that fellow who came to the house the night Brunner's went up. I'm right, aren't I? Blake? Dor's friend.'

'Yes.' A spark of hope. Mum is a good judge. 'Yes, that's him. He's not a bad man – you could see that?'

'He was polite enough, but I saw the way he looked at you. I sensed something was up. Never thought you'd be fool enough to fall for it. Alice and Teddy, have they met him?'

'Not yet.'

'So you'll introduce them at the weekend... Children, meet your new daddy.' Her voice cracks and tears spill over the red rims of her eyes. She takes a handkerchief from her sleeve. 'Can't you leave the kids here at least? I can't lose them too...'

'They're staying with me. Jen won't have them anyway.'

'But what about George? He'll want his children when he comes home. He adores those nippers. Have you told him?'

'No. I'll wait ... until I know he's coming home. There's no point–'

'No point upsetting him when he could be killed tomorrow? That would suit you just nicely, wouldn't it? Not a thought for his people, of course, his old dad.'

'He hasn't seen his dad for years! His people don't come into it.'

'That's true, because he's only got you. That poor man. You're right. It's better he was blown to pieces.'

We are both crying now. I reach for Mum's hand, but she pulls away.

'I'll make sure I'm out on Saturday. I'll be visiting your father.'

'And Dad might be coming home? There'll be a spare room at least...'

'You think there's a silver lining? I'm telling you there won't ever be one. When you leave, that's the end of it. Don't think you can come back when Mr Blake has had enough. You've cooked your goose now, girl. You're on your own.'

'Hear, hear.' Jen is standing in the doorway, tightening the belt of her dressing gown. 'And did she tell you the best of it? She wanted *me* to rear the little bastard. Pass it off as Alec's!'

Mum gasps, then collects herself, dabs at her eyes again. 'Go back to bed, Jen. We don't need your stirring. There's enough stirred up as it is.'

Jen slopes away and Mum walks over to the window. Pulling back the curtain, she looks into the black night, speaking quietly. 'He was Dor's feller too, weren't he? When Meena finds out ...

273

what a kick in the teeth. Meena's awfully fond of you. I didn't think you were capable of this, honestly I didn't. I brought you up proper. Granny took you to church. I suppose it's something inherited ... a weakness, like Beatrice...'

The windowpanes cloud with the warmth of Mum's breath. Her shoulders seem so slight and so pitiful. I want to put my arms around her, but I know she doesn't want me. All I can do is accept what's due, sit on my chair and weep.

32

He sorts through his books, stacking them into two separate piles: books that he can live without and books that he is determined to keep. The second pile is bigger than the first. He sorts a second time, attempts to be more ruthless, resists the temptation to open a novel at the ribboned page, or to read a stanza from a favourite poem. Now the first pile is a precarious tower, stretching up towards the sloping eaves of his lodging room. Near the top is *Lustra* by Ezra Pound. He removes it and places it on the bed, next to the folded clothes and the African hanging.

Mr Specterman has asked for two weeks' rent in advance. The books should fetch at least that amount, with perhaps some money over to buy necessaries when the baby arrives.

Daniel empties the contents of the tin trunk onto his bed. He stares at the letters and the photographs, the yellowed certificates and school reports, a *Boy's Own* annual he has kept for twenty-odd years. He picks up one of the small blue envelopes and traces Hannah's handwriting. *Mr D. Blake, 279 E. India Dock Road.* He smiles and ties the envelopes into a bundle. Soon there will be no need for letters and secret notes. He will miss them, no doubt. But to wake up next to Hannah each morning ... that will be worth a thousand letters.

Carefully he loads the books into the emptied trunk, then drags it out onto the landing and bumps it down the stairs. On the pavement, he lifts the trunk onto one shoulder and walks the short distance to Chrisp Street. It is Saturday morning and the roads are busy. A coalman's cart trundles ahead of him, the wooden wheels slanting outwards as if they might buckle at any moment. Two nuns pass and he nods them good day as best he can with the weight of the trunk on his shoulder.

The dealer is pleased to see Daniel and he looks after him, as Daniel knew he would, on account of the custom he's given him over the years. He leaves the stall with thirty shillings in his pocket.

He returns the empty trunk to his room and quickly repacks it, stuffing in the clothes and the African hanging and his remaining books. Everything else will go in his canvas bag. He checks his pocket watch. Better get a move on: he's meeting Hannah and the children in Whitechapel at eleven. Lovely kids, they are, and they seemed to like him well enough when they met at the rec on Thursday. Of course, it helped that he'd stuffed his pockets with sweets. Little Alice is a scamp all right, but Hannah has the measure of her. They'll rub along fine.

Sonia is still asleep. She likes a lie-in after a busy Friday night. He hasn't told her he is leaving, hasn't even told Mrs Browne. They'd only ask questions, badger him for a forwarding address, and he'd prefer not to discuss his situation. But he has a present for Sonia. From his trouser pocket he takes a piece of greaseproof paper and unwraps a small gob of moist putty. He divides it into two and rolls each section between thumb and forefinger, then pushes it into the two nail holes in the dividing wall. He smoothes over the putty with his thumb. A clean job of it. Good. He doesn't want some dirty-minded sod watching her.

As he leaves, he takes the Ezra Pound from his jacket pocket and pushes the book through the gap under Sonia's door. He thinks she'll enjoy *Lustra*. She appreciates the avant-garde.

He takes the tram to Whitechapel, and as the shops and the offices flash past the window, an image of Mr Specterman hovers in his mind, his expression when he opened up Daniel's registration card. What was it Mr Specterman had said? *Dry-dock worker, I see.* There was none of the disdain or the mockery that Daniel had come to expect, the suggestion that he was a shirker. There was just ... resignation, and when Mr Specterman said that his sons had died, Daniel was swept by an unexpected wave of guilt. That the Specterman boys – Jewish boys – had died for England, it humbled him, somehow. Still, there

276

was the urge to justify himself. He wanted to shout that he wasn't afraid, that joining up would be the easiest thing in the world now, the easiest method of escape.

He ain't a feather man, Hannah had said.

How can he be a coward? He is taking the most difficult path, a path other men wouldn't dare to tread.

33

Nettie is out of breath when I open the door, clutching her side as if she has a stitch.

'Those steps are a killer,' she says. 'Here, brought you these.' She holds out a bunch of daffodils, seven or eight of them, all different lengths and ragged at the stems. 'Well, you going to ask me in or what?'

She follows me into the living room and looks around without saying anything. I know it's not much, but I've done my best to brighten the place. The lace curtains are tied back, and the antimacassars are smooth and clean on the little purple sofa. I've hung up Daniel's African cloth, though the oranges and reds don't match too well with the pink hyacinths on the wallpaper. We tried to wipe the black stains off the ceiling above the gas lamps, but wiping only smeared them and now the marks look even worse.

The children are playing at arm-wrestling, lying tummy down on the rug in front of the fire. The fire isn't drawing well: it hisses and sighs because the coals are damp.

'Children, say hello to Nettie. My friend from the cafe.'

'Have you brought any buns?' asks Teddy.

'Sorry,' says Nettie, holding out her empty hands. 'Rations are so tight. We never get leftovers no more.'

'Don't be so cheeky, Teddy. Now go off and play in the bedroom, both of you. Go on, the blackboard's under the bed.'

Daniel has bought them a packet of chalk and a small blackboard. Noughts and crosses will keep them quiet for a while, so long as Alice is winning.

I put Nettie's daffs in a coronation jug on the mantelpiece and the room is more cheerful already. We drink tea from tin cups. The box of china broke in the van: my fault for packing everything in such a rush.

'You all right, then?' asks Nettie. She looks uncomfortable, shifting around on the edge of the sofa with her hands wedged under her thighs.

'Fine. It's strange, of course, being somewhere new.' Strange isn't the word. I feel giddy all the time, four floors up and a different world at my feet. 'The children think we're on holiday. Should've seen them last weekend, charging up and down the steps like the building was a fairground ride. Novelty's wearing off now, of course.'

'What about Daniel? They taken to him?'

'He's been ever so kind. More patient than me, he is. They seem to like him.' I don't tell Nettie that Alice has cried every night. She's happy enough during the day, cocky as ever, but at bed-time it's all 'Nana' and 'Auntie Jen' and 'When can we go back home?' Teddy misses his little cousin. I caught him talking to himself this morning, curled up with his thumb in his mouth as if he was a baby. 'Dee-dee,' he was saying. 'Dee-dee.'

'Alice starts school next week, two streets away, and Teddy can join after Easter.'

'So you'll have them off your hands when the baby's born.'

'Yes.' I put my hand to my belly. The baby has hiccups again, tiny jerks that set my teeth on edge. 'Did you find anyone, Nettie?'

She picks up her bag, bites her bottom lip. 'I asked around. This woman's supposed to be reliable. Mrs Moss. Delivered half the women in Whitechapel, my cousin says. Reasonable rates if she can see you're hard up. Not that I'm saying you're hard up, Hannah... Anyway, here.' She hands me a slip of paper with a name and add-ress written in smudged ink. *Agnes Moss, midwife.* I fold the paper and put it behind the coronation jug.

Nettie has a second cup of tea, but I can't face another with the baby pressing on my insides. And anyway, I'm trying not to drink much, because I'm too exhausted to go lumbering down the stairs to the ground-floor privies. I hate using the slop bucket during the day, makes me feel like an invalid, but there's no choice now.

She drains the cup and runs a finger round the rim. 'There was a bit of talk yesterday,' she says. 'At the cafe.'

'Oh yes?'

'Mr Cridge came out with it, called right across to Mrs Stephens.'

'Came out with what?'

'I can't remember the exact words. Something about you being knocked up. She nearly dropped her knife.'

'And what did you say?'

'Kept quiet, didn't I? Said I had no idea what he was on about. But then Mr Cridge said that by all accounts it was Mr Blake you'd run off with. I didn't know where to look. I went bright red – anyone could see.'

She expects sympathy from me, an apology for putting her in an awkward position. I tell her I'm sorry and she smiles grudgingly. There's an uncomfortable silence between us now. Why couldn't she have kept the cafe gossip to herself? It screws up my insides to think of them talking about me, to think there's a scandal to discuss and I'm at the centre of it.

Teddy comes in from the bedroom and tries to climb on my knee. 'I'm so 'ungry,' he says. 'When's tea?'

'Not long. I've got frumenty on.'

'A-*gain*.' He sighs and slithers down onto the floorboards. 'Is there jam?'

'You know we can't get jam, love. Now go and play in the bedroom, like I said. We're talking.'

'Want to stay here. Alice is mean.'

Alice's singing drifts through the open door. 'Little Teddy Tom Thumb landed on his bum-bum...'

When Nettie leaves, I lean against the kitchen

280

sink, staring at the dirty groove in the lino where the bottom of the door scrapes. From the bedroom comes the scratching of chalk, and Alice's commentary as she explains to Teddy why he's lost again.

I sit on the living-room sofa for a while, trying to gather strength to serve up the tea. The church clocks strike five and it's only then that I smell the frumenty, sharp and bitter: the smell of a pan burning dry. I've left the gas on too high.

I poke at the mush with a wooden spoon. The wheat grains have swollen into hard lumps, and the milky broth has gone stretchy like glue. Disgusting. Tears roll off my cheeks and splash into the pan. Damn, damn, damn. There are a few coppers in my purse set by for the meter. We'll have to go out for chips.

Daniel is lying on his back, arms linked behind his head, and I am in bed next to him, my chin resting on his shoulder. How peculiar it is: a Friday night together and instead of rushing away, I can lie beside him as long as I like.

'Sorry about tea,' I whisper.

His hand reaches out and closes over mine. 'Don't worry. You'll get used to the stove. We'll go shopping together tomorrow night. Get something special in for Sunday. Which reminds me.' He leans over to his jacket, reaches into the pocket and draws out a brown paper bag. 'Bought a little present for you.'

The bag is feather-light. I open it up and there are five teardrop-shaped seeds nestling in the bottom.

281

'Sunflower seeds,' he says.

'Wherever will we grow them?'

'Out on the landing. I'll plant them up on Sunday. We'll have one each – you, me, the children and the baby. We'll have a race – see whose grows highest.'

It sends a jolt through me, this mention of the baby. A real person, then, with its own little plant growing in a pot. 'Daft beggar.' I kiss his shoulder. 'The kids will love it.'

I lift my head from the pillow and listen out for the children. They sleep in the living room, top to toe on a palliasse that pulls out from under the sofa.

Do you think they're asleep?' asks Daniel.

'I reckon.'

He gets up from the bed and shuts the door with a soft click. From the architrave above the door he takes a key and turns it in the lock.

As he slides back into bed, he kisses my forehead and runs his hand along the side of my body: my waist, my hips, the tops of my thighs, even my belly, round and white as the moon. He wants me every night, kisses every part of me. I close my eyes and wonder how such pleasure is possible. The giddiness, the fear, it all dissolves when Daniel touches my skin.

34

The library windows blaze with sunlight. Daniel was alone for the first hour, but now a greasy-haired gent is seated opposite him at the large wooden table. The old boy is close enough for Daniel to hear his moist lips smacking as he reads, as if every page contains a morsel that must be savoured. At first Daniel found the noise distracting; now it seems almost companionable.

The baby is due in one month, at the end of May. Mrs Moss visited last Sunday, to check on Hannah's progress, and to collect her downpayment. Mrs Moss was flint-faced, with a harsh cough that came out as a single bark at the end of every sentence. She seemed more interested in pocketing her money than in Hannah's health. Still, Hannah didn't complain about Mrs Moss, so he didn't either.

He is rereading *Jude the Obscure*. It has fresh meaning for him now, the love affair between Jude and Sue, the judgement of their peers, the creeping tide of destitution.

It hadn't taken long for the men at Beaumont's to start talking. Many of them are regulars at the cafe: they would have devoured the rumours. 'Soldier's wife,' he'd heard Shears mutter one morning, and a group of men ahead of him in the crowd turned and stared. The same day a fragment of conversation had drifted over from the welding shop as he rolled a cigarette on a break. 'I'd've had a punt meself if I'd known she were easy.' His fists clenched, but he couldn't risk challenging them. They could have been talking about anyone, he reasoned. To start a fight would be madness.

In July his exemption runs out, and with every month the war drags on, the tribunals are getting more stringent. Christ knows how many were killed this spring: the army needs to replenish supplies. For Beaumont's to put his case, he must be a faultless employee. Yet the gossip has reached the foreman now, he's certain of that, because his shifts are shorter and fewer – too many half-days and never any overtime at the weekend. He is living in the twentieth century, the modern era, but the old codes have barely changed. There's nothing avant-garde about the lads at the docks, he thinks. Victorians through and through.

The worst of it is that he has lied to Hannah. She thinks he is at the yard now, but here he is, reading Thomas Hardy in Whitechapel Library with this scruffy old goat to keep him company. His mind races and he cannot concentrate on the chapter. Money. He'll have to get some or the rent will go unpaid. On Friday he will pawn Esther's jewellery – the ring and the bracelet he was saving for little Maddie. There are still a few books he could take to the dealer. He may as well sell them now, he thinks, with summer on the way. If they're still in the flat when winter comes, they might end up on the fire.

He turns another page and starts to read, but dread envelops him, the fear rising up as strong as it had done when he was a boy. He shuts the book and tries to erase the image of Little Father Time hanging limp in the closet. What on earth possessed him to pick this book from the library shelf? Why does he persist in reading at all? Books should bring escape, a sense of possibility. This book frightens him. It is too familiar now, like staring into a looking glass.

The old man opposite has fallen asleep, his chin resting on his chest so that his tangled grey beard sticks out at a forty-five-degree angle. His breathing is heavy, but he is not snoring. Daniel gets up from the table and walks over to the poetry section. He scans the titles and chooses a volume he does not know: *Poems* by Francis Thompson. When he returns to his chair, the man is still sleeping.

Daniel's back twinges from too much sitting. He circles his shoulders and stretches out his legs before opening the book at the first poem. A small piece of paper falls out, a sketch of a pretty girl, no more than twenty or so, with light falling across one side of her face. The name 'Lizzie' is written underneath the picture. On the back are some lines of scribbled verse. Many of the phrases are struck through, and at the bottom of the paper, '*Hopeless!*' is scrawled in thick pencil lead. He considers this word for a long time. In his mind, he sketches Hannah's face and it is filled with light. He imagines her sitting on a beach in Dorset, the dark cliffs framing her pale features. She is eating ice cream with a tiny wooden spoon. Behind her, their child is building a tower of shingle. Seven pebbles, ten. The tower rises and the child is

285

pleased. But with the final pebble the sky darkens and the sun is eclipsed. The cliffs begin to collapse and slide. Mud flows like smelted iron, choking Hannah and the child, swallowing them up. He runs to save them, but the mud traps him too. He looks out to the sea, to the tide flowing towards them. White gulls drop from the sky and disappear under the waves.

A woman with heeled shoes clacks into the reading room. Daniel starts awake. There is something in his fist. He opens out his hand and remembers the scrap of paper – the sketch of Lizzie, now screwed into a tight damp ball.

The man opposite has woken too. He turns a page and smacks his lips.

Daniel lights a cigarette and pulls back the curtain at the bedroom window. Though it is still dark, he can see the square silhouette of the German church, the crucifix rising from the bell tower. He would like to open the window, but Mrs Moss says she will not work in a draught.

He cannot stand the silence any longer.

'Is this normal?' he asks, his voice spiked with tension.

Mrs Moss turns to him with a weary look. Her sleeves are rolled up, and her arms are red with blood. Mrs Moss doesn't want him in the room – that much is plain.

'It's not unusual,' she says. 'The womb ain't closing fast enough.'

Hannah is lying back on the pillow. Her face is ashen, and around her eyes there is a hint of green. The baby is trying to suckle, but Hannah is barely strong enough to cradle her.

'Shall I hold the baby?' He takes a last drag of his cigarette and grinds the stub into the lid of an old paste jar.

'No, let her feed. It's feeding what keeps things moving.' She finishes the sentence with a cough, not bothering to cover her mouth.

'But ... there shouldn't be this much blood. She looks like ... she's fading.'

The labour had been fast, noisy, and woke the children in the living room. Daniel had tried to shush them back to sleep, but Alice was having none of it, so he took them outside onto the landing to see how the sunflowers were getting on. A gusty wind raged, and the children laughed as it lifted a pair of cotton drawers from a balcony washing line, over the rooftops and high above the streets. They watched the drawers as far as Mile End, until they floated down, ghostly, somewhere near the hospital. When Daniel and the children came back into the flat, there was the sound of a baby crying. Alice and Teddy were allowed the briefest glimpse of their new sister. Now they are tucked up again. Asleep, thank God.

This silence is so much worse than the screams of labour.

Two weeks early. Mrs Moss says not to worry, two weeks is nothing, but he feels as if they've been caught out. They weren't prepared.

Hannah attempts to sit forward, but her head sinks back to the pillow. The baby, waxy and bloodied, slithers to one side and lands in the gap between Hannah's arm and the side of her body.

Daniel rushes to the bed.

'How long do we let this go on? Surely there's something you can give her?'

He picks up the baby and realizes that it is still attached to the cord. It pulses pale yellow and blue, not pink as he would have expected. When Sam and Maddie were born, he was banished to the pub to drink beer with his brother-in-law. He never saw a thing.

Mrs Moss stands at the foot of the bed and lifts the sheet. She leans in and peers between Hannah's legs. 'Push, girl. *Push.*' She reaches her arms forward and lifts something. 'That's more like it. Final piece.'

Daniel turns and fixes his gaze on Hannah's face. Her eyes are shut. He would stroke her hair if only he wasn't holding the baby. Behind him, there is the sound of wet meat flopping into a tin pail. Tentatively he turns his head. Mrs Moss takes a large pair of scissors from her holdall and cuts the cord. He winces at the sound of metal slicing through the flesh. The remaining length of cord that hangs from the baby's navel changes before his eyes. It is paler now, the colour of a clouded moon. His mind casts back to the evening in Lady Tolland's garden, the smell of jasmine and the taste of ripe raspberries. Jesus. From that, to this.

The bleeding slows as the sun rises. Mrs Moss hurries off. At six Hannah drinks a little tea, but she is too weak to get out of bed. The baby sleeps next to her on the pillow. When she wakes, fussing, Daniel lifts her onto the breast and helps

288

to support the tiny body as she feeds. The baby is restless. She has the same dark lashes as Maddie, the same fuzz of brown newborn hair.

'The children?' asks Hannah.

'Still asleep.'

'They'll have to miss school.'

'I can take them.'

'And lose a day's work? No, you have to go. I'll see you tonight.'

'What if you take bad?'

She breathes two shallow breaths. He can see what an effort it is for her to speak. 'There's Mrs Tendler across the landing. She'll help out if I need her.'

In the kitchen, he splashes cold water onto his face. There is a small mirror resting on a shelf above the sink. As he shaves, he notices a circle of white hair in his black stubble, as if someone has pressed a piece of chalk to his chin. Perhaps the white patch is a family trait, a quirk inherited from his father. Aunt Winch had never been able to answer any questions about his father. Either she didn't know or she wouldn't say. It was the same with his mother, once she'd disappeared. 'Some feller from the West Country,' was the closest he ever got to an answer. 'Best you can do is forget all about her.'

He dries his face and ties his neck scarf in a loose knot as he creeps back into the bedroom. Hannah is dozing again. He bends to kiss her forehead, picks up his boots and carries them from the room.

Outside the front door, he bends to tie his laces. The sunflowers are in small stone pots against the balcony railings. Only three of the five seeds have germinated, and one of the seedlings is dying. Over-watering, most likely. He has told Alice that too much water is as bad as too little.

At the top of the staircase, he almost turns back. Can he really leave Hannah this morning, so feeble in the bed and the baby not eight hours old? He pauses with his hand on the cold banister and thinks of the new bed linen he must buy, the school clothes, milk and food. Red meat, Mrs Moss said, to build up her iron. Tomorrow is Friday and Mr Specterman will want his rent money. No, he has to take the work while it's there. Two ships have come into the yard and he's unlikely to be turned away.

35

I try to hide it from Daniel, the fact that I am terrified and lonely and desperate for him to stay. I listen to his footsteps fading down the staircase and tell myself it's only for a few hours and then he'll be back from work. My head is spinning and hammering. The light coming through the window makes me feel sick. Darkness is all I want. Black.

I'm bleeding again and the towel wedged underneath me is soaked through. The mattress must be ruined, and my head only hurts more when I wonder how we'll replace it.

The baby is sleeping. For the first time I have a

proper look at her. She's a good colour at least. Her squashed-up skin is wrinkly and red as last year's apples. I put out a hand to stroke her wavy brown hair. My hand is white and veined, so white it's almost see-through. She has sucked all the strength from me. Such power in so tiny a package.

I shut my eyes, lean back on the pillow and like a miracle the headache drains away. My body is heavy suddenly, as if I am sinking, disappearing. There is no pain at all, just a feeling of peace. It occurs to me that I may be dying. Not one ounce of strength is left in me: if someone asked me to open an eyelid, I couldn't do it. I am falling through warm air, and soft butterflies land on my skin. My thoughts are slow, floating down, slotting into place, and everything makes sense. I've had the baby. I've given her my milk. She has known her mother, if only for a few hours. Alice and Teddy will be all right when I die. They'll be back with their auntie and their nana and their cousin. It's what they want, what they've been asking for. George will get leave and it will be better for everyone when I am gone. I am sorry for Daniel, but he will survive it. He'll always know how much I loved him.

The doorknob rattles and someone comes into the room. I feel the butterflies lift from my skin, fly off towards the sun.

'There's somebody knocking,' says Alice. 'Shall I answer it, Mummy?'

'What?' The headache is back.

'Someone at the door.'

'Ask who is it.'

I hear Alice call out, then Nettie's reply.

The baby's fist pushes against my shoulder. I am still alive, then. She is still alive.

Nettie tries to pull the towel from under me, attempts to change the sheets. 'Leave me,' I whisper. 'Can you take the children out? Give them some breakfast.'

'It's two in the afternoon,' she says.

'What day is it?'

'Thursday.'

I think she does take them out because the flat is silent until the baby cries and somehow I manage to latch her on.

Mrs Moss comes, coughing. She gives me medicine and says it will cost another ten bob. Nettie hands over some coins and says the father will call by with the rest of the money.

The bleeding stops. Not the headache.

When Daniel arrives home, he talks in whispers with Nettie over by the window. If only dusk would come. I long for the dark.

By Sunday I am stronger. At teatime Daniel helps me from bed. I sit at the table for a few minutes and try to eat the soup he has put in front of me. Oat and potato soup, made by Nettie's mother. It's difficult to swallow because I am sobbing with every mouthful, thinking of my own mother and how I have betrayed her. Daniel comforts me, kisses my tears and tells me it's only natural to feel upset.

'Your mum'll get used to the idea,' he says. 'They won't cut you off forever.'

I try not to think of George, but he's impossible to ignore. Alice has just been asking: 'When Daddy comes home from the war, will we go back to Auntie Jen's? When Uncle Daniel gives you a kiss, is he my daddy too?'

The soup is getting cold now and I am sweating with the effort of holding the spoon. It's a warm evening and up here on the fourth floor there's no air at all. The children are squabbling in the living room and the screeching is more than I can bear.

'Let the kids play down in the yard,' I tell Daniel. 'Tell them to keep away from the pig bins.' I've seen rats slinking around there, bold as you like in the middle of the day.

It's a relief to have them out of the house. Daniel sits with me once I'm back in bed. The baby is hungry, and when she tries to latch on, I wince at the sharp pain. She fusses and cries, fusses and cries. I can't seem to settle her, and my milk won't let down. Daniel carries her around the room, jiggling her on his shoulder so that her little head wobbles. 'Little Lizzie,' he sing-songs. 'Little Lizzie Locket.'

He's been calling her Lizzie all day. That's what we'll name her, then. It suits her well enough.

I can't sleep for fretting. All this time I've been living from day to day, day to day with Daniel, doing my best not to think ahead. But the future is here now. It's here and I don't know what to do.

George will be missing my letters, sitting in his tent or his trench or wherever he is. He'll be wondering if we're all right, waiting for news of the

293

children. I haven't dared write since we moved. It's been over two months now. Perhaps there is a letter from him, propped up against the button box in Sabbarton Street.

That night there's another raid over London. Daniel and I stand at the window, watching the searchlight beams fingering the sky. Bursts of shellfire from the anti-aircraft guns rattle the windowpanes and we can feel tremors in the floorboards beneath our feet. To the north, a fire blazes. 'Bethnal Green,' Daniel says, and all I can think is, Thank God it's not Canning Town.

Somehow the racket seems to have calmed Lizzie and she sleeps soundly on the bed. Not a peep from Alice or Teddy either. Daniel's arm is tight around my shoulders. I won't shelter in the Tube station – I'd rather we were all up here than trapped underground – and Daniel doesn't argue. Cheating bombs is a dangerous pastime. Everything is down to chance. If you run outside, you're as likely to be killed by red-hot shrapnel from our own falling shells.

On Tuesday I manage to take the children to school. I strap the baby to my chest with a shawl and somehow I get down the stairs, one step at a time. Alice runs on ahead. She knows the way now; it won't be long before they can walk themselves to school.

Teddy clings to my skirt when we reach the school gate. 'Got tummy ache,' he says. 'Do I have to go?'

'You don't want to be stuck indoors with the

baby, do you, Teddy? Get into school now. Good boy.'

He sniffs and trails in after Alice.

Two mothers are standing at the gates, chatting in low voices. They both stare at me as I pass, no pause in their conversation, just the eyes following.

The post office is on the corner of Whitechapel High Street and Osborn Street. Thankfully the queue is not too long, because if I don't sit down soon, my legs will give way.

I hand over my ring paper and watch Mr Feldman count out the money. He's taken to chatting, though over the weeks I've done my best not to be friendly.

'Ah, Mrs Loxwood. You've had the baby, yes? Beautiful!'

I nod and smile, my hands gripping the edge of the counter.

'More babies, more shillings, Mrs Loxwood. I give you the form? Send it to your husband to fill in.'

He slides the form across the counter with the money and the stamped ring paper. ARMY SEPARATION ALLOWANCE, FORM W632. WIFE WITH DEPENDANTS. My hands are shaking as I collect the coins and drop them into my purse. The form stares up at me. I paw at it, but I can't seem to lift it. It may as well be stuck to the counter.

'Mrs Loxwood, you are ill? I can call for my brother. He's a doctor, nearby. Here...' He rushes from the counter and pulls a stool from behind a stack of boxes. Just in time. My legs buckle and I fall awkwardly onto it. Lizzie slumps forward, almost tipping from the sling.

'I'm very tired, that's all. Thank you.'

A girl appears with a glass of water, and then a man with a stethoscope is crouching in front of me, his fingers feeling for the pulse at my wrist.

'The baby is how old?'

'Four days. No, five.'

'Any problems?'

I wonder whether to tell him about the bleeding. He might suggest more medicine. More money.

'No, it's my third. I'm tired, that's all. I can go home now, back to bed.'

'You live far?'

'Adler Street. Two minutes.'

'Take your time. If you need me, send a neighbour.'

When Nettie visits on Thursday, she's grinning like a menagerie monkey. I was hoping she'd take the baby out for a while, but all she wants to do is chat. She has plenty to talk about. Her husband has turned up, begging forgiveness.

'I did my best to give him the cold shoulder, but honestly, Hannah, when he brought me this, I didn't have the heart to turn him away.'

She sticks out her hand and shows off a ring with a tiny green gem set in a gold claw.

'Semi-precious stone, it is. Fancy!' She flutters her fingers as if to make the gem sparkle, but there's nothing sparkly about it. It's quite a dull sort of stone, colour of bread mould. 'He's seen the error of his ways, he says, taken the pledge.

Now he's got some money together and we're going to look for our own place. Where's the baby?'

'She's over there. In the cot.'

Nettie laughs. A quick, high-pitched laugh that grates as much as her voice. 'Oh, that? The soap box with cushions in.' She walks over and strokes the baby's head. 'Bless her.'

'We've had to make do. My sister's got the proper cradle.'

'Course.' She chews her lip as she looks around the room. 'Sorry, Hannah, I know how hard it must be for you. I've said to Spencer that when we're looking for rooms, I'm not going any higher than the second floor, and there has to be a shelter in running distance.' She takes off her hat and fans herself with the brim. 'Phew, it's ever so hot up here. I don't know how you stand it.'

I stand it because I have to, but I keep the sharp words in my head and gulp a mouthful of tea. I don't think Nettie means to be thoughtless. I must try to be happy for her.

She natters on about the cafe, tells me all about the new girl and how she's having trouble adding up the figures. 'I know Mrs Stephens misses you, but she won't have your name mentioned. And if I so much as smile at a customer, she bustles up, telling me to drain the potatoes or some such. Gets on your nerves.' She gives a little gasp and reaches into her bag. 'I nearly forgot. A woman came into the cafe and asked me if I'd forward this. She rushed off, wouldn't stop to chat.'

Nettie hands me a crumpled envelope. It's addressed to Mrs George Loxwood.

297

Daniel tells me to burn the letter. He grabs a box of matches from the mantelpiece and strikes a flame.

'I'll do it myself. Put it in the grate.'

We watch the paper catch light. The words turn scorch-brown, then yellow, then orange – *slut, shame, traitor, Ada* – and finally they are flakes of quiet grey ash.

'She's a bitch,' Daniel says. 'I always knew it. Dora thought she was a hoot, but I never liked her.'

Ada knows; the factory girls know. Of course they do. Only natural that the gossip should spread. I've let down the war effort – that's what they think. Might as well be shot as a traitor. *We girls have to stick together.* But if you don't do your duty, don't conform, you can forget it. You're on your own.

I kneel on the hearth tiles and the ash shifts in the draught. 'What if Ada tells her husband? He's in the same battalion as George.'

'He has to find out somehow.'

'And then what? I don't know what he'll do. I really don't. He might come after us. I mean, he ain't one for fighting, but ... he'll stop the allowance. That's the first thing.' I pause to think for a moment. My mouth feels cracked and dry, and I can taste the burned letter, the words turned to ash. 'I can take in some work. Shirt-finishing, I could do that, used to help Mum...'

'I'm working, aren't I?'

'But it ain't enough – you know it ain't enough, the price of everything. If only I had someone to look after the kids, I could get a job in a factory… The money's good in munitions.'

Daniel takes my face in his hands. I try to find comfort in his eyes.

'We'll face the troubles as they come along. We can get through it, Hannah – I know we can. George won't come after us, not while this war carries on.'

I swallow down my tears. Think straight, Hannah, think straight. There's a drawer full of clothes in the bedroom. Dora's clothes. Nice blouses, a good hat. It mangles me with guilt just to look at them, let alone wear them. Dora would forgive me for pawning her things, I'm certain of it. She loved me, didn't she, her oldest friend?

36

Most evenings he comes home to find Hannah crying. No wonder, the way Lizzie screams every night. There's something wrong with her, Hannah says. She'll only feed for a minute or two; then she breaks off, fussing and yelling. When Lizzie finally sleeps, they both stare at her, lying in the cot, their ears ringing in the fragile silence. He wants to love his daughter; sometimes a feeling of tenderness breaks across his chest and he places his hand, lightly, on her soft hair. But if she twitches as though she might wake, he draws back and turns away. There is more fear than love.

The yard is busy yet the foreman has cut his

hours. Last week he was hired only for three half-days. On Friday he left Adler Street and walked the short distance to Aldgate East Station, took the underground train to Westminster. He stood on Westminster Bridge for an hour, watching the river traffic in the shadow of Big Ben. Then he wandered up to Trafalgar Square and sat in the June sunshine with the drunken out-o'-works and the maimed soldiers. It took all his strength not to go into the beer shop himself.

He hasn't sent money to his sister in over a month. She has probably been writing to him at Mrs Browne's. Not that Ellen and Alf need the money. It strikes him that they may even be pleased if he stopped contributing. They wouldn't feel obliged to invite him to Kent. They could have the children to themselves, bring them up in comfort, in a way that he never could.

The foreman appears on the workshop floor. He saunters towards Daniel. The other men carry on working, but they are watching, exchanging glances.

'Blake, see me at the end of your shift,' the foreman says.

At two o'clock he finishes the welding job and walks over to the foreman's cabin next to the engine room. Daniel has to stoop to get through the door, and even when he is inside, he is unable to stand upright.

'About your exemption,' says the foreman. He is sitting behind a narrow desk, fingering a sheaf of papers. 'The next tribunal is 22nd July. That's–' he looks at the calendar nailed to the wall '–three weeks' time. Just so's you know: Beaumont's is going to release you.'

'What?'

'Thought it was time you joined the ranks, Blake. We can do without you here because, anyone can see, your mind hasn't been on the job. Not this job, anyway.' He almost smirks, then thinks better of it, clears his throat and stands to pat Daniel on the shoulder. 'Still, we got the Yanks on our side now, eh? Bloody boatloads of 'em. Reckon we might win this war yet.'

Daniel steps back, shrugs off the foreman's hand. The trenches. Christ, this is it. He needs to make a case for himself, some kind of appeal. 'If you could just give me another six months,' he says. 'Things are ... difficult at home.'

'So I hear. I'm afraid that's your lookout, ain't it? Beaumont's has to do what's right for the firm. And the country.' He puffs his chest, warming to the theme. 'You could look at it this way, Blake: it's a kind of balancing act. You took a step in a new direction. Difficult territory. Tipped yourself over the edge, in a manner of speaking.'

Daniel bows his head. Smug little fucker. He'd like to swing for him. Instead he looks up and attempts a smile. 'And till the tribunal? Can you give me some extra hours?'

'I'll see what we can do, Blake. In the circumstances.'

He wanders along East India Dock Road, past the statue and Mrs Browne's lodging house. He cannot go home to Hannah, not yet. She'd be beside herself if she found out he's only worked a

301

half-shift.

He turns into the recreation ground and follows the pathway, weaving between the prams and the children, the scolding grandmothers in trailing skirts. A young boy slips behind the railings that edge the flowerbeds. The boy picks a posy of marigolds and pelargoniums, then runs off towards the bandstand to hand the flowers to his mother. Daniel remembers doing the same when he was young, scooting home to Aunt Winch with a posy and getting a clip round the ear for taking what wasn't his.

In the shade of a maple tree, there is an empty bench. He sits down and shuts his eyes. The wind feels cold, now that he is out of the sun. The scent of roses reminds him of Greenwich. Has Lady Tolland found another gardener, he wonders, or has the garden grown to seed?

Children's footsteps shuffle along the path in front of him. He looks up to see a crocodile of silent workhouse girls holding hands in pairs. They wear bleached white aprons over calico dresses; several have shaved heads. One of the girls turns to look at him with her large brown eyes.

'Keep in line,' shouts their mistress, a tall woman with an old-fashioned black bonnet tied tightly under her chin. The girl with brown eyes shrinks back, and her little fist clenches at her side.

He shivers again in the wind. Is the sun shining in France? It cannot last. Autumn will follow soon enough. He thinks of the trenches, the winter rain stirring up the mud.

37

Alice and Teddy aren't happy. Their school's all right; they don't seem to mind that so much. It's being in the flat they can't stand. I thought Alice would be pleased to have a baby sister, thought perhaps she might even be a help. Instead she looks at Lizzie as if she's her sworn enemy, a stranger who's brought nothing but evil.

The weather's getting hotter. It's so stifling up here some nights I'm tempted to sleep out on the stone landing just so I can breathe. The children are baking in the living room. There is only the tiny window to offer a wisp of a draught if the wind gets up.

Another hour till I have to collect them from school. For once I want the baby to wake up. I've got bread soaking in milk and she needs to eat it before the milk goes sour. She's had a rotten tummy for days now. I can't turn the nappies round quick enough. What I wouldn't do for the luxury of our own yard, a proper washing line. When I think of Sabbarton Street, it's as if my body is hollowed out. It's what you call home-sickness, I suppose. I can cope whenever Daniel is here. But when he's not with me, the dizziness takes over. It's as if I'm suspended up in these dead-air rooms: dangling and ready to drop.

No choice but to wake Lizzie for the sops. I manage to get a couple of spoonfuls in her mouth, but then she turns her head away, stiffens her body and starts to cry. Her muscles are strong for such a tiny scrap. I scoop up another spoonful and try to hold her head, force it in, but her face screws into a furious yell and I know it's no use. Something flips in me and I sweep the bowl off the table. It crashes onto the lino and the milk and soggy crumbs spew across the floor.

'Sod you, then,' I shout. 'You'll be screaming hungry in an hour and then it'll be too late.' It's as much as I can do not to throw her down into the cot.

Lizzie cries even harder and in the next breath I am shaking with guilt. I rock her in my arms, try to soothe her with a kind voice. The other two tested me, but nothing like this. Maybe Jen was right, after all. I'm an unnatural mother. I don't deserve this poor baby. She was born from love, love like I never knew could exist, yet love won't flow between us. It's as if the lock gates are fastened shut, the water rising higher and higher with nowhere to go.

I have to get outside, away from Union Buildings, down onto solid ground. I tie a sling and put Lizzie into it, hold her close to my body and sway from side to side until her crying stops. When I step out onto the landing, Mrs Tendler is there, watering a tomato plant by her front door.

'Got a good pair o' lungs, eh?' she says, straightening up.

'You could say.'

'Makes me glad mine are grown. I don't envy you. 'Specially when it's hot like this.' She's looking me over, sizing me up. 'You keeping well?' she asks.

'Not too bad.'

'And your husband?'

There's an edge to her voice, a note of suspicion. She'll have heard Alice call him 'Uncle Daniel' – that's what it is. Alice shouts at him from the landing. *Uncle Daniel, my sunflower's the tallest! I'm beating Teddy!* Well, I'll put Mrs Tendler out of her misery. I'll tell her outright.

'We're not married. Perhaps you guessed.'

'Over the brush, is it? Mr Specterman won't like that, sweetheart.'

'I don't suppose anyone will tell him.'

'No, I don't suppose.' She folds her arms and the little watering can dangles from her wrist. A few drops leak out onto the stone.

Might she be a friend to me? Maybe she'll be flattered if I confide. Offer to lend a hand. I can't count on Nettie, as it turns out. She hasn't visited for nearly a month, now she has the perfect husband and rooms of their own on the Old Ford Road.

'My people don't approve, you see. I ain't got any help...'

'Just you and him against the world, eh?' says Mrs Tendler.

'That's about right.'

'You want to go and see your family. We all have our troubles. They'll melt when they set eyes on the baby – I'd put money on it.'

'That's what Daniel says. You don't know my sister, though. I think she's grateful to have me out of the way.'

'You got a mum?'

305

'She's not taken it well either.'

'Churchy, are they?'

'A bit. Not really. Just ... respectable.'

'I've got a little granddaughter myself, but she's in Norfolk with my daughter-in-law's people. While my boy's at the front.'

Her son is at the front. How can I tell her I have a husband fighting? If I don't get away this second, she'll ask more questions. *And what about the older kids? Their dad still around?* Mrs Tendler can never be my friend.

Soon the school will close for the summer holidays. All those weeks cooped up with the children, all those extra dinners we'll have to buy.

How trapped I used to feel in Canning Town, hemmed in by the creek and the factories and the railway lines. Yet I haven't escaped anything here. I'm more trapped than I've ever been.

I start to wonder whether Mrs Tendler is right. If I call round to Sabbarton Street, Jen and Mum might relent. I wouldn't be asking for forgiveness – there'd be no point – just for a little understanding, for the children's sake. When I tell them how much Alice and Teddy miss their auntie and nana, they might see things differently. If the children could pop round on a Sunday, perhaps stay over now and then during the holidays, it would make all the difference. For Alice and Teddy's sake. Jen couldn't say no to that, surely.

There might be letters at Sabbarton Street. I told Jen to forward anything on to Nettie, care of the cafe. But there's a good chance Nettie has left the cafe, now she's moved in with Spencer. She said he was earning pots of money, playing jazz trumpet at Dixieland dances, so much cash she might not need to work at all.

The warm spell has broken and rain is chucking down. I can barely see out the tram windows for the muck and the spray kicked up from White-chapel Road. The tram stops and starts, stops and starts, the carts, the motor vans and the bicycles tense with morning energy. Words jumble in my head and my pulse races. Lizzie is asleep on my chest. A woman next to me smiles down at the baby, but I turn away, back to the dirty windows.

Along East India Dock Road, past Daniel's old room. I stare up at the narrow terrace and there's a new lace curtain draped in a crooked line across his window. Jealousy needles me. Somehow it feels wrong that someone else should be living there. With all my heart I want Daniel back in his lodging room. I want our old life back, the Friday nights when our happiness was a secret thing, a beautiful miracle we didn't have to share.

At Blackwall, the tram terminates. 'Last stop,' shouts the clippie, one thumb hooked through a belt loop at the waist of her skirt. We edge off the tram, and when I reach the pavement, the smell of the docks smothers me, tar-stained and wind-whipped. So familiar it hurts to breathe.

The steps up to the iron bridge are slippery. I grasp the wet railing and Lizzie stirs, her head turning back and forth, nuzzling against my chest. I've covered her head with a handkerchief, but the cotton is already soaked through with rain. Over the bridge, the sleeping giant. The moored boats knock their greeting against weed-slimed piers.

At Sabbarton Street, a muddy stream is flowing along the gutters, down towards the creek. A cold wind pummels my back. Number nineteen, number seventeen ... almost there. My hands are numb. I wonder if there has ever been a July day so drear.

Number fifteen.

The whitening on the step is smudged and grey with rain. Will Jen be inside, putting baby Alec down for his morning nap? Will Mum be sitting in front of the stove, drinking her tea? Please let Mum answer the door. Mum, not Jen. Please God.

I knock twice, take the handkerchief from Lizzie's head. With the cuff of my coat I try to dry her hair, softly, so that she doesn't wake.

The man who opens the door is small and bent. His hands shake. He is wearing pale blue pyjamas, which gape around his chest.

'Dad?'

The man looks up, straightening his spine a little. I am sure now: it is my father. His face is creased in confusion. He doesn't know me. He's clean-shaven, but there's a razor cut close to his ear, dried flakes of blood stuck to the wound. He doesn't have his teeth in.

'Dad, it's Hannah. You're back, then. That's good...'

There's not a scrap of recognition in his eyes; he simply turns his back on me while I am speaking and shuffles along the hall towards the scullery.

Jen appears in the scullery doorway, drying her

hands on a tea towel. In the poor light, I can see only the silhouette of her, the mad curls springing from her bun.

'Dad! What are you doing down... Oh.' Jen flicks the towel over the door handle. 'You.'

She takes Dad by the arm and guides him towards the stairs. 'I'll be down in a minute,' she hisses, staring at my boots rather than look me in the eye. 'Come in and shut the door. I don't want the street seeing.'

I close the door and stand in the dark hall, my skirt dripping onto the lino.

Upstairs, the bed creaks as Dad gets back into it. He's in my old room, then. Jen moves across the landing and closes the door to the front bedroom. I can picture baby Alec in his wooden cot, fast asleep under the summer eiderdown.

At last Jen comes downstairs. The sling is dragging on my shoulders now and I'd do anything to untie it, sit down in the armchair with a cup of hot tea.

'Well?' says Jen.

Lizzie starts to stretch her fists and I can tell she's building up to a yell. I put one arm under her bottom and try to rock her back to sleep.

The speech I'd prepared won't come to mind. Instead I gabble, and as I gabble, I start to sob, so that my words come out in stupid splutters. 'It's the children ... if they could just come round ... and you'll need my address... My friend at the cafe, I hardly see her no more. I hardly see anyone... I know I've done wrong ... but won't you just let the children visit?'

Jen listens with a couldn't-care-less attitude on

her face. When I finish, she sighs, as if she can barely be bothered to speak.

'And what was the last thing I said to you?' she asks, like she's a schoolmistress set on humiliating a disobedient child. 'Don't come crying when it all goes wrong – that's what I said. Six months, I gave it. How old is this?' She waves her hand towards the baby.

'Six weeks.'

'Six weeks old. And the father's had enough, I take it?'

'No! He won't leave me. I've told you.'

She snorts. 'You mentioned all this to George yet?'

'I'm going to write soon. Are there any letters?'

'You'd better have them, I s'pose.' She disappears into the scullery and I can hear her prising a lid from a tin. She comes back with half a dozen or so letters in army envelopes. It looks as if the envelopes have been opened.

'He's getting worried about you,' says Jen. 'Can you blame him?' She gives me the letters, then wipes her nose with the back of her hand.

'You've read them?'

'Why not? Didn't know if we'd ever see you again. Thought my only option was to write back and spill the beans.'

'And have you?'

'Not yet.'

I open my bag and drop the letters into it. From my purse I take a small square of card and hold it out to her.

'You should have my address. We're in White-chapel.'

She shakes her head and takes a step backwards. 'We don't want your address, Hannah. Can't you understand that? You made your choice. Alec feels the same, so don't think you can start batting your eyelashes at him when the war's over. Like I said, he knew all about your fancy man. He ain't surprised. Said you always did have slutty eyes.'

I clench my fist. The card crinkles and digs into my palm. Alec? She thinks he's a saint? Christ, he'll be first in the queue at the French knocking shops. I can't rise to it, though. Can't risk making things worse.

'Is Mum here?'

'No.'

'What about Dad? I'd like to go up and see him.'

She shakes her head. 'He's come home to die. They did some more tests. Turns out he has a tumour in his brain. Nothing more they can do, and God knows they need his bed for the poor soldiers.'

A tumour in his brain. All along, a tumour growing, growing, stealing my dad. Lizzie's mew turns into a proper scream. Shush, shush. Not now. Please, not now.

'Can I see him?'

'He won't know you.'

'Can I *see* him?'

I step towards the staircase, but Jen moves sideways to block me.

'He. Won't. Know. You.'

She talks at me like I'm the local idiot. I could fly at her, tear out handfuls of her stupid hair, but she would just push me away with her leg-ofmutton arms. I turn round and try to open the front door. The wood has swollen in the rain and it takes a strong heave to shift it from the frame.

Jen steps forward and holds the door by its handle. 'One last thing,' she says. 'We had Meena Flynn round here last week. She wants Dor's things back. She knows all about you and Dora's sweetheart. Spitting feathers, she was. I won't repeat the language.'

She closes the door softly, so as not to wake her baby.

I stumble to the end of the street, squinting through rain and tears, sheltering for a moment in the alley, under the brick arch where Daniel and I stood on the night of the explosion. I cry for my dad and I cry for Dor. Dor, what must you think of me? The pawn tickets are in my purse. Five shillings for the hat, twelve for the clothes. Never a hope of buying them back.

Lizzie screams as I press on towards the creek. Last time I thought too hard. I stood on the bridge and I pictured myself climbing up and over, imagined myself falling. Why stand on the bridge at all? That was my mistake, of course. Far easier to wander down the bank, wade in through the slimy grasses.

The creek is in sight now, the path that leads down to the bank, the boats knocking against the piers. The water is flowing fast. Tide's going out, rushing downstream.

'Dear? Is that you?'

It's an old lady, her wide-brimmed hat tipped low on her face. Her hand is on my arm. Mrs Hillier.

'It *is* Hannah, ain't it?'

I can't speak for weeping. Just a nod, a forced smile, and I hurry past before the questions start.

I take George's letters from my handbag. The first letter is dated 18th March 1918: *We've had a hell of a show here. Can't say too much, but our lot come through all right. Strange not to have heard from you.* Then on 21st April: *Must be some problem with the post. Queer, though, because the other lads have been getting their letters.* On 5th May: *Write as soon as you can. I am getting worried, but I tell myself no news is good news. The boys soon get wind when there is a problem at home.* And 19th June: *We are on our way back to France and our battalion has joined the 89th Brigade, 30th Division. Thought I would let you know, if you're still interested. I know it has been an awful long time, but I still think of you every day and I am longing to hear news of you and the children. I have sent a note to your mum, but no reply as yet.*

So many letters. More in three months than he's written over the last year. I stuff them under the pillow and lie down on the bed. I can't leave George wondering anymore. I'll write tonight, when Daniel is home. We'll do it together.

Daniel's clothes are sodden. We hang them on the wooden dryer, then stand the dryer in the tin bath to catch the drips. I light the burners on the gas stove to try and get some heat in the kitchen. Impossible to get anything dry.

Alice and Teddy fall asleep by eight. Daniel and I shut ourselves in the bedroom. He has the baby on his shoulder, rubbing her back. I stand at the window, looking down into the courtyard of the German church. There is a circular flowerbed with a rose bush in the middle. The rose blooms have been battered by rain and red petals lie bruised on the earth among clumps of valerian. An old priest emerges from a side door, takes a key from his robes and locks it. As he walks towards the high street, he stares up at Union Buildings and seems to gaze straight at me. I turn from the window.

'I went back to my sister's today.'

Daniel stops rubbing Lizzie's back.

'How was it?'

I shake my head, my eyes stinging as the tears come. 'She can't stand the sight of me. Says everyone feels the same; I'm never to come back. Dad's home, but he's dying. A brain tumour. And she gave me these.' I move towards the bed, take George's letters from under the pillow and drop them on the blanket. 'I feel so guilty, you can't imagine...'

He places Lizzie in the cot, puts his arms around me and says he is sorry. I weep into his chest, clinging to him, wishing I was a child again, wishing for a strange moment that it was Dad's arms I could feel, the smell of liquorice instead of peppermint.

Dad is lost to me now. Only Daniel can make me safe. Yet even with his arms around me, I feel uneasy. Weightless before the fall.

Daniel breaks away, picks up one envelope and slides out the notepaper. It's George's most recent letter. His eyes flit across the words, stopping every so often as he deciphers the writing.

'He's going back to France, then.' He sighs and returns the letter to its envelope.

I sink down onto the bed, gather the envelopes together and shove them back under the pillow. 'I'll have to reply. I don't need to tell him anything much. Just let him know that Alice and Teddy are fine. Give him the new address.'

Daniel sits next to me on the bed and takes my hands. 'You're sure?'

'It's too cruel, ignoring him like this, and I can't have him writing to Sabbarton Street again. Jen's opening my post. Says she might write to him herself.'

He drops his hand and chews the nail on his little finger. Lizzie snuffles in the cot. Daniel opens his mouth as if he's about to say something, then changes his mind and kisses my hands.

'You're right. You send him the letter.'

It's after midnight and I'm on my third attempt. Daniel has fallen asleep; his breathing is steady, slower than the tick of his pocket watch lying on the chest of drawers next to a packet of damp tobacco. His eyes flicker beneath the lids. I think he must be dreaming.

My back hurts from sitting so long on the sagging mattress with my knees up and the note-paper resting on one of Daniel's books. The pile of books gets smaller every week. He lends them to a man at work, he says. They like to discuss poetry on their fag breaks.

I read through the letter again, blushing at the lie, although it's not a bad one. It will comfort him, in a small way.

12 Union Buildings
Adler Street
Whitechapel E.

July 11th 1918

Dear George,
I'm sorry you haven't been getting my letters. I've written several times. Perhaps there's a problem at the local office here, or else they've gone down with a boat. We've moved, as you can see. I won't write much more in case this one gets lost too. If you still don't hear, I will have to send a telegram.
The children are well and send their love.
Yours affectionately,
Hannah

I fold the paper in half and tuck it inside the book. Daniel rolls onto his side, facing me, and a hand comes to rest on my thigh. I look down at him and his eyes flicker open. He smiles, half asleep, and his fingers move across my thigh, the gentlest of strokes. I cannot give him what he wants, not yet. Daniel is understanding for now.

A letter drops through the box and skits across the kitchen lino. Alice dashes over to pick up the envelope.

'It's a Daddy letter!' she says, hopping from one foot to the other. Her little face is so joyous my heart could break. 'Daddy! Can I open it?'

'Not now, Alice – you'll be late for school. You

don't want to get a late mark, do you? Right before the holidays? We'll open it after school. Wash your face.'

I stuff the letter into my pocket as she stamps over to the sink. I take Lizzie into the bedroom and quickly rip open the envelope. He must have replied by return. Three days, only three days since I posted my own letter! I scan down the page. It's nothing but a list of questions: why have I gone to Whitechapel? Have I quarrelled with Jen? Is it fair on the children to move them so sudden? And then the last line: *Now we are in France, our battalion has started allowing men to come to England on leave. If I'm lucky, I could be home in a week or two. If I'm unlucky, I might have to wait some time.*

He could be home in a week. A week or two. He knows our address. For a lunatic moment I wonder if I can tidy away Daniel's things, hide the baby. I dismiss the idea, then, ten minutes later when I'm walking the children to school, I resurrect it. I itemize everything in the flat, then work out where I can conceal it – the baby with Mrs Tendler, the cot in the kitchen cupboard, Daniel's clothes in the trunk under the bed. But what if Cole Buckley has told George? George might have known all along. Might be planning revenge. My mind races, faster and faster, and I can't control my thoughts, the wild ideas that ricochet until I think they could burst from my skull.

'Daddy, Daddy,' Alice sing-songs, skipping ahead.

38

The problem is how to tell her. Already it is 15th July. He will be before the tribunal in one week. Now that Beaumont's has refused to back him, he could have his call-up papers that day. He might be in uniform by the end of the month.

Hannah was half frantic when he came home from work last night. She met him out on the landing, sobbed as she thrust George's latest letter into his hands. *If I'm lucky, I could be home in a week or two.* He couldn't mention the tribunal after that. No choice but to wait for another day.

He has lain awake since dawn. Sunlight strays through the lace curtains at their bedroom window. Sparrows chatter in the guttering. He gazes at Hannah's sleeping face and thinks how beautiful she is, even with her face still puffy from crying and the shadows under her eyes. He had tried to calm her. 'We'll face it out,' he'd said. 'It's better to get it over with,' all the while knowing that when George crosses the Channel on leave from France, he, Daniel, could be sailing in the other direction.

She's frightened about money. And for all his reassurances, he is frightened too. Hannah's army allowance will stop when George finds out. She says she'll take in work – ironing or shirt-finishing or sewing umbrellas – but they both know she'll earn a pittance, and in any case she's not strong enough. Her face is still so pale, and the headaches last for days. It's as much as she can do to get up and down the stairs to take the children to school.

Perhaps they could afford a single room somewhere, in the tenements at Spitalfields? He shudders at the thought of Hannah there, with the whores and the thieves: vulnerable as a wren in a rookery.

Lizzie cries and Hannah starts awake. He lifts the baby from the cot and carries her to Hannah as she sits up in bed. She unbuttons her nightdress and the baby begins to feed.

'Beautiful morning,' he says, walking over towards the window.

'Don't pull the curtains. Not yet. I can't stand it too bright.'

He sits on the edge of the bed and inhales the warmth of Hannah's body. Today is the day. He has to find a way. 'Let's have our tea out this evening,' he says. 'We can all go to the pie shop, then the gardens over at St Dunstan's.'

'St Dunstan's?'

'Stepney High Street. Five minutes on the tram. The kids can have a run around. A walk will do us good, clear our heads.'

'If you like.'

'I'll be finishing early today. Home by four.'

Her face falls. 'Short time again? However shall we afford tea out?'

'I've got a few bob put by.' He kisses her and leaves the room before any more questions are asked.

There are eight books left in the box on the kitchen floor. On his way out, he sorts through them, leaving just one behind. Mr Layman doesn't give the best prices – hasn't a clue what's valuable and what's not – but his shop is convenient. No need for a tram fare.

He watches as Hannah chases gravy around her plate with a spoon. The mash must be cold by now. She has barely eaten a thing.

'Do you want my leftovers?' she asks Daniel.

He shakes his head. He hasn't much of an appetite himself. It doesn't help that little Lizzie is fidgeting in the crook of his arm.

'I think Lizzie wants more of the milk and mash,' he says. They all look at the baby. She has turned her head towards Daniel and gazes up at him with hopeful eyes. 'Yes, you do, don't you?' he says to her in a gentle voice. 'More mash, is it, Lizzie? More mash?' She blinks and then smiles: an unmistakable smile, the first of her life.

'Oh, look,' says Hannah. She bites her lip and her eyes glisten with tears. 'Bless her little heart. She's a pretty thing. Ain't you, pretty thing?' Lizzie smiles again, and Teddy pulls a funny face, hoping to make his baby sister laugh.

Alice drops her cutlery on the plate with a clatter. 'Can I have your leftovers, Mum?' she says.

'Share them with Teddy.' Hannah spoons pie crust and dollops of greyish mash onto their plates.

'Daddy will like to see her smiling, won't he?' says Alice. 'He'll be coming home just in time.'

Hannah looks down. Daniel is not sure how to

react. He has never spoken of George to the children, never tried to explain anything. Hannah says they won't understand – it's best to say nothing at all. But he thinks Alice is cannier than her mother realizes.

'Don't get your hopes up, Alice,' he says, attempting to sound casual. 'There's only a chance of home leave, the letter said. Nothing definite.'

'When he comes home, will it be to Auntie Jen's or to here?'

'Oh ... both, I expect,' says Hannah. 'Now eat up. We want to get to the park while it's still warm.'

'*When* can we go back to Auntie Jen's? Please, Mummy. I don't want to live 'ere no more.'

Alice looks so confused and broken it makes him wretched with pity. He has tried his best with Hannah's children, all the while knowing his own kids are far away, having a fine time in Kent and forgetting all about him. It's still early days, he tells himself. Still only four months since they moved in together, only six weeks since Lizzie was born. He thought the baby might bring them all together, unite them like a proper family, but so far she seems to have achieved the opposite, poor little mite. Lizzie can smile all she likes, but she has splintered their lives. Sent them all spinning.

The gardens are busy. Alice and Teddy pal up with a gang of Jewish kids and they dart around the oaks and the beeches playing a game of hide-and-seek. Mothers and nannies push babies in their prams and Daniel knows what Hannah is

321

thinking. What she wouldn't give for a pram. Lizzie is putting on weight and the sling is getting heavy.

'Here, let me carry her,' he says, lifting the baby from the swathe of grey linen criss-crossed over her chest. People will stare, he knows: a man carrying a baby. Let them stare all they like. He wishes he could link arms with Hannah – the baby in one arm, Hannah on the other – but he knows she wouldn't like that, not with the children so close by.

They talk about George, and Hannah does her best to be brave. She tries to reason things out, echoes Daniel's own reassurances from the previous night. George might not be home for a good while, she says. And yes, they can face it if they have to. They can face it so long as they're together.

'Hannah.' He stops still and she walks half a pace in front of him. Her shoulders stiffen and she turns awkwardly to look at him. 'There's something I need to tell you,' he says. 'It ain't good news.'

There is a bench up ahead. He takes her elbow and guides her to it. He brushes some grass seeds from the wooden slats; then they sit together, a few inches apart, the baby on his lap.

'Got my tribunal next week,' he says.

'Oh?'

'Beaumont's are letting me go.'

She leans forward on the bench, covers her face with her hands.

39

We leave St Dunstan's and ride the bus back to Whitechapel in silence. Even the children are quiet, and Lizzie falls asleep in Daniel's arms. It's a strange sort of calm, a calm that comes when you know that the worst has happened and you might as well be dead. I wipe a smear of mash from Teddy's chin, comb out the tangles in Alice's hair with my fingers. I even plait a braid into her hair, though with nothing to fasten it, and the rocking of the bus, the braid soon starts to drop away. An old man looks on, smiling. He sees a happy family, and I am glad.

The gas lamps are all off now, and only one candle burns on the bedroom mantelpiece. The lace curtain is drawn across the open sash. The wind wisps through the window, playing with the curtain, sucking and billowing.

We are so high up here. So high.

We sit side by side in bed, hands clasped, until finally it is time to speak. Every nerve in my body is keen. It's as if my voice has its own power, like I'm raised on a pulpit, reciting the Truth.

'All this time I've been waiting, Daniel, waiting for something to happen. I tried to believe in fate. George might be killed, or a bomb would drop on us. And after Lizzie was born... I thought I was dying and I wasn't scared. I was happy, in a way, to die. It seemed a fair punishment, for our sins.'

Daniel breathes in sharply. 'But it's not a sin, is it? We said it wasn't a sin to love someone.'

'It's a sin to cause pain. Our pleasure causes pain. It hurts so many people. And so when I thought I would die, I felt relieved, somehow. But it wasn't to be. Fate didn't let me die. I wasn't brave enough for the river.'

'The river? Christ, Hannah, I couldn't live without you. I couldn't lose you—'

'You don't have to live without me. We have to make fate happen; that's what I've realized. It's up to us. It has been all along.' I pause. 'It's the only way we can be together. It's better for Alice and Teddy. They can go back to their nana.'

He falls silent. I think he understands.

'And Lizzie?' His voice is low and steady, but I can feel a tremor in his fingers as he grasps my hand.

'She comes with us. I won't have her in the workhouse.'

A storm rips the sky that night. We cling to each other, one body, in union. Hailstones crash down onto the rooftops and the street. I climb from the bed to stand at the open window. Giant hailstones, the size of pigeon eggs. I put out my hand to catch one and it strikes, flat and heavy in my palm.

When the candle gutters, we light another. Daniel uses the flame to light a cigarette. He stands at the fireplace, smoking. I sort through the papers in my toffee tin, the trinkets and the keepsakes, the buttons in a twist of white tissue paper.

40

Next morning he goes to Beaumont's for his final shift. The sleepless night has sharpened his senses. The gull's cry is louder; the engine fumes are stronger; the gravel on the pavement pricks at his worn soles. As he walks along the dock road, he remembers the passage in *Tess of the d'Urbervilles* when Tess thinks of all the years she has lived through her death date, 'a day which lay sly and unseen among all the other days of the year, giving no sign or sound when she annually passed over it'.

How strange to know the date of his own death.

All his hopes, his dreams of their being together lie useless and broken, frail as feathers on the tide. He has failed Hannah, failed his children.

Oxalic acid was Hannah's idea. "'Found naturally in rhubarb leaves,'" she read to him from her herb book. Her voice was determined, no hint of hysteria. "'A mild laxative if taken moderately, but in concentration it is highly toxic.'" He uses oxalic acid most days at work; a few drops on a rag cleans the rust from bolts, shines up a ship's hull like nothing else.

After his shift he calls into the post office to send a package. He is returning his last book to Lady Tolland. It is *Jude the Obscure*, a first edition that went missing from her bookshelves fifteen years ago. Let her call the police now.

His throat is so dry. He finds a pub on a Limehouse backstreet, almost empty. The landlord looks half drunk, and when he pulls Daniel's pint, he places it on the bar and declares it's on the house. 'I'm celebrating,' says the landlord. 'My daughter just had a baby. Our first grandson.'

Daniel smiles and looks around in case there is anyone he recognizes. Is it worth the risk? He checks himself: there is no risk. He can say what he likes now. 'I'll drink to that. My wife's had a little girl.'

'Is that so? We'll wet both babies' heads. Your good health!'

The certainty of death, the bizarre euphoria of the previous evening – all that dissolves as he sits at the bar drinking his pint of stout. It is surreal. Here they are, celebrating, when tomorrow his baby will be dead. Tomorrow his two children will be orphans. Alice and Teddy will have lost their mother, their little sister. He allows himself to believe, momentarily, that this pact he and Hannah have formed is nothing but monstrous fantasy. Perhaps they can find a way through the problem. Perhaps there is an alternative.

His thoughts hurtle and collide. He grips the tiny bottle in his pocket, the cork bound tightly in rags in case the acid should leak.

Self-sacrifice, Hannah calls it, not suicide. God knows it is commonplace enough. *Body in the dock!* – when the shout goes up, it gathers a crowd, but the interest soon seeps away, even as the corpse's clothes dry in the breeze.

Hannah says she saw a drowned woman at the

age of six, the body of her own aunt. But now she understands Auntie Beatrice, admires her courage.

It is the right thing to do, the honourable thing. Alice and Teddy can go home to Sabbarton Street. Sam and Maddie will be happy in Kent. Their children will thank them in the long run: the shame will be forgotten.

The alternative? He finishes his pint and sets out the likely sequence of events as though he were placing dominoes on a board. Daniel, drowning in the mud of some godforsaken shell hole. Hannah, destitute, forced into the workhouse, where her children would be wrenched from her. All of them dying, alone, apart.

He wanted her entirely, didn't he? Nothing could be more complete.

There is no alternative.

The landlord pours him another pint and he is grateful for this small ceremony.

In the midst of life we are in death.

41

'We'll have a chat tonight,' I tell the children. I sit down in the middle of the palliasse and pat the sheet either side of me. 'Come for a cuddle with Mummy.'

They wriggle up, Alice on my left side, Teddy on my right. I feel their heads resting against me, the heat from their hair. This is good, they're thinking. A cuddle with Mummy. A chat.

Can they feel my body trembling? I gulp a deep breath, try to chase down the wild vibration in my chest, the cry that would bellow and roar if I let it escape. I must keep my head. I must give them this tiny gift.

'You miss Nana dreadful, don't you?'

Alice nods. Teddy strokes his cheek with his Ducky.

'Hasn't it been a funny adventure, moving up here, changing schools? But if it don't work out for the best, well … perhaps you'll go back to Auntie Jen's after all.'

Alice's head jerks up. 'Really?' she says. 'Soon?'

'Quite soon, maybe.' I grip them tighter to me. 'I want you to be happy. You have to remember that. Alice, Teddy? I want you to be happy.' They both nod and snuggle in firmer.

How can I ever explain it to them? How can I say goodbye without saying goodbye? I close my eyes and think of Auntie Bea.

'I had an auntie once, who died when I was a little girl. Auntie Beatrice was her name. Grand-dad White's sister. When she died, people said bad things about her, but I know she weren't bad. Sometimes people die because that is the best thing. They still love the people around them. They always go on loving them.'

'From heaven?' asks Alice.

'From heaven, yes.' Or wherever they are.

I reach in my apron pocket and take out the twist of tissue paper. Inside there are two enamel buttons, each one painted with a miniature cat. 'These are special buttons, from Auntie Bea's favourite dress. Alice, you have this one.' She takes it as if it were a precious jewel, traces her finger over the Siamese's green ribbon. 'And, Teddy, you can have the sleepy tabby.' Teddy smiles and rubs the button against his cheek.

'It's getting late now, children. I'm ever so tired. I think tomorrow we'll have a lie-in. Don't come into the bedroom, will you? Let me have a long sleep.'

'What about school?' says Alice.

'Well ... one day off won't harm.'

They give a little cheer and it rips my heart.

I kiss Alice and Teddy and tuck them in, top to toe on the palliasse. My beautiful children.

In the kitchen, I leave out a small pot of jam I queued two hours to buy, plus four slices of bread under a tea towel. I write out a note in printed letters: *Do not come into Mummy's room. If I am still sleeping, call on Mrs Tendler across the landing. Love from your mummy xxxx*

I stare down at the note and add another line: *xxxxxxx These kisses are from Daniel and Baby Lizzie.*

There is a rushing in my ears, the sound of water crashing, pressing down. I can cheat the water. I will not fall. Daniel is waiting for me in the bedroom. One small drink and I'll always be his. We shall be free.

Part Four

Leman Street Police Station

20th day of July 1918

Police Report
Police Constable Michael Chambers

I beg to report that at 10 a.m. on the morning of 18th July I was sent to number 12 Union Buildings, Adler Street, Whitechapel.

The door was opened by Alice Loxwood, age six years, and her younger brother, Edward Loxwood, age four years. The latter was crying. When questioned as to the whereabouts of their mother, Alice replied that she was still sleeping. I entered the kitchen of the flat and asked the children where their mother was sleeping. They pointed to a set of double doors and said that she was in the front bedroom. I attempted to open the doors, but found they were locked.

A note in the kitchen, apparently from the children's mother, suggested that they should call on a neighbour, Mrs Tendler. I knocked on Mrs Tendler's door at number 10 Union Buildings and asked whether she would take charge of the children. She said that she would.

I re-entered number 12 and forced open the locked bedroom door. I entered the bedroom and found a woman and her female child, age two months, lying dead upon the bed. The woman was lying upon her back, dressed in chemise and nightdress, being covered, with the exception of her face, with a sheet, double blanket and bed quilt. The infant, with the exception of shoes and socks, was fully dressed and was lying on her face tightly wrapped in a double blanket, with a linen handkerchief tied loosely round her neck, one end of which was in her mouth. She was also covered over with the sheet and bed quilt, a pillow lying on the top. Both bodies were discoloured and they appeared to have been dead some hours.

On a table, I found six addressed and sealed envelopes, one of them having stamps affixed. Upon opening them, I found jewellery in two and letters in all, the contents of which go to show that the deceased and the prisoner Daniel Blake had agreed to take their own lives and die together the previous night.

I also saw a cup and a glass on the table, the cup containing what appeared to be paste, the glass bearing signs of having contained crystals. On the mantelpiece was a small bottle, the cork stopper removed. I then communicated with Leman Street Station. Dr Clarkwell, divisional surgeon, attended, shortly afterwards followed by Chief Inspector Aherne.

Later that day I went to 15 Sabbarton Street, Canning Town, an address that was written on two of the envelopes, apparently in the handwriting of the deceased. I informed the deceased's mother, Mrs Susan White, and the sister of the deceased, Mrs Jennifer Danks, of the events that had occurred. I asked if they would be able to care for the deceased's two children. They said that they would.

I returned to 12 Union Buildings to collect the children's clothes and keepsakes. The children travelled by police motor car with me to 15 Sabbarton Street, where they were welcomed by their grandmother and aunt.

I then arranged for a telegram to be sent to the husband of the deceased, Private George Loxwood, a soldier in the London Regiment, currently serving in France.

The Times
23rd July 1918

SOLDIER'S HOME-COMING.

Wife And Her Baby Found Dead.

An inquest was opened at Stepney yesterday on the bodies of Hannah Louise Loxwood, wife of a soldier, and her baby daughter, formerly living at Union Buildings, Adler Street, Whitechapel, where the woman and her child were found on Thursday. In the room was a cup which had contained oxalic acid, and tied round the baby's neck was a handkerchief, its head being wrapped in a blanket.

It was stated that last Thursday morning a man had thrown himself in front of a moving train at Aldgate East Station. The man had a marvellous escape. He was conscious when picked up and gave the name of Daniel Blake. He told the police that they would find the dead body of Hannah Louise Loxwood at Adler Street, adding that he had been living with her, and, as she had had a child of which he was the father, and had heard that her husband was coming home on leave, they decided to take poison.

Private George Alfred Loxwood, of the London Regiment, the husband, said he and the woman were married in 1912, and there were two children. His wife and he had been thoroughly happy, and when he went away, they parted on the best of terms. He had been to Salonika and Egypt, and latterly in France, and had not seen his wife for two years, but her letters had been affectionate.

The following letter in the dead woman's handwriting was read:-

Dear Husband – Just a few lines hoping you will forgive me for what I have done, but I cannot help it, as I have loved this man and he has loved me from the first time I met him, and as we cannot have one another, we are going to die together. Whatever a man does he gets out of it, where a woman has to suffer all her life for one wrong. I hope you will see the children looked after for me. I do not want to live without this man. From your wife Hannah.

The inquest was adjourned.

Metropolitan Police

Reference 3/257B

13th day of September 1918

I beg to report that on the eleventh of this month the prisoner Daniel Blake was arraigned before Justice Darling at the Central Criminal Court indicted with the wilful murder of Hannah Louise Loxwood and her female child, further with attempting to commit suicide, the prosecution being conducted by Sir Daniel McMann, the prisoner being represented by Mr Lecount.

The prisoner was tried for the murder of the woman, found guilty and sentenced to death.

42

Pentonville Prison, February 1919

Ludston is sleeping at last. Daniel listens to his vile breathing, the grunts and the mutters and the occasional dull scrape of toenail against coarse bedding. The bedsprings shift in the bunk above as Ludston turns onto his side. A small mercy. He is quieter on his side.

Daniel opens the Arnold collection at the ribboned page. He cannot see the words. Candles are confiscated after lights-out and there is no window in the cell. No moonlight. He traces a finger along the right-hand page, feels the delicate impress of black ink on smooth paper. The words echo through his mind:

Ah love! Let us be true
To one another! for the world, which seems
To lie before us like a land of dreams,
So various, so beautiful, so new,
Hath really neither joy, nor love, nor light,
Nor certitude, nor peace, nor help for pain;
And we are here as on a darkling plain
Swept with confused alarms of struggle and flight,
Where ignorant armies clash by night.

Let us be true to one another. He had tried to be true to Hannah. He had held her as she lay, curled in pain. He held her tightly because there was nothing gentle about her death. She clawed at him. There are scars on his chest. And yet she never screamed out. The children slept soundly.

They had planned to take the poison together, but at the last moment she said she would like to go first. *Stay with me until the end.*

Afterwards he washed her and dressed her in clean nightclothes. He laid her on the bed and kissed her beautiful face. She looked calm.

It was his turn. He stared at the cup on the table. It had taken a long time for her agony to end. Twenty minutes, was it, half an hour? They had thought it would be seconds.

He picked up the cup. No one would be there to hold him, to lay him out, to clean up the vomit and the rest of it. The door was locked, but what if he screamed, if the children managed to open the door and found him writhing? He returned the cup to the table, sat on the bed and held Hannah's hand. The warmth had drained from her fingers, and her skin was slack. Was Lizzie cold too, under all those blankets? He looked at the small, pitiful mound under the bed quilt, next to Hannah's body. Little Lizzie. Dear Christ, could this be real? Oh, it was real. The horror of it smashed at his guts, his bowels. He vomited into the slop bucket.

He stood facing the window, rocking on his feet, swallowing down nausea. Is this what his life amounted to? He had striven for so much more. He thought of his mother and the love she wasn't able to give, the father he had never known. Esther and her distant moods, the children, so happy now with his sister. Only one woman had loved him purely, a love so pure she would rather die than lose him.

He must be true to Hannah.

It was dawn now. Morning sun speared through the lace curtains. Carts would be trundling to the haymarket outside Aldgate East. The underground trains would be running. He dressed quickly. They had left all their money next to the letters. He counted out enough change for a single fare.

Ludston calls out in his sleep. 'Stickfor now fire', some such gibberish.

He is allowed one visitor per fortnight, and one letter a week. Lady Tolland comes regularly. Each time she brings him a book and each time he is suitably grateful.

Ellen writes with all the news. Sam and Maddie are getting on grand, no need to worry. They have a new puppy, a brown spaniel called Treacle. Her last letter was longer than usual:

I've been chatting with a friend, Mrs Green. She has family in Canning Town. It's hard to know whether you will want this news, but I hope it might bring you some comfort. By all accounts Alice Loxwood is a bright little spark, ten out of ten in all her spellings, and she won the prize for art. Their uncle is demobbed, and the aunt is expecting another baby. Alice tells everyone she hopes it's a girl.

He should be dead. He should have jumped two seconds sooner. A woman had sauntered onto the platform, distracting him, breaking his nerve.

For a moment he'd thought it was Sonia, the same skinny body and too-big feet.

He might be dead, had it not been for Lady Tolland and her wretched petition. Two thousand two hundred signatures. The world and his wife had made up their minds. The home secretary was convinced. Even the king agreed. Daniel Blake should not hang.

Penal servitude for life.

He shuts the book and closes his eyes.

Some nights he dreams of her, and when he wakes, he can still conjure her face. He can see her beautiful skin, white as apple flesh.

On these nights he feels lucky.

Epilogue

Her friends are at a cocktail party in Knightsbridge, but Alice has decided to stay home to finish packing. The boat for New York leaves on Sunday morning. A six-month trip, her first ever sea crossing. She packs sketchbooks and magazines, a volume of American poetry, which was a gift from one of her actress clients.

Standing at the opened wardrobe, Alice runs her fingers along the clothes pressed together on the rail. She takes out the green day dress and holds it up against her body, turning to face the full-length mirror fixed to the inside of the wardrobe door.

The dress is a talisman, a reminder of her good

fortune. When she entered the drawings into the competition, she was working as a clerk in the windowless back office of a solicitors' firm in Holborn. Of course, she heard nothing about the competition for weeks, chastised herself for indulging such fanciful dreams. Then one evening she arrived home to find a thick cream envelope standing against the button box. The judges admired Alice's design for a stylish day dress – the puffed sleeves, the slim black belt and especially the chartreuse-green satin bow, tied voluminously at the throat and printed with silhouettes of Siamese cats. She was awarded first prize, and a commission from a London salon.

The outfit is dated now, over four years old, but she decides to pack it, for luck. She tucks a lavender bag inside each sleeve, folds the dress in tissue and places it inside the trunk.

On the dressing table is a photograph in a wooden picture frame. Nana gave it to her before Christmas, when Alice visited Sabbarton Street for Sunday tea. Nana had waited until Auntie Jen was in the scullery and Uncle Alec was in the yard fetching coal, and then she produced the frame from the bottom of her knitting bag. 'I've been having a sort-out,' she had said. 'Thought you might like this.'

Alice studies the photograph again, as if she may discover something new this time, some clue that has eluded her these past few weeks. Her father leans against a polished mahogany pillar, his face pale and unlined, impossibly young. Her mother is cradling Alice on her lap, grasping the soft baby shoe on her tiny foot. There is amusement in her mother's wide eyes: a look of calm pride. Why wasn't Dad enough? wonders Alice. What did he do so wrong?

She decides not to put the photograph in the trunk. It is small enough to fit inside her handbag. She would like to keep it close.

The handbag is on her eiderdown. She opens the inside pocket, takes out Auntie Beatrice's enamel button and closes her fingers around it. *Sometimes people die because that is the best thing.* Her mother loved her; she feels certain of that. But still there are questions: strands of memory, fragile as frayed silk. A little sister, crying in a soap box. Sunflowers in jam pots. A bedroom door that would not open.

One day she will find the answers.

16 Chapelhay Street
Weymouth
Dorset

2nd June 1934

Dear Alice,
Thank you very much for your letter, which my sister has forwarded on your request. It was a great surprise to hear from you, but a very pleasant surprise indeed.

I am pleased to learn that you and Teddy are in good health. It is hard to imagine Teddy as a motor mechanic: of course, he was only four years old when I last saw him. And you are a fashion artist – how interesting that sounds.

Dear Alice, I have no idea how much you know or remember of the circumstances... But as to the present, since my release I have been employed as a welder in a small boatyard. My lodgings are comfortable, and I like to walk the cliffs and the surrounding countryside when time allows. I have a cat, Toby, who seems to tolerate my company. As I write, he is stretched on the best armchair, curling his claws into a crocheted cushion.

With regard to the last paragraph of your letter, I do understand that you must have many questions, and I am willing to answer them if this is your definite wish. I have thought carefully about how best to respond and I must confess that I am not sure of the right course. But if you would like to meet with me, naturally I will be very pleased to see you.

Rest assured I think of your mother every day. But this is not the time to discuss matters. If you would like to meet, then I will tell you our story.

Yours sincerely,
Daniel Blake

Acknowledgements

With thanks to:

Sophie Orme at Mantle for her warm encouragement and insightful editing.

Maria Rejt, Mantle publisher, for enjoying the poetry.

The team at Mantle and Pan Macmillan for their professionalism and expertise.

Hellie Ogden, my agent at Janklow and Nesbit, for her tremendous talent, enthusiasm and sound advice.

Alison MacLeod and the creative writing staff at Chichester University. Here be miracles.

Librarians and archivists at the Museum of London Docklands, Tower Hamlets Local History Library and the National Archive. Historian Keith Grieves at Kingston University for his detailed reading of the manuscript. Eve Hostettler at the Island History Trust for advising on Docklands history. Any inaccuracies are my own.

Writer friends, Isabel Ashdown, Elayne De-Laurian, Jane Osis and Sandra Walsh for helping to sharpen the manuscript. Thanks also to my mum, Angela West, and my sister, Alison Laurie, for valuable comments on the first draft.

Eric Williams and Phil Hollis *(in memoriam)* for boosting my confidence with their writerly wisdom and good humour.

Yvonne Phillips and all at Horsham Writers' Circle for kindness, support and friendship.

Joan Ward, granddaughter of the 'real-life' Hannah Loxwood. Your blessing for this project is greatly appreciated.

My children Isobel, Jessica and James, for keeping me in the real world.

Finally, love and heartfelt thanks to my husband, Steve Wilson, who makes everything possible.

The publishers hope that this book has given you enjoyable reading. Large Print Books are especially designed to be as easy to see and hold as possible. If you wish a complete list of our books please ask at your local library or write directly to:

Magna Large Print Books
Magna House, Long Preston,
Skipton, North Yorkshire.
BD23 4ND

This Large Print Book for the partially sighted, who cannot read normal print, is published under the auspices of

THE ULVERSCROFT FOUNDATION